Alphonse Jules Wauters

Stanley's Emin Pasha Expedition

Alphonse Jules Wauters

Stanley's Emin Pasha Expedition

ISBN/EAN: 9783337325572

Printed in Europe, USA, Canada, Australia, Japan

Cover: Foto ©Andreas Hilbeck / pixelio.de

More available books at **www.hansebooks.com**

EMIN PASHA

EXPEDITION

BY

A. J. WAUTERS

CHIEF EDITOR OF THE MOUVEMENT GEOGRAPHIQUE, BRUSSELS

WITH ILLUSTRATIONS

NEW YORK
JOHN B. ALDEN, PUBLISHER
1890

CONTENTS.

LIST OF ILLUSTRATIONS.

INTRODUCTION.

In February 1883 Dr. Junker had penetrated so far into the heart of Africa that he found himself at the zeriba Ali Kobo, on the banks of the Welle Makowa, in a region hitherto traversed by no other European.

For three years this indefatigable traveller had been exploring north and south, east and west, the districts watered by the Welle, in the hope of finding a definite solution to the important geographical problem propounded by his friend Dr. Schweinfurth, thirteen years previously, as to whether the Welle was connected with the Shary and thence with Lake Tchad, or whether it flowed into the Congo.

It needed only a few more weeks of perseverance and progress towards the west, and the explorer would have attained his end and reaped the reward of his labors. He was within a few days' march of the Congo and was about to push onwards, when letters from Lupton Bey brought news of startling import and put an end to further investigations.

Dr. Junker had for a considerable time been quite aware how the country around Khartoum was harassed by the revolutionary action of an agitator who professed himself to be the "Mahdi," that is, a deliverer invested with a supernatural mission. He had been apprised that the powerful tribe of the Dinka had taken arms, and was threatening the military settlements and zeribas on the Bahr-el-Ghazal; and had further learnt from Lupton Bey, who was the representative of the Egyptian government in that province, that the route between the Niam-niam country and the landing-place of Rek on the Bahr-el-Ghazal was completely blockaded, while the Mahdists were at the same time making an alarming progress. Lupton Bey's advice to him was that he should endeavor forthwith to return to Egypt; and letters received at Semmio, his station in the Niam-niam country, as well as those which came to hand some weeks later, so far from representing the outlook in a more reassuring light, pictured it as dark and overclouded. The Dinka round Meshra-er-Rek, and the Mahdi's forces about Khartoum, were steadily gaining ground, so that the northern route was ever becoming more and more impracticable. The conviction, therefore, could not fail to take hold on his mind that he would be obliged to remain in the south for the repression of the two revolts before he could carry out his design of returning to Europe by way of Egypt and the Nile.

A certain presentiment of the hard times which he would have to face had already occurred to him. In his journal of August 1, 1883, he made the entry:— "All hope of seeing my country this year is fading away. Thanks to frequent communications from Lupton Bey, I have been kept informed of the events on the Bahr-el-Ghazal. Our gaze is fastened on the north, whence with the utmost anxiety we are looking for relief. The Khartoum steamer is expected. The last news from Lupton is urgent; Hassan Mussa has been killed; sixty more guns have fallen into the hands of the rebels: the road to Meshra-er-Rek is again closed, and 900 soldiers are about to make an effort to reopen it. My fears for the population of the Rohl and for the station of Rumbek are verified, for Lupton writes, 'Rumbek is destroyed, only six soldiers managing to escape,' while he further announces the desertion of about thirty Dongolese, drawn over by some fakirs to the Mahdi. If the disasters that I forebode should come to pass, and the Arabs, driven down from the north, should invade the Bahr-el-Ghazal, I foresee that there will be no alternative for us but to retreat by the south. O that help may arrive from Khartoum!"

But the hope was in vain. There was no longer any chance of relief from the north. Neither Meshra nor Lado was again to welcome a steamer from Khartoum. The northern road was closed, and the entire situation in the Soudan was critical to a degree of which Dr. Junker in his remote station in the Niam-niam country could form no conception.

The situation, in fact, was more than serious. In Kordofan and the Bahr-el-Ghazal district the Arab and the negro were persistently joining the rebels; Sennar and El-Obeid were threatened; the Egyptian corps in Darfur, as well as the detachments under Lupton and Emin, was absolutely cut off from the rest of the Sou-dan, and the Mahdi, whose audacity increased with his prestige, had under him an army of at least 100,000 men. Moreover, the government troops had met with sanguinary reverses, and were reduced to such a state of alarm that symptoms of rebellion had begun to appear in their ranks. The governor-general, Abd-el-Kadir, was almost overpowered, and compelled no longer to send for a few battalions from Cairo, but to implore that an army might be despatched to his aid. Altogether, things were becoming desperate.

It was in this emergency that the British govern-ment, rousing itself from its protracted reserve, de-termined to substitute its own action for the inadequate efforts of the Khedive, and proceeded to equip 10,000 soldiers who should start from Suakin, make forced marches, and re-establish order in Kordofan.

All along, throughout this time, at Lado, at Meshra, and at Semmio, anxious eyes were turned towards Khartoum awaiting help. But no help was forthcom-ing. The drama of the Soudan had commenced.

On a stage of which the scenery extended from the Red Sea to Lake Victoria, from the frontier of Abys-sinnia to the remote confines of Darfur, scenes wild and bloody were about to be enacted. Face to face with the invincible Mahdi and his fierce general Osman Digna were now to appear successively Hicks Pasha, Baker Pasha, General Graham, and Admiral Hewett; in his turn should follow General Gordon, the hero *sans peur et sans reproche;* and then finally a second British army under the command of the renowned Lord Wolseley, the victor at Tel-el-Kebir.

And so for three years along the Nile there ensued a series of terrible struggles, of brilliant, sanguinary, yet futile engagements, of which the eventual results were alike disastrous to the cause of civilisation and damaging to English prestige.

The drama came to an end. When Baker was worsted, Khartoum captured, Gordon massacred,

Wolseley in retreat, and the Soudan abandoned to the hands of the Mussulman and slave-hunter, it seemed as if civilisation was arrested, the hope of years was extinguished, inasmuch as not an individual remained who could give effect to the counsels of Europe. The Khamsin, which at the bidding of a fanatical leader had arisen in the desert, had made all things retire before it, and the region of the Nile-sources must again relapse into the gloom of night.

Such, at least, for a considerable time was the general conviction, until, one day, from beyond the domain of the bloodthirsty tyrant of Uganda, from Msalala, the Christian mission station by the southern shore of Lake Victoria, suddenly there rose the voice of Junker.

He announced that he was safe, and that Emin with the soldiers who had remained faithful to him was safe also; so too was the Italian explorer Casati. All three had succeeded in securing their liberty amidst the break-down of the Egyptian authority in the Soudan.

The time had come for Dr. Junker to realise the truth of what in 1883 he had written in his diary, that if the events he dreaded should come to pass, there would be no alternative but that he must take a southern route.

After two years and a half of suspense, of struggle and privation, the explorer resolved to attempt his retreat by this southerly route, that he might make Egypt and Europe aware of the existence and critical position of these last defenders of the lost Soudan. It was another year before he succeeded in reaching Zanzibar. Europe was stirred by his appeal, and this time, without hesitation or delay, England undertook to organise an expedition of relief.

But the difficulty was great: the obstacles were many. What forces would be requisite to break through the enemies by which Emin was environed? What route towards Wadelai should be chosen? The hordes of the Mahdi barred all access from the north; the warlike Masai and the battalions of Uganda held the east and the south; the regions to the west were utterly unknown. Beyond all there lay the further question as to who should be the leader of such an enterprise. The way into the heart of that mysterious region was over mountains and valleys, through deserts, virgin forests and marshes, amidst savage and relentless tribes, beneath the rays of the equatorial sun. Who should be found competent to conduct a caravan made up of numerous and promiscuous followers, equally ready to quarrel with nature and with their fellows, yet indispensable for the conveyance along that weary route of the double cargo of victuals, ammunition, and supplies?

The answer was forthcoming. Then it was that for the fifth time Central Africa was to behold the hero, at once the discoverer and deliverer of Livingstone. Stanley was ready for the task. He chose the Congo route, which he had himself opened up for the commercial enterprise of Europe, while the opposition of the Mahdi was closing all access by the Nile. More fortunate than Wolseley, who only reached Khartoum in time to register its fall and the slaughter of its defenders, he accomplishes his arduous undertaking, and after three years' undaunted perseverance he has brought back Emin and Casati, with their faithful adherents, in safety and triumph to Zanzibar.

It is the history of this ever-memorable expedition and of the dramatic events that led up to it, together with the important geographical discoveries resulting from it, that forms the subject of the ensuing pages.

CHAPTER I.

Project of Mehemet Ali—Khartoom—Meeting of Baker, Speke, and Grant at Gondokoro—First explorers of the Upper Nile—Ismailia, and expedition of Baker against Fatiko slave-traders—Exploration of the Bahr-el-Ghazal and discovery of the Welle by Schweinfurth—*Zeribas* on the Bahr-el-Ghazal—Ivory trade and kidnapping—Gordon's government—Europeans at the King of Uganda's court—Gessi Pasha on Lake Albert—Conquest of Darfoor, Chekka, and Dar-Fertit—Revolt of Suleiman-Zebehr—The Egyptian Soudan—Deposition of Ismail Pasha and recall of Gordon—Raouf Pasha at Khartoom.

At the date of the earliest events which it is the purpose of this book to narrate, M. Louis Vossion, then French Vice-Consul at Khartoom, wrote the following description of the place :—

" Khartoom, the capital of the Egyptian Soudan, stands on the left bank of the Blue Nile just at its junction with the White Nile.

" Any traveller arriving at the town for the first time could not fail to experience much surprise. After passing what is called the Ras-el-Khartoom at the confluence of the two streams, a low tract of alluvial soil, covered with thick herbage relieved by occasional clumps of palms, the boat, all sails set, glides into the Blue Nile. A few minutes more and, hailed by the vociferous shouts of the Nubian boatmen, the town rises suddenly into view, with its palm-trees, its lines of little houses along the shore, its white mosques, with their pointed minarets, all standing out sharply against the clear blue sky. Heavy boats called ' nuggers,' laden with durra-corn, wood, and gum-arabic, are ranged for nearly half a mile along the river-bank. The stone buildings of the Roman Mission of Verona and of Marquet's factory are conspicuous above the dwellings of Nile mud to which they are in proximity.

" Upon landing, the stranger will find himself surrounded by a whole swarm of inquisitive negroes, and his astonishment will increase at every step; he will at once be struck by the variety of the types of the tribes of the Soudan into which he is thrown so suddenly. There are the Dinka, Shillooks of the White River, Bari from Gondokoro, people from Unyoro, Niam-niam from Makraka, Monbuttoo, Nueir, Dyoor, Bongo, Ferteet from the Bahr-el-Ghazal, Galla, Abyssinians, negroes from Djebel-Nooba, Dongola, Darfoor, and Kordofan; add to these Arabs of the various semi-independent tribes, Bishareens, Hadendowas, Chookries, Kababishes, Baggaras, Jews, Syrians, Greeks, and it may be imagined what a strange and well-nigh unique spectacle is presented by such an agglomeration of nationalities, all retaining their own traditions and marked out by their peculiar costumes!

"The general impression is intensified when it is remembered that Khartoom is on the very fringe of the civilised world, and is the threshold of that mysterious Africa which holds so many secrets in its bosom."

When, in 1838, the energetic Viceroy Mehemet Ali made his journey into the Soudan, Khartoom was a mere fishing village; but with a quick appreciation of its importance as a geographical position, he determined to rear upon its site a town that should become the capital of the new equatorial province over which it was his dream that he should reign. His successors, one after another, added a stone to the edifice by increasing the area of the new city, to which it was found that traders, not only from Egypt but from Europe, were ready and eager to flock.

The increase of the population of Khartoom, thus rapid, was altogether beyond and out of proportion to the progress of its internal appliances. Sir Samuel Baker, who saw it for the first time in June 1862, describes it as one of the most dirty, miserable, and unhealthy places that could be imagined. Built of sun-dried bricks, it stood upon a low-lying flat, which was often quite under water at the period of the floods. Notwithstanding that the houses were overcrowded with a population exceeding 30,000, there was no drainage nor sanitary arrangements of any kind. The streets were full of filth of every description; the bodies of the dead animals that lay about were so many centres of corruption and disease. The entire aspect was that of utter misery.

In matters of administration things were even worse. Musa Pasha, by his deplorable misgovernment, was ruining the country. From the highest to the lowest of his officials, dishonesty and fraud were the common characteristics; every one cheated according to his rank. Slave traffic, with all its abominations, was the leading business of the place, a fact which has been demonstrated alike by Baker and Schweinfurth, who, at separate times, had ample opportunity of studying the matter upon the very scene of the misdoings.

It was the laudable ambition to ascertain the true sources of the Nile that took Baker into regions south of Khartoom that had previously been unexplored. Accompanied by his courageous wife, on February 2, 1863, he reached Gondokoro, then a miserable group of turf-cabins occupied only for two months in the year by the Khartoom traders whose "*dahabiehs*" could go no farther. He landed there to meet Speke and Grant, who, weary, ragged, and destitute, were on their way back from the interior along the Nile, of which they had just discovered the real springs. The meeting was a memorable epoch in the history of the Soudan; it marked a new stage in the progress of the opening up of Equatorial Africa, betokening at the same time a fresh extension of Egyptian rule towards the south.

In his own lively manner Baker gives a description of the incident:—" Shots in the distance. The ivory-bearers that I have been expecting have arrived. My people are running frantically towards my boat and shouting that two white men from the sea are with them. Is it possible that they can be Speke and Grant? Away I start. True enough, there they are! Hurrah for old England! Returned they have from the Victoria Nyanza; thence it is that the Nile flows forth; . . . the mystery of the ages is solved.

" At the same time, with all the excitement of joy there is mingled a sense of disappointment. It would have pleased me better to meet them farther on. However, it was satisfactory to know that I had made such arrangements as would have ensured my meeting them in case they were in any difficulty, as I ascertained that they had returned by the very route which I had proposed to follow.

"My people are mad with delight: in firing a salute they have managed to kill one of my donkeys, a melancholy sacrifice in celebration of the accomplishment of the great geographical discovery!

"When I first caught sight of them they were approaching my boats. At the distance of some hundred yards I recognized my old friend Speke; my heart throbbed with ecstacy, and raising my cap, I called aloud, 'Hurrah!' and ran towards him. At first he did not know me; a beard and moustache of ten years' growth had so altered my countenance that, not expecting to meet me, he did not comprehend my sudden apparition. There was no need for Speke to introduce me to his companion, as we already felt like intimate friends. When the first transports of this propitious meeting were over we all proceeded to my *dahabieh*, through a cloud of smoke raised by the continuous salutes of my people."

A year after the exploration of Lake Victoria by Speke and Grant, Baker made his name illustrious by the discovery of Lake Albert. Thenceforward an increasing interest was centred on these regions, and Gondokoro, from being the mere halting-place that it was when the three English travellers met there, became a new centre for the commercial activity of the Khartoom traders, as well as a starting-point for various scientific expeditions, the history of the Soudan becoming from that time intimately connected with the history of discovery.

Antecedent to the enterprises that were undertaken by the three great Englishmen, there had already been various expeditions, half scientific, half commercial, which had partially raised the veil that concealed the inland regions of Africa from the curiosity of European eyes. William Lejean and Petherick had visited the Upper Nile; Piaggia had explored the Dyoor country and the Bahr-el-Ghazal; Dr. Peney had reached Mount Gniri; Dr. Cuny had penetrated to Darfoor, Poucet to Dar-Ferteet, and Munziger to Kordofan.

Greedier than the vultures and hyenas of the desert, the Egyptian troops and Government officials **had** followed in the wake of the explorers and traders, so that, little by little, the political limits of the new province were extended, while the native populations (their opposition and outbreaks being promptly suppressed by relentless bloodshed) successively submitted to the conqueror.

In 1870 the extension of Egyptian territory towards the south was pushed forward by a larger and more rapid impetus. During that year Ismail Pasha, alarmed no doubt by the reports that reached him that the Soudan was becoming overrun by the Bashi-Bazouks, who, beyond control, were making perpetual incursions into it, made an appeal for European assistance to strengthen him in completing the conquest of Central Africa. Baker was accordingly placed in command of 1200 men, supplied with cannon and steamboats, and received the title of Governour-General of the provinces which he was commissioned to subdue. Having elected to make Gondokoro the seat of his government, he changed its name to Ismailia. He was not long in bringing the Bari to submission, and then, advancing southwards, he came to the districts of Doufilé and Fatiko, a healthy region endowed by nature with fertile valleys and irrigated by limpid streams, but for years past converted into a sort of hell upon earth by the slave-hunters who had made it their headquarters.

From these pests Baker delivered the locality, and having by his tact and energy overcome the distrust of the native rulers, he established over their territory a certain number of small military settlements, by means of which communication could be kept up with Egypt, and its authority over the country be maintained.

This expedition was accompanied by M. de Bizemont, a lieutenant in the French navy, as scientific attaché; but in spite of the favourable auspices which attended it at its outset, it can hardly be said to have fulfilled the expectations that had been formed about it. From the very first Baker had protested too strongly that he had come to the Upper Nile to destroy the slave-trade, and the consequence was, that he made himself enemies at once amongst the Viceroy's officials, who were all more or less interested in the negro traffic, and con-

spired accordingly to frustrate his plans and to impede
his progress.   The result was, that he found himself
unable to carry out his design of advancing as far as
Lake Albert, and had to stop short at Masindi, the
residence of Kamrasi, the native king of Unyoro.

Baker returned to Europe flattering himself with the
delusion that he had put an end to the scourge of
slave-dealing.   It was true that various slave-dealers'
dens on the Upper Nile had been destroyed, a number
of outlaws had been shot, and a few thousand miserable slaves had been set at liberty; but beyond that
nothing had been accomplished; no sooner had the
liberator turned his back than the odious traffic recom-
menced with more vigour than before through the region south of Gondokoro.

This, however, was only one of the slave-hunting
districts, and by no means the worst.   To the west
the basin of the Bahr-el-Ghazal was far more infested.
Nowhere throughout the Soudan had the negro trade
been more hideous and disastrous in its working than in
the fertile and populous plains inhabited by the Dinka,
the Dyoor, the Bongo, and the Niam-niam.   While
Baker was at Cairo organising his second expedition,
Dr. Schweinfurth was exploring all this fine and interesting country, pushing forward to the Monbuttoo
land, where he discovered the large river Welle.   The
story of his journey, which claims to be remembered
as one of the most important scientific records of
Equatorial Africa ever published, has thrown light
upon districts in which for the last quarter of a century the Khartoom traders have established a series of
fortified depôts.   As this eminent traveller points out,
these depôts were originally brought into existence for
the sake of the ivory trade.   They were set up in
places where elephants were most abundant, and in the
midst of peaceable populations, devoted to agriculture
and cattle-breeding, and every year were visited by
the Khartoomers, who carried back the ivory that had
been procured.   The men who were armed and despatched on these annual expeditions were composed
of the very scum of the people.   Ascending the Nile
as far as Lake No, they spread themselves over the
lands adjacent to the Bahr-el-Ghazal, the Bahr-el
Arab, and their affluents, and having thus gained a

footing, proceeded to apportion the country amongst them. They reduced the natives to a state of subjection, and for the purpose of securing a base for further operations and obtaining free access to the surrounding districts, they established isolated settlements, which they enclosed by palisades and thornhedges, and which hence were called *zeribas*. The whole line of the various watercourses was thus studded with these *zeribas*, which usually bore the names of the traders to whom they belonged, and are so distinguished upon the maps.

But although originally designed purely for mercantile purposes, the settlements became gradually transformed into centres for slave-hunting. They were (and, though in a diminished degree, they are) the starting-points for expeditions of armed marauders, who made sudden attacks upon the native villages, to which they set fire, and then, having reduced the terrified residents to a condition of helplessness, carried off the women and children, along with the ivory and the cattle. Destined to be bartered by the slavers for either money or merchandise, the miserable captives were yoked two and two together, and dragged in long caravans to some place of embarkation, where they were crammed down into the holds of the *dahabiehs*, and conveyed to the markets either on the coast or in the interior.

Such was the way in which the ill-fated districts of the Egyptian Soudan, and especially those of the Bahr-el-Ghazal, Darfoor, Kordofan, and Djebel-Nooba, became, as it were, the nursery whence were supplied more than 30,000 slaves every year to satisfy the requirements of Oriental luxury and debauch.

But the eyes of the civilised world were at length opened to the atrocities that at the close of the nineteenth century were thus being perpetrated in the Soudan with the knowledge, and often by the connivance, of the Egyptian authorities. Under European compulsion, therefore, the Khedive Ismail undertook to promote measures to put a stop to the scandal. He entered into various conventions with England on the subject; and in order to convince the Powers of the sincerity of his intentions, he consented to put the equatorial provinces under the administration of an

European officer, who should be commissioned to carry
on the work of repression, conquest, and organisation
that had been commenced by Baker. His choice fell
upon a man of exceptional ability, a brilliant officer
trained at Woolwich, who had already gained high re-
nown in China, not only for military talent, but for
his adroitness and skill in negotiation and diplomacy.
This was Colonel Gordon, familiarly known as "Chinese Gordon," who was now to add fresh lustre to his
name in Egypt as Gordon Pasha.

Gordon was appointed Governour-General of the
Soudan in 1874. With him were associated Chaillé-
Long, an American officer, who was chief of his staff;
the German, Dr. Emin Effendi, medical officer to the
expedition; Lieutenants Chippendall and Watson;
Gessi and Kemp, engineers; two Englishmen, Messrs.
Russell and Anson; and two Frenchmen, MM. Au-
guste and Ernest Linant de Bellefonds, sons of an
engineer who had been Minister of Public Works under Mehemet Ali.

Thenceforward the territories, of which so little had
hitherto been known, became the continual scene of
military movements and scientific excursions.

Colonel Chaillé-Long, with a mission from Gordon
to Mtesa, the king of Uganda, reached the residence
of that potentate without hindrance, and was entertained with much magnificence. He availed himself
of the opportunity to explore the northern section of
Lake Victoria, and descending the Somerset Nile, not
without some conflict with the native tribes, he discovered on his way the lake which he designated by
the name of Ibrahim Pasha. He rejoined Gordon at
Gondokoro, and was subsequently despached by him,
in company with Marno, the Austrian naturalist, to
make an exploration on the Makraka district.

Shortly after Chaillé-Long had taken his departure
from Uganda, Mtesa received other European visitors.
M. Ernest Linant de Bellefonds arrived at the court,
and was much surprised to find that the king had
already welcomed another white stranger, who was
seated at his side. His first impression was that
this must be Cameron, but it proved to be Stanley,
who, having started from Zanzibar to make further in-

LUPTON BEY.

CAPTAIN CASATI.

GENERAL GORDON.

DR. JUNKER.

vestigations at Lake Victoria, had been for some days the guest of the black chief.

Subsequently there arrived the German, Dr. Schnitz- er, then known as Emin Effendi, but afterwards as Emin Bey. In the mission with which he was charged by Gordon to Mtesa he exhibited such diplomatic skill as to attract the approbation of his superior, and to mark him out for the important duties which he would afterwards be called to fulfil.

All the time that Gordon was thus negotiating with Mtesa, and endeavouring to secure him as an ally who would acquiesce in his schemes, he was likewise laying himself out to extend his own authority in the direc- tion of Lake Albert. Two others of his party, the Englishmen Chippendall and Kemp, were sent out to explore the unknown portion of the Nile between Gon- dokoro and the lake, and succeeded in launching, above the rapids, a steam vessel, the " Khedive," and two iron-plated boats. On board one of these, the Italian engineer Gessi, accompanied by his fellow-countryman Piaggia, made his grand circumnavigation of Lake Al- bert in March and April 1876, taking possession of it in the name of the Khedive.

Two years previously, after Ismail Ayoub's smart campaign, Darfoor, Chekka, and Dar-Ferteet had been annexed, Colonels Purdy, Colston, and Mason having, by a series of military advances, united the new con- quests to Dongola and Khartoom.

In that Darfoor campaign the Government had been backed up by a rich trader, Suleiman Zebehr, the owner of numerous *zeribas* and of large companies of armed slaves in the Bahr-el-Ghazal district. Having been rewarded for his support with the title of Bey and Mudir of Chekka, he seemed to be able to set no bounds to his ambition. Dazzled by his power, and irritated by the request of the Government that he should desist from his slave-raids, he broke out in re- volt, and making alliance with the dethroned Sultan of Darfoor, he attacked the Egyptian outposts, and fostered an insurrection which very nearly led to the loss of the province and that of the Bahr-el-Ghazel.

Had it not been for the energy and courage of Gessi, whom Gordon despatched with all speed to quell the rising rebellion, there is every probability that not only

the Bahr-el-Ghazel and Darfoor, but part of Kordofan
also, would have repudiated the authority of the Khedive, and relapsed into the control of the slave-hunters. Gessi, however, was equal to his task. Although
without provisions, and almost without ammunition,
and supported by a comparatively small force, he made
an intrepid advance, and by his resolution not only
succeeded in preventing the two enemies from effecting
a junction, but routed them separately before they
could combine. Zebehr and his chief officers were arrested and executed, Gessi taking up his quarters in
the Bahr-el-Ghazel, of which he was appointed Governour.

Under Gessi's administration the province was en-
abled to enjoy a period of peace and prosperity. Owing to his energy and skill, ways of communication
were opened, forsaken villages were repopulated, lands
were brought afresh into cultivation, slave-raids ceased,
the natives regained confidence, and agriculture and
commerce began to take a new start.

In the meanwhile Gordon Pasha, on his part, was
vigorously carrying on the work of organisation in the
equatorial provinces. Leaving Gondokoro, which was
situated in a bad and unhealthy locality, exposed to
the miasma of stagnant water, he crossed over to Lado,
on the other bank of the Nile, and there established
the seat of his government. The storm which had
broken out at the time of his arrival seemed now to
have subsided into a calm; hostilities had been overcome, and the Soudan was so far conquered as to be
held by about a dozen military outposts stationed
along the Nile from Lake No to Lakes Albert and
Ibrahim.

In 1876 Gordon went back to Cairo. Nevertheless,
although he was wearied with the continual struggle of
the past two years, worn down by the incessant labours
of internal organisation and geographical investigations, disheartened, too, by the jealousies, rivalries,
and intrigues of all around him, and by the ill feeling
of the very people whom the Khedive's Government
had sent to support him, he consented to return again
to his post; this time with the title of Governour-General of the Soudan, Darfoor, and the Equatorial Provinces. At the beginning of 1877 he took possession

of the Government palace at Khartoom, at the gate of which, eight years afterwards, so dire a tragedy was destined to be performed.

Egyptian authority, allied with European civilisation, appeared now at length to be taking some hold on the various districts, and the Cairo government might begin to look forward to a time when it could reckon on some reward for its labours and sacrifices.

The area of the new Egyptian Soudan had now become immense. Geographically, its centre included the entire valley of the Nile proper, from Berber to the great lakes; on the east were such portions of the valleys of the Blue Nile and Atbara as lay outside Abyssinia; and on the west were the districts watered by the Bahr-el-Ghazal and the Bahr-el-Arab, right away to the confines of Wadaï. Politically, it consisted of Upper Nubia, the ancient island of Meroe, Sennaar, Baggara, Kordofan, Darfoor, Chekka, Dar-Ferteet, the lands of the Shillook, Nueir, Dinka, Bongo, Bari, Latooka, Madi, and Aloori, with the northern part of Unyoro.

The dream of Mehemet Ali was in a measure realised. The foundations of a great Soudanese empire under Egyptian rule had been laid upon the Upper Nile, and the little fishing village which the first conqueror, with far-seeing augury, had destined for its capital, had grown into a flourishing town, with a population of more than 45,000, and was the seat of government and the general trade-centre of the entire region.

Unfortunately in 1879 Ismail Pasha was deposed, and, to the grievous loss of the Soudan, Gordon was recalled. As the immediate consequence, the country fell back into the hands of Turkish pashas; apathy, disorder, carelessness, and ill feeling reappeared at Khartoom, and the Arab slave-dealers, who had for a period been kept under by Baker, Gessi, and Gordon, came once more to the front.

It is only too obvious that the slave-trade must for a long time be the great obstacle to any true progress in the Soudan, preventing its taking its own proper part in the movement which will ultimately result in its civilisation. The Arab merchants, to the present day, consider the traffic in slaves to be perfectly legitimate, and detest not only the Egyptian government, but especially the European officers in its employ, for obstructing their operations, seizing their boats, liberating the negroes, and otherwise damaging their abominable trade. This detestation is made manifest on every conceivable occasion.

Year after year had Gordon, as Governour-General, to deal with the hordes of Arab slave-dealers; and although he succeeded in suppressing their rebellions and punishing their misdoings, he was never able to quench the spirit of revolt, which, nurtured by fanaticism and hatred to the infidel, secretly brooded underneath all outward appearance of submission, keeping up amongst them the hope that some accident would open up for them an opportunity to overthrow the administration which they hated, and bring back the old *régime*, under which they could continue their nefarious practices free and uncontrolled.

It was Raouf Pasha who, in 1879, succeeded Gordon as Governour-General. He had three Europeans as his subordinates—Emin Bey, who, before Gordon left, had been placed in charge of the province of the equator; Lupton Bey, an Englishman, who had followed Gessi as Governour on the Bahr-el-Ghazal; and Slatin Bey, an Austrian, in command at Darfoor.

Raouf had barely been two years at Khartoom when the Mahdi appeared on the scene.

CHAPTER II.

REVOLT OF THE SOUDAN.

The Mahdi, his programme and military successes—Disaster of Hicks Pasha —Osman Digna and engagements near Suakim—English intervention— Gordon at Brussels; starts for Khartoom—Hesitation of England—Further success of the Mahdi—Capture of Berber—Blockade and siege of Khartoom—Organisation of relief expedition under Lord Wolseley—Engagements at Aboo-Klea and Metammeh—Fall of Khartoom and death of Gordon.

PROMPTED either by personal ambition or by religious hatred, the idea of playing the part of "Mahdi" had been acted upon by many an Arab fanatic. Such an idea, at an early age, had taken possession of a certain Soudanese of low birth, a native of Dongola,. by name Mohammed Ahmed. Before openly aspiring to the *rôle* of the regenerator of Islam he had filled several subordinate engagements, notably one under Dr. Pency, the French surgeon-general in the Soudan, who died in 1861. Shortly afterwards he received admittance into the powerful order of the Ghelani dervishes, and then commenced his schemes for stirring up a revolution in defence of his creed. His proceedings did not fail to attract the attention of Gessi Pasha, who had him arrested at Chekka and imprisoned for five months.

Under the government of Raouf he took up his abode upon the small island of Abba, on the Nile above Khartoom, where he gained a considerable notoriety by the austerity of his life and by the fervour of his devotions, thus gradually gaining a high reputation for sanctity. Not only offerings but followers streamed in from every quarter. He became rich as well as powerful, and married a large number of wives, whom he took care to select from the most influential families of the country, principally from those of the opulent slave-dealers in Kordofan and Baggara.

Waiting till May 1881, he then assumed that a propitious time had arrived for the realisation of his plans, and accordingly had himself publicly proclaimed as "Mahdi," inviting every fakir and every religious leader of Islam to come and join him at Abba.

So skilfully was his proclamation conceived that it could hardly fail to attract to him a large number of adherents. From a religious point of view, he fascinated his devotees by his announcement of the imminent fulfilment of prophecies, always popular, declaring the destined supremacy of the reformed religion of Mahomet. In a socialist aspect, he secured the sympathy of the disinherited classes by promises of universal equality and community of goods. On the other hand, he attracted the good-will and support of the traders by reminding them of the tyranny and rapacity of the officials of the Egyptian Treasury, and by declaring that, although it was tabooed by an European Governour, the traffic in slaves was perfectly legitimate. Finally, he appealed to the nationality of all classes of the Soudanese, and exhorted them to

rise in insurrection against the invaders, and to fight
for the independence of their country.

Convinced that it was impolitic to tolerate any
longer the revolutionary intrigues of such an adventurer at the very gates of Khartoom, Raouf Pasha resolved to rid the country of Mohammed and to send
him to Cairo for trial. An expedition was accordingly
despatched to the island of Abba, but unfortunately
the means employed were inadequate to the task.
Only a small body of black soldiers was sent to arrest
the agitator in his quarters, and they, inspired no
doubt by a vague and superstitious dread of a man
who represented himself as the messenger of Allah,
wavered and acted with indecision. Before their officers could rally them to energy, the Mahdi, with a
fierce train of followers, knife in hand, rushed upon
them. and killing many, put the rest to flight;
then, seeing that a renewed assault was likely to
be made, he withdrew the insurgent band into a retreat of safety amongst the mountains of Southern
Kordofan. Henceforth revolt was openly declared.
Such was the condition of things in August 1881.

Chase was given, but every effort to secure the person of the pretended prophet was baffled. A further
attempt was made to arrest him by the Mudir of Fashoda with 1500 men, only to be attended with a still
more melancholy result. After a desperate struggle
the Mudir lay stretched upon the ground, his soldiers
murdered all around him. One single officer, with a
few straggling cavalry, escaped the massacre, and returned to report the fatal news.

The reverse caused an absolute panic in Khartoom,
an intense excitement spreading throughout the Soudan.

" The Governour-General "—so writes M. Vossion,
the French consul at Khartoom—" perfectly terror-
stricken, telegraphed to Cairo for reinforcements, and
his request was urgently supported by all the European
consuls. On the 23d of December a telegram from
the Khedive announced that reinforcements had been
granted, and it was stated, moreover, that Abdellal
Bey's negro regiment had received orders to start; but
the military party, then all-powerful (it was just the
time in which Arabi's *pronunciamento* appeared), be-

lieving that it was a mere pretext for packing off some of the compromised troops out of the way into the Soudan, flatly refused to allow Abdellal Bey and his men to go. In this way the Soudan was left to shift for itself."

Meantime the Mahdi's prestige was ever on the increase, and he soon felt sufficiently strong to assume the offensive. His troops overran Kordofan and Sennaar, advancing on the one hand to the town of Sennaar, which they set on fire, and on the other to El-Obeid, which they placed in a state of siege. In the following July a fresh and more powerful expedition, this time numbering 6000 men, under the command of Yussuf Pasha, left Fashoda and made towards the Mahdi's headquarters. It met with no better fate than the expeditions that had gone before. Unable to withstand the impetuous cavalry charge of the Baggara rebels, it was cut to pieces on the battlefield, all the wounded being massacred and the prisoners beheaded.

The way to Khartoom lay open. There the confusion and dismay were beyond description. Dreading an immediate attack from the rebels, the Government in all haste threw up fortifications, and despatched still more urgent demands to Cairo for assistance, making no concealment of the critical situation in which the 11,000 Christian inhabitants of the town and its garrison of 6000 soldiers were placed. But Cairo was powerless to make any effective movement.

And then it was that the English Government, discerning danger for Egypt in this insurrection of Islam, set to work to act for the Khedive. It told off 11,000 men, and placed them under the command of Hicks Pasha, an officer in the Egyptian service who had made the Abyssinian campaign. At the end of December 1882 this expedition embarked at Suez for Suakim, crossed the desert, reached the Nile at Berber, and after much endurance on the way, arrived at Khartoom.

Before this, El-Obeid had fallen into the Mahdi's power, and there he had taken up his head-quarters. Some trifling advantages were gained by Hicks, but having entered Kordofan with the design of retaking El-Obeid, he was, on the 5th of November 1883, hemmed in amongst the Kasghil passes, and after three days' heroic fighting, his army of about 10,000 men was overpowered by a force five or six times their superior in numbers, and completely exterminated. Hicks Pasha himself, his European staff, and many Egyptian officers of high rank, were among the dead, and forty-two guns fell into the hands of the enemy. Again, not a man was left to carry the fatal tidings to Khartoom.

Rebellion continued to spread. After being agitated for months, the population of the Eastern Soudan also made a rising. Osman Digna, the foremost of the Mahdi's lieutenants, occupied the road between Suakim and Berber, and surrounded Siukat and Tokar; then, having destroyed, one after another, two Egyptian columns that had been despatched for the relief of these towns, he finally cut off the communication between Khartoom and the Red Sea. The tide of insurrection by this time had risen so high that it threatened not only to overthrow the Khedive's authority in the Soudan, but to become the source of serious peril to Egypt itself.

The English Government was consulted, and gave the advice that the Egyptian Government should relieve the beleaguered garrisons, and retiring as quickly as possible from the districts threatened by the Mahdi, should concentrate its forces in the rear of Wady Halfa at the second cataract. Promise of the assistance of English troops was held out, if this line of defence should in its turn be threatened.

Added to this, Colonel Coëtlogon, who had been sent by the Khedive to Khartoom under a commission to report upon the condition of the town, recommended a speedy retreat. According to his account, a third of the soldiers in the garrison were disaffected, the whole of the soldiers were on the worst terms with the population, and the entire situation was most critical. Moreover, unless the retreat were made at once, it would before long become impracticable, and great disaster must ensue.

Thus compelled by stress of circumstances, the Khedive's Government adopted the resolution of concentrating at Khartoom all their troops that were dispersed over the Soudan, and of ultimately evacuating

the town; but at the same time an intimation was
forwarded to the English Government warning them
of the immense difficulties that were involved in the
execution of the measures which were being undertaken in conformity with their advice. Where was
the man who would volunteer to conduct so hazardous
a retreat, through a district given over to revolt and
overrun by bands of rebels? Who was there in all
the Soudan of sufficient influence to negotiate with the
Mahdi, and to secure some guarantee of safety or
some facilities by which the retreat could be accomplished? Raouf Pasha, who, with unwarrantable in-
justice, had been held responsible for former reverses,
had been recalled a year ago; and Abd-el-Kader, who
had succeeded him, had not been in any respect more
fortunate, and was, moreover, quite bewildered by the
complication of dangers which continued to increase.

And now it was that England bethought herself of
the versatile and famous general who once before for
four years had held rule in the Soudan, gaining an
uniform popularity alike with the European residents
and the natives of the place. For the second time
Gordon Pasha should appear upon the scene.

Since 1879, when he had been called upon to resign
the Governour-Generalship of the Soudan, Gordon had
successively occupied posts in India as secretary to
the Viceroy; in China, where he settled the dispute
about Kashgar between Russia and the Celestial Empire; in Mauritius, where he had been the very life-
spring of British influence; at Suez, whither he went
to meet his brave and devoted friend Gessi, who died
there of fever in March 1881; and at the Cape, where
he had been entrusted with the settlement of the
Basuto-land question.

On the 1st of January 1884 he arrived at Brussels,
having been summoned by a telegram from the King
of the Belgians, which reached him at Jerusalem while
he was making a pilgrimage in Palestine. The King
at once gave him an audience, and explained to him
that, as patron of the Congo Association, he was
anxious to renew negotiations that had been opened
some years previously, and that he had sent for him
to induce him to go to Africa and to share with Stanley the mission of introducing European influence into

the districts along the upper part of the river. It was
a task altogether in unison with Gordon's tastes, and
he did not hesitate to accept it, undertaking to be
ready to set out by the steamer on the 6th of February so as to arrive at Vivi as soon as possible to relieve Stanley, who for some months past had been
applying for leave to return to Europe.

But although it was thus arranged that Gordon should
go to Africa, his destination was to be elsewhere than
on the Congo.

Returning for a brief visit to England to take farewell of his sister and friends, he was " interviewed "
at Southampton by one of the staff of the *Pall Mall
Gazette*, which was forthwith published with a sensational article containing Gordon's views on the Egyptian difficulty with the Soudan, a subject which was
very near to his heart, and of which there was no one
more capable of forming a practical judgment than
himself.

Again in Brussels, on the 16th of January, he was
suddenly recalled to England by a despatch from the
Government at home. On the following day he submitted to King Leopold the fact that he had been summoned to go to the Soudan that he might, if possible,
effect the deliverance of the Egyptian troops, making
no concealment of his sentiments that a soldier's first
duty was to his own country, when it appealed to his
devotion. The king at once released him from his engagement.

Not an hour was lost. On the evening of the 18th
he left Charing Cross station, where he was attended
by the Duke of Cambridge, Lord Granville, and Lord
Wolseley, and reached Cairo on the 24th. On the
second day after his arrival, refusing all escort and
accompanied only by his adjutant, Colonel Stewart,
he started for Khartoom by the quickest possible route,
along the Nile to Korosko, and thence by camel-ride
across the desert to Berber. Exactly one month after
quitting London, on the 18th of February, he came
within sight of Khartoom, where he was hailed by the
population as a deliverer, and entered the town amidst
the wildest enthusiasm.

From the very first moment of his entry he displayed
the most prodigious energy ; he held public audiences ;

he instituted a council of notables ; he visited the pris
ons, where for years some hundred wretches, most of
them unjustly, had been huddled together in the most
abject misery ; he administered justice ; he provisioned
the white troops at Omdurman, on the left bank of
the Nile ; he entrusted the defence of Khartoom to the
Soudanese regiments ; he abolished tolls and remitted
payment of arrears of taxes ; he placed boxes in various quarters of the town for the reception of claims
and complaints, and finally issued a proclamation announcing that henceforward the Soudan would be independent, and recognising as legitimate that slavery
which, according to a former decree of the Khedive,
had been definitely prohibited, from November 1889,
through all the districts between Assouan and the great
lakes.

Great was the consternation excited by the latter
clause of this announcement. It was interpreted as
the official re-establishment of the slave traffic and regarded as a scandal by Europe, where it seems to be
imperfectly realised that domestic slavery has from
time immemorial existed, and will continue to exist
for a long period yet to come, in spite of all the de-
crees in the world. It is obvious that if Gordon were
to fulfil his object of evacuating the Soudan, there
must of necessity be involved an acquiescence in this
kind of slavery, and therefore it is altogether beside
the mark for the European philanthropists to criticise
his words without regard to the practical view of the
case.

Months elapsed. There was a continuous inter-
change of despatches between the defender of Khartoom and the English Cabinet in London, carried on
by the intervention of Sir Evelyn Baring, the British
representative at Cairo. They bear evidence of the
indecision of the Government as to the course to be
pursued. The questions were various and complicated.
Should an effort be made to retain the Soudan at any
price? Should it be entirely abandoned? Should any
of the equatorial provinces be reserved for civilisation?
No one seemed competent to give an answer or sug-
gest a policy. So involved and disorderly was the
state of affairs that even Gordon himself, with the best
opportunity of forming an opinion, does not appear to

have had altogether settled views as to what was
best. At first he declared his intention of presenting
himself personally in the camp of the Mahdi, and of
seeking to negotiate with him directly terms upon
which the western provinces might be definitely surrendered. He was forbidden, however, by the authorities at home to persevere in this step, because, it was
alleged, it would entail serious political inconveniences.

He next demanded that after the withdrawal of the
Egyptian troops the office of Governour-General should
be conferred on Zebehr Pasha, formerly a merchant in
the Bahr-el-Ghazal, and the father of Suleiman Zebehr,
who had been taken and executed by Gessi. This
Zebehr, then in confinement in Egypt, Gordon believed was the only man to be found with anything
like sufficient influence to counterbalance the power of
the Mahdi; he was a direct descendant of the Abba
sides, and had obtained a high reputation all through
the country. This proposition was rejected by the
English Cabinet, notwithstanding Sir Evelyn Baring's
approval of it, on the ground that public opinion
would not tolerate its being carried into effect. As
matter of fact, " the Anti-Slavery Society " indignantly
protested against the idea of either seeking or accepting the co-operation of one who had been so actively
concerned in the slave traffic.

Failing thus to obtain authority to execute his mission by means of the only men in the Soudan who
were able to assist his purpose, Gordon appealed for
foreign intervention. He asked that 200 English
soldiers should be sent to Wady Halfa, for the simple
sake of showing that he was really supported by European military influence; he likewise advised that
the route between Suakim and Berber, which was still
occupied by Osman Digna, should be reopened by the
employment of Indian troops.

No reply came to his application, and Gordon almost began to think himself forsaken by those who
had sent him out. He next proposed, without further
delay, to move all the troops and the Egyptian officials
to Berber, under the command of Colonel Stewart;
and feeling that his presence would then be no longer
requisite at Khartoom, he tendered his resignation,
intimating his own intention of retiring, with the steam-

ers, ammunition, and Soudanese troops, to the provinces of the Bahr-el-Ghazal and the Equator (then under the government of Lupton Bey and Emin Bey), and placing them under the protection of the King of the Belgians, whose possessions on the Congo were adjacent.

" Quick ! " wrote Gordon on the 11th of March 1884 — " Quick, or we shall be blockaded."

Sir Evelyn Baring could only answer that the English Government were not contemplating any military movement, at the same time making Gordon understand that he must manage to remain at Khartoom, and that under no pretext whatever was he to betake himself to the south.

Thus time was lost; and while all this tedious circumlocution was going on, the power of the Mahdi and the number of his partisans were being continually augmented; the circle of the rebels was drawing in, closer and closer, around the town, and Osman Digna was still holding the Red Sea route, having on the 11th of February worsted Valentine Baker at Trinkinat and slaughtered more than 2000 of his men, and subsequently captured both Sinkat and Tokar. Some bloody successes, indeed, were gained by General Graham at Teb on February 29th, and at Tamanieh on March 13th, but they were altogether futile in displacing Osman from the mastery of the road.

The advances of the Mahdi's people towards Khartoom became more and more daring. On March 12th the town was completely invested. Four days later a sally was made by a bevy of troops, but they were betrayed by five of their officers, and, stricken with panic, fell back in confusion and with considerable loss. Thenceforward the place was exposed to continual assaults from the besiegers; the blockade became closer, and soon the bombardment was almost incessant, shells falling into the centre of the town, though without doing serious damage or creating much alarm.

On the 27th of April the outlying station of Mesalimmeh, with all its ammunition and a steamer, made a surrender. At the end of May Berber fell into the hands of the enemy, whereby all communication between Egypt and the Soudan was interrupted. There was no longer any question about evacuating Khartoom. The sole consideration was by what means to rescue its defenders.

Impossible was it for England any longer to remain a passive looker-on ; the demand for military interference was imperative. The voice of the press, enforcing public opinion, cried vehemently for the deliverance of Gordon, and the British Government decided upon sending out an expedition of relief. Parliament voted £300,000 towards the expenses, and Lord Wolseley, the hero of Tel-el-Kebir, was appointed Commander-in-Chief, and started for Egypt, where his forces arrived during August 1884.

There had been no cessation of the fighting at Khartoom ; for months not a day had passed without a skirmish. The garrison soon reckoned a loss of 700 men. During an attack upon Gatarneb upon the 10th of July, Saati Bey, one of Gordon's bravest associates, was killed, with three of his officers, while Colonel Stewart, who took part in the engagement, escaped only with the utmost difficulty.

Hope now began to flag and misgivings to arise lest help should not arrive in time. As a consequence, symptoms of disaffection became too apparent, not only amongst the besieged troops, but especially amongst the Egyptian officers.

Military matters in Lower Egypt were pressed forward with all possible despatch. Portable steamers and whale-boats manned by Canadians, accustomed to their own rapids, were launched upon the Nile. The expeditionary forces, composed of picked troops and a volunteer camel corps, were not long in starting, and Lord Wolseley, with his staff, arrived at Wady Halfa on the 5th of October. The first cataract was passed, and by the beginning of December the advanced guard reached Debbah, forty miles from Dongola.

By the end of the month an entrenched camp was formed at Korti, and from thence were despatched two columns—one, under General Earle along the river, to entice the enemy towards Berber ; the other, under General Sir H. Stewart, across the desert straight for Khartoom, in order to assist Gordon to hold out until the main body of the troops should arrive.

So opened the fatal year 1885. The situation at Khartoom had become desperate.

On the 17th of January Stewart first fell in with the Arabs, and gave battle at the wells of Abou-Klea, which were defended by 7000 of the Mahdi's men, against 1350 under the English general. At the outset the engagement was indecisive, but ultimately the Arabs were out-manœuvred, and the column proceeded on its march. The next day a second battle took place at Metammeh, where Stewart was killed, with several of his leading officers, as well as Messrs. Herbert and Cameron, the correspondents respectively of the *Morning Post* and *Standard* newspapers.

The command of the column devolved upon Colonel Wilson. Notwithstanding its heavy losses, it was still victorious, and continued its way, reaching El Gooba the same evening, where it entrenched. This was on the Nile, about seventy-five miles below Khartoom. It had been a forced march, skilfully conducted and brilliantly accomplished; but the end seemed in view, and the courage and energy of the British soldiers rose nobly to the occasion.

On the 23d four iron-plated steamers hove in sight. What could these be? and whence and for what purpose had they come? The explanation was not far off; Gordon had sent them from Khartoom. Although the town had been besieged for months, the assailants continually increasing in numbers and ferocity, it still held its own. The Mahdi had taken up his position before its gates, superintending the operations of the siege, and himself leading an attack upon the entrenched camp at Omdurman, in which, although he was repulsed, he took one of his adversary's boats. Gordon, however, did not give in; with a presence of mind that never failed, he persevered in facing every danger from without, whilst all along he had perpetually to be upon his guard against the inertness and still worse, the treacherous spirit of mutiny of a portion of his own troops. And now the announcement came that the long-looked-for succour was at hand; he would hasten to send some recognition of its advance, and accordingly he sent out, laden with provisions, the four steamers that had appeared in view.

Without losing time, Sir C. Wilson and Colonel

Stewart, with twenty men of the Sussex regiment, embarked on two of these steamers, and on the next day
left the entrenchments at El Gooba and started for
Khartoom. It was a time of deep suspense. On the
28th they came in sight of the beleaguered town. All
was silence. There was no sound nor sign of welcome.
Uneasy and in bewilderment, they at once hove to, but
only to find themselves under a close fire from the ram-
parts, over which, floating from the Government palace, was seen the green banner of the Madhi.

Too late ! The relief had indeed come too late. Eight-
and-forty hours before, Khartoom had been surrendered
by treachery to the rebels ; the great and blameless hero
was dead, shot down under the acacias of the Government buildings, on his way to the Austrian Consul's,
to take his last farewell of his good friend Hansal.

CHAPTER III.

THE EQUATORIAL PROVINCES.

The land of rivers—The Bongo—The Dinka—Roumbek—Meshraer-Rek and
Amadi—Lupton Bey—The province of the Equator—Rapids of the Upper
Nile—Paradise of botanists—The Makraka—The Bari—The Latooka—
Lado, Doufile, and Wadelai—Emin Bey.

THE two most southern provinces that had been
brought under the dominion of Egypt, and entrusted
to the subordinate rule of European pashas and beys,
were those of the Bahr-el-Ghazal and of the Equator.
The former of these had come under the command of
Lupton Bey, and the latter had been assigned to the
charge of Emin Bey.

By the victorious progress of the Mahdi's bands,
both provinces alike had been cut off from communication with Khartoom, and consequently with Cairo
and Suakim.

The authority of the Khedive had hitherto been sufficiently maintained by the establishment of a limited
number of fortified stations defended by small garrisons, varying from 100 to 200 men. Placed along
the watercourses in positions selected either for their
political or strategical advantages, these stations were

for the most part merely enclosures protected by palisades or by trenches, to resist any sudden outbreak on the part of the natives. The majority of the men composing the garrisons were liberated slaves belonging to the various Soudanese tribes, and were commanded sometimes by Egyptian, sometimes by native officers.

The province of the Bahr-el-Ghazal, as its name implies, includes the larger portion of the basin watered by that important tributary of the Nile. Eliseé Reclus was quite justified in designating it "the land of rivers," inasmuch as the Gazelle, with its great affluents, the Rohl, the Rua, the Dyoor, the Bahr-el-Arab, and the countless sub-affluents which run into them, extends over a vast triangular area, and forms a perfect labyrinth of streams. The soil is exceptionally fertile, the flora is rich and rare, the crops are abundant, elephants abound in the virgin forests, and herds of cattle swarm in the populated parts. It may be avowed that there are few regions in Africa tha hold out greater promise for the future, when the time shall come for the culture of the natural products of the earth to supersede the traffic in flesh and blood, and when a systematic communication for commerce has been opened between its three or four millions of inhabitants and the civilised world.

First amongst the explorers of the Bahr-el-Ghazal were the Frenchmen Pency, Lejean, and Poncet, the English Petherick, and the Italians Miami and Piaggia ; but although their discoveries were diversified and interesting, they must be reckoned as comparatively incomplete. It was Dr. Schweinfurth who could first lay claim to a really scientific delineation of the country, of which his elaborate work, "The Heart of Africa," must long be regarded as the standard of geographical knowledge. He devotes several chapters to the description of the various tribes, including the Nueir, the Agar, the Dinka, the Dyoor, the Bongo, the Moroo, the Galo, and the Sheir. Of these the most considerable are the Bongo and the Dinka.

It was about 1850 when the Khartoomers first made their way among the Bongo. They found the country split up into small independent communities, all in a state of anarchy ; consequently there was little dif-

ficulty in reducing it to subjection, and in establishing
settlements in the divided territory, so providing for
a system of raids to secure both ivory and slaves for
traffic.   Reduced by two-thirds, the population has
for the most part concentrated itself around the *zeribas*,
where it is devoted almost exclusively to agriculture,
contributing largely to the support of the garrisons.

No doubt it is to the scantiness of the larger kinds
of cattle that the Bongo, in their subjugation, owe
much of their comparatively peaceable relations with
" the Turks," as they ordinarily call the owners of
the *zeribas;* and the same reason may probably account
for the feeble resistance that they made.   Their domestic animals, in fact, include little beyond goats,
dogs, and poultry.

So essentially are they agriculturists that they may
be said to depend entirely upon the products of the
soil for their subsistence.   Men and women alike
labour in the fields, cultivating sorghum as the principal crop, although tobacco is grown well-nigh everywhere throughout the country.   They have a singular
aptitude for smiths' work.   Iron is abundant, and almost by instinct the people have learned to utilise it.
Their tools are of the rudest description, yet they produce a large variety of articles, such as spear-heads,
arrows, rings, bells, buttons, clasps, pins, and knives,
that for workmanship might compare not unfavour-
ably with any that are made in Europe.   The smelt-
ing season commences when the harvest is housed and
the rainy season is over.   To their skill in the manipulation of iron must be added, although in an inferior
degree, a certain dexterity in the carving of wood, as
is exhibited in various utensils and articles of furni-
ture, notably in the little four-legged stools with which
every household is provided.

As regards their phsyical appearance, the Bongo are
of medium height.   Their skin is of a reddish brown,
not dissimilar in colour to that of the soil on which
they reside.   The men, as a rule, wear nothing but a
little apron of skin or other material attached to their
girdle, the women contenting themselves with a leafy
bough, or not unfrequently with a tuft of grass.   Van-
ity induces some of them to load themselves with neck-
laces, whilst on any occasion of a feast they deck the

head with feathers, the rest of the body being entirely unclothed.

North of Bongo-land lies the territory of the Dyoor, situated in which is the *zeriba* of Ghattas, one of the largest in the whole country. Still farther north is the district occupied by the Dinka, a tribe which has recently played a prominent part in the history of the province.

So numerous are the Dinka, and so extensive are their lands, that in all probability they will continue to hold their own, whatever may be the confusion of the various tribes by which they are surrounded. They may be classed amongst the tallest and strongest as well as the darkest of negro races. Tattooing is practised, but only by the men. The observation made by Barth, that many heathen tribes consider clothing more necessary for men than for women, is not applicable to them, inasmuch as, according to their views, any attire, however limited in quantity, is unworthy of the stronger sex; whilst, on the other hand, their women are scrupulously covered with two aprons of skins reaching to their ankles. It is to be remarked that bows and arrows are unknown among them; their most effective weapon is the lance, although they frequently arm themselves with sticks or clubs.

The Dinka do not live in what are ordinarily known as villages, their dwellings consisting of small groups of huts scattered in farmsteads over the cultivated plains, the huts for the most part being solidly built and spacious, frequently forty feet in diameter. The people are clean in their homes, and in culinary matters better skilled than the Arabs, or even than the Egyptians themselves; in fact, in the choice and preparation of their food they are in advance of all other African tribes. Crocodile flesh they refuse to eat; iguanas, frogs, and mice they never touch; but, like true European connoisseurs, they use the turtle for making soup; the hare is considered a great delicacy. As to cannibalism, they would have as great a horror of it as ourselves.

Their domestic animals are oxen, sheep, goats and dogs; but, for some unexplained cause, they have no poultry. The oxen are of the zebu kind, of small size, and for the most part white, or nearly white; they are

brought together from separate districts into one large
enclosure, and the sole ambition of the owner seems to
be to increase his stock ; they are regarded with a sort
of reverence, and whenever a Dinka has been robbed
of one of them, either by rapine or by death, there is
hardly any sacrifice which he is not ready to make to
repair his loss.

So far as regards their race, their mode of life, and
their customs, the Dinka have all the elements of national unity ; but they fail on account of their several
tribes making war upon each other, and submitting to
be enlisted as instruments of plunder by foreign intruders. Nevertheless, the Khartoomers have hitherto
been unable to bring them into subjection. A considerable number of Dinka slaves, remarkable alike for
their fine stature and native courage, were enlisted
into the army of the Soudan ; and Adam Pasha, who
in 1870 commanded the Soudan forces, was himself a
Dinka by birth.

Of all the *zeribas* established in the country by
Khartoom traders the most important is Roumbek,
formerly the headquarters of an Egyptian *Mudirieh*.
The population of the settlement is estimated by Dr.
Felkin to be about 3000, whilst he further reckons the
adjacent villages to make up an aggregate of hardly
less than 30,000 inhabitants. It is peculiar to the
district that the wearing of clothes is regarded as a religious privilege, and no woman, except she is married
to an Arab, has a right to appear with any kind of covering whatever. A fortified post named Bor defends
the eastern portion of the settlement.

On the north is situated the cluster of warehouses
known as Meshra-er-Rek (or landing-place of the Rek),
which is the starting-point for all caravans proceeding
on their way to the basin of the Bahr-el-Ghazal. Up
to the date of the recent wars a steamer from Khartoom
periodically ascended to this point.

South of the Dinka territory, in the country of the
Monoo, situated amidst extensive fields of millet and
sesame, is another important trade-centre, the fortified
village of Amadi, on the banks of the Yeï. It is one
of the chief ivory-depôts ; at one time it had the am-
biguous reputation of being the *zeriba* whence the ha-
rems of Egypt and Arabia were supplied with eunuchs.

The first European Governour of the Bahr-el-Ghazal was Gessi Pasha, who in 1878, after suppressing the revolt of Suleiman Zebehr and purging the country of its hordes of slave-dealers, took up his residence, in the very camp of his adversary, at Dehm Suleiman, which has since developed into the largest township on the Upper Nile. Dehm Idrees, to the east, in the Golo country, has also of late grown into a store of such proportions that at the end of 1883, when Bohndorf, the companion of Dr. Junker, was passing along that way, he was informed that the accumulated stock of ivory exceeded 200 tons.

In 1881 Gessi was succeeded in the government of the province by Lupton Bey.

Frank Lupton, a native of Ilford, in Essex, was born in 1853. Being of an adventurous nature, he entered the navy at an early age. In 1878, having been in command of a steamer on the Red Sea, between Suakim and Teddah, he formed a resolution that he would visit Central Africa. By the advice of a friend he tendered his services to Gordon, who invited him to Khartoom, and there offered him the charge of a flotilla that was about to be sent to the relief of Emin Bey and Gessi Pasha, who were in the south, shut in by " the Sett," that notorious grass-barrier which blockades the Upper Nile.

This mission accomplished, Lupton was associated with Emin in the administration of the Equator, and afterwards, upon Gessi's removal, was raised by the Khedive to the rank of Bey and appointed to the Governourship of the Bahr-el-Ghazal, where, such were the activity and intelligence that he brought to bear, he made that rich district, which had hitherto been a heavy burden to Egypt, become a source of profit, so that his budget for 1883 showed a surplus for the year of nearly £100,000. Unfortunately the events of the year's close put a check for an indefinite time upon that promise of prosperity.

The other province—the province of the Equator—next demands to be described.

Extending along both banks of the Nile from its egress from Lake Albert right away to Lado, this includes the northern portion of Unyoro and the territories of the **Shooli**, Madi, Bari, Latooka, Makraka, and Moroo.

Travellers seem to be unanimous in representing the Equator province as a picturesque, fertile, well-populated, fairly healthy, and promising reigon. Its productions are caoutchouc, various kinds of gum, wax, vegetable butter, cotton, skins, fruits, grain, and vegetables, in addition to the ivory which is to be obtained in large abundance. Europeans can stand the climate provided they lead an active life, and would be even more likely to maintain good health if opportunities were secured for periodical recruiting in sanatoriums which might easily be erected in the hills to the south and east.

From north to south the Equator is traversed by the Nile, receiving the Assua on the right and the Yeï on the left, and affording all the way from Lake Albert to Doufilé a channel from fifteen to thirty feet deep, capable of being navigated at all seasons by the largest boats. Between Doufilé and Lado navigation is arrested by a succession of rapids at Fola, Yerbora, Gudji, Makebo, Teremo-Garbo, and Djenkoli-Garbo, which, although they may permit boats to be carried over in the time of floods, are utterly impassable when the water is low.

Westward from the Nile, at some distance, the chain of the Blue Mountains is in sight, stretching towards the north, and forming the boundary of the Congo basin. The range is not lofty, but it presents a number of conspicuous peaks, which have been severally named after Schweinfurth, Junker, Speke, Emin, Baker, Gordon, and Gessi. On its western slope are the sources of the Welle. Its soil gradually rises through the country of the Shooli and Latooka until it is finally overhung by granite crags elevated more than 3000 feet above the level of the river.

Considered as a whole, the province may be described as one prolonged productive valley, divided into broad plains rich with luxuriant pasturage for the innumerable flocks, studded over with forests of splendid growth, adorned with natural parks, where the trees are fine and the glades are open, and relieved ever and again by undulations, every eminence of which is crowned by a well-placed village. The

land of the Shooli, or more especially the district of
Fatiko, has been called " the paradise of botanists," so
diversified and so abundant is its flora.

Most important amongst the native tribes are the
Makraka and Madi, on the west of the Nile, and the
Bari and Latooka, on the east.

The Makraka really belong to the powerful Niam-
niam people, whose vast territories extend south-west-
wards as far as the Congo basin. They are most ex-
pert cultivators of the soil, and their substantial prosperity has secured them a foremost standing amongst
the tribes. Their courage is notorious, although a
suspicion that they are given to cannibalism has caused
them to be regarded with a certain degree of terror.
When the Egyptian rulers are enlisting soldiers they
prefer, as a rule, the Makraka to any others.

Like the Makraka, the Madi, their neighbours on
the same bank of the Nile, are mainly occupied in
agriculture. They grow excellent tobacco, in addition
to the many kinds of fruits and vegetables that have
been introduced by Arabs and Europeans, whilst
around their villages the fields of sesame and sorghum
stretch away far as the eye can reach. Characterised
by hospitality, they have ever a ready welcome for a
stranger, and amongst them, as indeed with the Makraka, the traveller's safety is so assured that he may
approach them, cane in hand, with no other escort
than his porters.

More warlike as a tribe, the Bari soldiers are re-
puted to be the bravest and fiercest of all the river-
settlers along the Nile. Both Gondokoro, the first
residence of Baker when he was Governour, and Lado,
subsequently built by Gordon, are situated in their
territory. It is probable that the atrocities perpetrated
against them by the Khartoomers have inflamed their
animosity towards the invaders of their home, as for
a long period Gondokoro was a pandemonium, a perfect den of thieves and assassins, glutted with the
cattle and the slaves that they had carried off in plunder from the surrounding parts. The arrival of Europeans happily put a limit to this state of things, but
it must be long before the memory of the enormities
can be entirely obliterated.

Similarly to the Dinka in the Bahr-el-Ghazal, the

Bari in the Equator are a pastoral people, being owners of large herds of diminutive cattle; they likewise regard the cow with a species of reverence, and, like the Dinka too, they go unclothed, esteeming the wearing of any garment a degradation of masculine dignity. The French traveller, Peney, observes that they have a dread of clothing, and relates of himself that in order to secure a good reception at their hands he was obliged to divest himself of every garment. As a rule, no doubt, they are a fine race of men, remarkable for well-proportioned limbs and for dignity of carriage. Their villages and the interior of their huts are models of cleanliness, the huts very frequently having granaries attached, made of wicker, protected by thatch, and raised upon a kind of platform.

Away to the west dwell the Latooka, a tribe which in the opinion of most travellers is of Galla origin. Ravenstein remarks that their dialect resembles that of the Masaï. Baker, during his residence amongst them, visited several of their largest villages, and considers that the people are the finest savages he ever met with; their average height is six feet, their physiognomy is pleasant, and in comparison with neighbouring tribes their manners are polished. They are open-hearted, cheerful, and always ready for a laugh.

A peculiarity of the tribe that arrests attention is the *coiffure* of the men. It is arranged in the form of a helmet, and is most delicately manipulated with burnished copper and bits of red and blue glass, intermixed with shells, and surmounted by a plume of ostrich feathers. European ladies might be astonished to learn that a period of eight or ten years is scarcely sufficient for the arrangement and adorning of a Latooka's hair.

Tarrangole, the capital of the country, was also visited by Baker. It is quite a town, and at that time contained 3000 houses. Not only was the whole place environed by a palisade of iron-wood, but separate dwellings were protected by small fortified enclosures of their own, and raised platforms three stories high were erected at intervals to serve as watch-towers whence sentinels might give alarm in time of danger.

With the Latooka, as with the Dinka and the Bari, cattle is the staple of their wealth, and thousands of heads may be seen around every important village; they are kept in huge kraals. A Latooka's main possessions are his wives and his oxen; of these, in time of battle, he will make languid efforts to protect the former, in contrast with the desperate energy with which he will defend the latter.

It is in the Equator province that the exertions of European Governours have attained the best and apparently the most lasting success; here it was that Baker, Gordon, and Emin alike established many civilising centres, the majority of which are still in existence. Lado, the station by which Gondokoro was replaced as the Governour's residence, is quite a good-looking town; its buildings are of brick, roofed with iron, and it boasts an ample quay and promenade. Redjaf, Bedden, and Kirri lie to the south, all of them on the left bank of the river.

Several fortified settlements have been made among the Madi, the foremost being Doufilé, in an excellent strategic and commercial position, a little above the confluence of the Assua. This is the extreme point which steamers can reach from Lake Albert and the Upper Nile, as farther progress is barred by the Fola rapids. Below the rapids, on the river-bank, are the small forts of Laboré and Muggi.

There are also several important stations in the district of the Shooli. On the bank of the river is Wadelaï, which for the last two years has been occupied instead of Lado as the abode of the Governour, and which will henceforth be associated with the name of Emin Bey. In the interior are Fatibek, to the east of Doufilé; Faloro, a populous mart, one of the granaries of the Egyptian Soudan; and Fatiko, in the heart of a picturesque and healthy country.

Formerly the Egyptians had a settlement in the north of Unyoro, inhabited by the Lango tribe, named Foweira, which they abandoned; but they still retain Magungo, in a situation overlooking the spot where the Nile, after forming the imposing Murchison Falls, flows into Lake Albert. In the Aloori country, on the western shore of the lake, they have Mahagi, near which are some hot sulphur springs; and at a considerable distance to the west, in the middle of the Makraka country, close to the sources of the Yeï, are the

two small outposts of Uandi and Makraki-Sougaire.
All these stations owe their establishment to Baker or
Gordon, Englishmen, or to Emin, the German, who
have successively been Governours since 1872.

Emin Effendi, whom Gordon, on leaving the Soudan
in 1879, raised to the rank of Bey, and placed in
charge of the province of the Equator, was born at
Oppeln, in Prussian Silesia, on the 28th of March 1840.
His real name is Edward Schnitzer. After completing
his studies at Berlin, Vienna, and Paris, and having
obtained the degree of doctor both in medicine and in
natural science, he went in 1869 to Albania, where he
found an engagement in the Ottoman service at Scu-
tari. Some years later, when Gordon assumed the
government of the Soudan, Dr. Schnitzer, under the
name of Emin Effendi, accompanied him as medical
officer, and never failed to distinguish himself in any
business that was entrusted to him. Under commission of the Governour, he was sent to Mtesa, king of
Uganda, and to Kabrega, king of Unyoro, and succeeded in securing them both as allies. In all his expeditions he diligently made scientific notes, the substance of which appeared at intervals between 1878 and
1883 in the " Mittheilungen " of the Geographical Institute of Gotha.

Under his administration the province of the Equator went on well. He assiduously continued the work
that Gordon had begun, opening fresh communications,
making new settlements, stimulating the industry of
the population, and securing their support in the suppression of abuses. Last but not least, he was successful in gaining for the Egyptian Government a surplus revenue where hitherto there had been only a
deficit.

In a letter to Dr. Felkin at Edinburgh in 1883, Emin
Bey said that although for some years he had not received any assistance from Khartoom, yet he had persevered in insisting on the cultivation of cotton, indigo,
sugar-cane, and rice, and had established numerous
farms for ostrich-breeding and cattle-breaking; and
that, in spite of the heavy outlay entailed by the formation of new roads, his budget for 1880 showed for the
first time a surplus of £8000. " If only," he added, "I
could get a few Europeans to support me, and a small

EMIN PASHA.

subsidy for the purchase of seed and agricultural implements, I have not the slightest doubt that in four or five years I could realise an annual profit of £20,000, exclusive of ivory, which is the monopoly of the Government."

Such were the hopes he cherished. The disastrous events at Khartoom checked them all. From the first Emin had his forebodings. In March 1882 he went to Khartoom to put Raouf Pasha on his guard, and even offered to go and try to conciliate the Mahdi in a personal interview; his alarm was regarded as exaggerated, his proposal was declined, and he was instructed to return to his post and to do his utmost for the interests of the province. He left Khartoom on the 15th of June, not again to return.

Results have demonstrated how great was the error of distrusting his far-sightedness; it was a mistake not to attempt, while perhaps there was still time, to avert catastrophe by making use of his talents for negotiation.

CHAPTER IV.

JUNKER AND CASATI.

The Welle—Biography and travels of Dr. Junker—The Niam-niam—Dr. Junker and the Niam-niam chiefs—Captain Casati—The Monbuttoo—Cannibalism—Dr. Junker in the Aruwimi basin and at Ali-Kobo's *zeriba*—Bad news from the north—Junker and Casati with Emin Bey at Lado.

EMIN BEY and Lupton Bey were not the only Europeans who were blocked in the heart of Africa by the Mahdi's victories. At that period the Russian, Dr. Junker, and Captain Casati, the Italian, were still farther south, investigating the basin of the Welle.

The Welle is the name given in its upper course to the most important of the right-hand tributaries of the Congo; it is a powerful stream, which, in length and volume, may be compared to the Danube; it receives nearly all the water from the region situated between the northern Congo and the ridge-line whence the Bahr-el-Ghazal, the Shary, the Benwé, and their several affluents take their source.

As the result of the explorations of recent years its

upper section is beginning to be fairly well known. It has been ascertained that, under the name of the Kibbi, it has its source on the western slope of the low range of the Blue Mountains, somewhat to the west of Wadelaï ; that it then flows from east to west for nearly 1000 miles, taking a slight curve, and being parallel to the Congo. Amongst many affluents, the principal are the Garamba, the Duru, the Bomokandi, the Werré, the Mbima, and the Mbomo.

What becomes of the Welle after its confluence with the last of the above tributaries must as yet be held as an open question. Various solutions have been suggested during the last fifteen years. It has been stated that it finds an outlet into the Shary, into the Ogoowé, or into the Aruyimi ; it has been asserted that it flows into a Lake Liba, the existence of which is enigmatical, a second Lake Tchad ; and finally, it has been maintained that it joins the Itimbiri and the Mongalla, inferior affluents of the Congo. A conclusive answer to the question has still to be awaited ; future observation can alone decide ; nevertheless geographers are now almost unanimous in accepting the hypothesis promulgated nearly three years since by the writer of this volume, which would identify the Welle of Schweinfurth and Junker with the mighty Wbangi, whose confluence with the Congo a little south of the Equator the Belgian Captain Hanssens was the first to discover, and which was ascended by Grenfell, a missionary from England, beyond the Zungo rapids. "It may fairly be believed," says M. Elisée Reclus, "that the Welle continues to flow from east to west below its confluence with the Mbomo, and that, after describing a southwesterly curve parallel to the Congo, it joins the Wbangi about 250 miles from the spot where Junker left its course." *

It must be added that Dr. Junker, during his explorations of the river-basin, extending over three years, has done much to verify this hypothesis ; he has, moreover, by his numerous itineraries, provided the material for a map of this unknown region, and has amassed such valuable scientific information as must make the history of his travels, now in preparation, a geographical contribution of the highest importance.

* A. J. Wauters, *Le Mouvement géographique*, 1885-1887.

This eminent explorer, Wilhelm Junker (to whom the present volume is dedicated), was born at Moscow on the 6th of April 1840. He studied at Gottingen, St. Petersburg, Berlin, and Prague. His earlier travels were in Iceland, but in 1874, abandoning the frozen zone for tropical Africa, he made various excursions into Tunis and Lower Egypt, whence he proceeded to the Natron Lakes and Fayoum, and crossing to the Red Sea, went in succession in Suakim, Kassala, and Khartoom; then, having explored the Sobat, he made his way to Gondokoro. The year 1877 found him in the basin of the Bahr-el-Ghazal and the Yeï.

After four years' wanderings, with many useful results, the Doctor returned to Europe for rest; but the attraction of African life was too strong to be resisted, and in 1878 he started again by way of Suakim for Berber, going on to Khartoom, where he arrived in January 1880.

This time he had a definite purpose in view: he had determined to explore the almost unknown regions that were watered by the Welle, and set his mind on following its course as far as possible to the west, that he might put to rest the dubious question of its ultimate issue. Accompanied by a specialist in natural history, M. Frédéric Bohndorf, and by a young negro whom he had taken with him to Europe after his first journey, he made his way to the heart of the continent, halting at the *zeribas* Meshra-er-Rek, Dyoor-Ghattas, Uau, Dehm Suleiman, and Dehm Bekir, and finally taking up his quarters, as the base of his operations, at the residence of Ndoruma, a powerful Niam-niam chief in the Congo basin.

The Niam-niam are that strange people whose existence, surrounded by mystery and legend, was attested by the very earliest adventurers into the Soudan. They were the famous "men with tails" in whom certain *savants* imagined that they had discovered the missing link between ape and man; and such was their weird repute that Soudanese and Nubians alike associated their name with all the savage devilry that imagination could conjure up. The apellation by which we distinguish them is borrowed from the dialect of the Dinka, and signifies "great eaters," an illusion only too suggestive of cannibal propensities.

Dr. Schweinfurth was the first to give any detailed particulars about the Niam-niam, whose general aspect excited his repeated wonder. He writes :—" No traveller could possibly find himself for the first time surrounded by a group of true Niam-niam without being almost forced to confess that all he had hitherto witnessed amongst the various races of Africa was comparatively tame and uninteresting." He thus describes a Niam-niam warrior :—" The stranger, as he gazes on him, may well behold in this true son of the African wilderness every attribute of the wildest savagery that may be conjured up by the boldest flight of fancy. . . . I have seen the wild Bishareen and other Bedouins of the Nubian desert, I have gazed with admiration upon the stately war-dress of the Abyssinians, I have been riveted with surprise at the supple forms of the mounted Baggara, but nowhere in any part of Africa have I ever come across a people that in every attitude and in every motion exhibited so thorough a mastery over all the circumstances of war or of the chase as the Niam-niam. Other nations in comparison seemed to me to fall short in the perfect ease, I might almost say dramatic grace, that characterised their every movement." *

Equally well may the Niam-niam be described as a nation of hunters or a nation of agriculturists. As with most African races, the cultivation of the soil is carried on by the women ; not that this involves any excessive labour, inasmuch as the natural productiveness of the soil, the exuberance of which in some districts is unsurpassed, makes all culture exceptionally easy. The whole land is pre-eminently rich in many products that conduce to the direct maintenance of life, and eleusine, sweet potatoes, yams, manioc, and colocasiæ may be said to grow all but spontaneously.

Speaking generally, it may be said that they have no cattle ; cows, goats, and sheep are hardly known otherwise than by report. The acme, however, of human enjoyment for a Naim-niam would seem to be *meat*, every one is a hunter, and it may be, within certain limits, a cannibal. The cry that resounds in all their campaigns is, " Meat, meat ! "

As to cannibalism, there is no doubt that it has been

* Schweinfurth, " Heart of Africa," vol. ii. p. 12.

attributed to them by all the surrounding nations, and perhaps few could venture to dispute this widespread testimony ; on the other hand, it must be acknowledged that travellers have met with Niam-niam chiefs who vehemently repudiate the idea of eating human flesh. At the same time, it is asserted of other chiefs that they have openly and without reserve, if not ostentatiously, confessed their predilection ; whilst it is stated, in addition, that they adorn themselves with the teeth of the victims they have devoured, and exhibit their skulls conspicuously among their hunting-trophies. Moreover, it is said that the fat of the human body is in general use.

The country inhabited by the Niam-niam is so immense that as yet it has been but partially explored. The ridge between the basins of the Nile and the Congo forms pretty nearly a central line through the whole. Eastwards their population extends to Lake Albert and the Nile ; westwards they probably reach to the north of the French Congo, to the sources of the Benwé ; and to the south they occupy the greater portion of the Congo Free State, on the banks of the Welle.

They have no national unity. Schweinfurth counted no less than thirty-eight independent chiefs in the country north of Tankasi, and a still larger number was visited by Junker, whose travels carried him along both banks of the Welle ; he makes special mention of Ndoruma and Semio, well-known rulers, in whose domains he established stations, and further speaks of Bankangaï and Kanna, who reside in the Bomokandi basin within the limits of the Congo St; te, as the most powerful chiefs that he came across throughout his entire journey.

Of towns in an ordinary sense, or even of villages, the Niam-niam have none. Their huts are grouped in little clusters, which are scattered about the cultivated lands and separated from each other by tracks of wilderness more or less extensive, broken by forests and savannahs that are the haunts of innumerable herds of elephants and antelopes. The country everywhere is picturesque, and in the valleys, where heat and moisture are combined, the scene is often charming as fairy-land.

M. Bohndorf pronounces the climate to be superior to that of Java or India, and considers that when the

ameliorating appliances of civilisation shall have been
introduced, the mortality of the white man will be
comparatively small.

Personal security is nowhere more assured than in
the majority of the districts farther north. The European has only to use a little tact and he may travel
quite unarmed. Except on a few excursions when he
obtained an escort either from Gessi Pasha or from
Soudanese traders, Dr. Junker made all his journeys
accompanied only by a few lads and porters. His sole
precaution, before entering the territory of an unknown chief, was to send some messengers in advance
to announce his arrival, and to declare that his intentions were quite peaceable. A few presents went
far to conciliate the favour of the chief, not only obtaining permission for the white man's entry, but
procuring the loan of guides to conduct him onwards.

By such prudent policy, and probably through the
absolute want of anything like military display, Junker was able to travel for more than two years in the
Niam-niam country, going southwards beyond the
Bomokandi, and westwards to a little above the confluence of the Mbomo, in the Bandchia tribe, where
Ali Kobo, a merchant, has established a *zeriba* for the
ivory-trade. To the east he penetrated into the abode
of the Monbuttoo, where, in August 1882, at the village of Tangasi, he met the Italian explorer, Casati.

Gaetano Casati, a native of Monza, in Upper Italy,
was serving as a captain of *Bersaglieri*, when it was
proposed to him by M. Camperio, the founder of the
Italian Society for the Exploration of Africa, that he
should join his countryman, Gessi Pasha, in the Bahr-
el-Ghazal, as correspondent to the geographical review, *L'Exploratore*.

The offer was accepted ; and on December 24, 1879,
Casati embarked at Genoa for Suakim, whence he
continued his way to the interior, where he has resided ever since, staying successively in the lands of
the Dyoor, the Dinka, and the Makraka, and proceeding, after Gessi had taken his departure, westward of
Lake Albert into the district of the Monbuttoo.

This interesting negro race, the Monbuttoo, thirty
years back, was not even known to have an existence ;
it has now been brought into notoriety by Dr. Schwein-

furth, the first European to make his way so far in that direction. According to the estimate he formed about them, they are a people that must take a foremost rank amongst African tribes. They are a noble race, with a higher grade of culture than their savage neighbours. They exhibit a public spirit and a national pride, and certainly possess an intelligence and judgment such as few Africans can boast. Their word is sure, and their friendship lasting. The Nubians who reside among them can never say enough in praise of their fidelity, their military qualities, and their personal courage.

A marked development characterises their capabilities ; and as potters, wood-carvers and boat-builders, they are second to no tribe on the entire continent. It is, however, in their architecture that the versatility of their artistic faculty most reveals itself. Alike in size, in arrangement, and in decoration, their buildings excel all that travellers in Central Africa have found elsewhere ; the great hall in the palace of Munza, who was king of the Monbuttoo at the time of Schweinfurth's visit, was not much short of a hundred feet long, fifty feet wide, and forty feet high ; not unlike the central portion of a large railway-station, its vaulted roof being supported on three long rows of pillars formed of polished wood.

The Monbuttoo sovereigns enjoy far higher prerogatives than the rulers of the Niam-niam. Besides the monoply of ivory, they claim regular contributions, levied upon the products of the soil. In addition to his bodyguard proper, Munza was always attended by a large *suite*, never leaving his residence without being accompanied by a retinue of some hundred men, and preceded by a long array of trumpeters, drummers, and couriers with large iron bells.

And yet, advanced as they seem in some respects towards civilisation, and eminent as travellers declare them to be for hospitality, they are a people amongst whom the practice of cannibalism is most flagrant. They are skilled sportsmen, and hunt elephants, buffaloes, and antelopes ; they take the guinea-fowl, the francolin, and the bustard in snares ; but there is no game for which they have a keener relish than for human flesh.

Living in a state of perpetual warfare with the inferior tribes of the Aruwimi basin, their neighbours on the south, they have hunting-grounds which are inexhaustible in the supply of this coveted food. The dead bodies of those who fall in battle are immediately distributed to be cut up, and are dried upon the field, preparatory to being carried away. Every family would seem to have its supply, and human fat is universally employed for domestic purposes. According to Schweinfurth, children are regarded as a special delicacy, and are reserved for the table of the king.

It is now accepted as a fact, established by the testimony alike of transient travellers and of agents permanently residing in the Congo State, that all the tribes inhabiting the vast region between the Congo and the Welle are adicted to cannibalism: but if Schweinfurth's impression be correct, the cannabalism of the Monbuttoo is the most inveterate of all; he had no difficulty in getting two hundred skulls of their victims to be submitted to him, of which he selected forty to bring away.

Nothing short of European occupation, with the introduction of cattle and the suppression of internecine wars, can ever avail to put an end to the revolting practice.

Situated as it is between Emin Pasha's province and the Congo Free State, it is to be hoped that the Monbuttoo country can hardly be long before being brought under European influence. From a politico-economical point of view, it holds out a promise of great importance; its fertility, its population, its wealth, its comparative salubrity, and its picturesqueness attract the interest equally of travellers and traders. "The Monbuttoo land," says Schweinfurth, "greets us as an Eden upon earth. Unnumbered groves of plantains bedeck the gently heaving soil; oil-palms, incomparable in beauty, and other monarchs of the stately woods, rise up and spread their glory over the favoured scene; along the streams there is a bright expanse of charming verdure, whilst a grateful shade ever overhangs the domes of the idyllic huts." *

Like the Niam-niam, the Monbuttoo have no real villages. To quote Schweinfurth again :—" The huts

---

* Schweinfurth, " Heart of Africa," vol. ii. p. 85.

are arranged in sets following the lines of the brooks along the valleys, the space between each group being occupied by plantations of oil-palms. The dwellings are separated from the lowest parts of the depression by the plantain grounds, whilst above, on the higher and drier soil, extend the fields of sweet potatoes and colocasiae." †

Notwithstanding his efforts to make further progress to the south, Dr. Schweinfurth, in 1871, found himself unable to advance beyond a spot within King Munza's dominions, on the left bank of the Welle, the present site of Tangasi.

Captain Casati was more fortunate. Taking a south-westerly course, he succeeded in passing beyond the Monbuttoo frontier, and reached the residence of the Niam-niam chief, Bakangaï, who, being afraid that he might be held responsible for the death of a European traveller, refused to allow him to penetrate farther west into the country of the fierce Ababua.

About the same time as Casati, Dr. Junker also arrived at the quarters of Bakangaï. Not to be deterred, he made a bold dash from Tangasi towards the south, and managed to get across the southern ridge of the Welle basin, and having passed through the Mabode country into the Aruwimi valley, reached the quarters of one of their chiefs named Sanga, a prince of Monbuttoo origin.

This spot, on the banks of the river Nepoko, was destined to be the farthest point that was reached in the adventurous enterprises of that date.

Both Junker's and Casati's investigations were now to be interrupted, and finally to be altogether checked, by the disquieting intelligence from Khartoom that was forwarded to them by Lupton and Emin Bey.

In November 1882, just as he was leaving Semio for the west, Dr. Junker received a warning from Lupton that, instigated by the Arabs, the Dinka had risen in revolt, and that the route towards Meshra-er-Rek was quite unsafe. Persevering, however, and not allowing his schemes to be frustrated by the tidings, he pursued his way into the unknown regions to the west, resolved, if possible, to ascertain the real direction of the course of the Welle-Makua. He traversed the territory of the

Bandchia tribes, and arrived at the *zeriba* Ali-Kobo, in the Bassange country, the extreme point hitherto reached on the great river.

It was, however, only for four days that he could remain there. He had hardly arrived when letters from Lupton overtook him, forwarded in urgent haste, announcing the rapid progress of the Mahdi's revolt and the rising of the natives in the Bahr-el-Ghazal. There was no alternative for him but to return at once ; at the very moment when he seemed to have the immediate prospect of being able to solve the question of the Welle, he was obliged to abandon his undertaking and beat a retreat.

By the following May he was back in Semio. After waiting in doubt and anxiety for six months, and still despairing of finding any way open to the north, he set out towards the east in the direction of the province of the Equator, where Emin Pasha was pressing him to come and join him without delay. He reached Lado on the 23d of January 1884. Casati had arrived there some months previously.

It was high time ; the crisis was at hand ; stern action must be taken.

CHAPTER V.

PRISONERS IN THE SOUDAN.

Native rising in the Bahr-el-Ghazal—Fall of Roumbek, Ghaba-Chambil, and Bor—Lupton Bey a prisoner—The Emir Karam-Allah—Siege of Amadi—Heroic conduct of negro troops—Transfer of seat of government from Lado to Douille—Letter from the Mahdi—Battle of Remio—Emin Bey at Wadelai—Dr. Junker amongst the Lango—Emin Bey's army, fortifications, and boats—Dr. Junker prepares to start for the coast.

It was in Lupton Bey's province of the Gazelle that the insurrectionary movement first broke out. The Dinka betook themselves to arms, and for eighteen months waged a determined and sanguinary war against the Government troops ; and in spite of Lupton making a levy of all the force at his disposal, he was unequal to the task of suppressing the revolt.

The Nueir, the Agar, and various other tribes of the Rohl River, were not long in following the lead of the Dinka, and the Egyptian station at Roumbek was captured and destroyed.

With reference to this trying period, speaking on the 20th of May 1887 at a meeting of the Geographical Society of Paris, Dr. Junker said—" Throughout the critical circumstances of that time Lupton Bey's conduct was most admirable. His letters, dated from every quarter of the province, attest that he was ubiquitous in pursuit of his fugitive adversaries. The details of that arduous struggle are not well known in Europe, and consequently the general public has never duly appreciated Lupton's merits. That war of the Dinka for eighteen months against the Government troops, was more desperate and murderous than the subsequent encounters with the Mahdists in the province of Emin Bey."

Within a year Lupton was engaged in more than twenty battles. To aggravate his difficulty, the Arabs, who favoured the rebellion, sent reinforcements to maintain the conflict, and in spite of the most heroic efforts to suppress it, the insurrection kept on spreading until it reached the western tribes of the Equator province. At the end of 1883 the Bari began to make a movement, and at the beginning of the following year the station of Ghaba-Chambil, with its entire garrison, fell into the hands of the rebels, a loss which was quickly followed by that of Bor.

Henceforth, Emin's province lay open to the encroachments of the insurgents.

It was just at this time that Gordon arrived at Khartoom, and the blockade of that town was commencing. Communication with the north was already cut off, as Fashoda, situated on both sides of the Nile at the confluence of the Sobat and the Bahr-el-Ghazal, was in the hands of the Mahdi's followers, who kept continually advancing to the south.

Deserted by a portion of his troops, Lupton was unable to hold out. In May he was reduced to extremities and compelled to surrender himself a prisoner. He was taken to Kordofan. No long time elapsed before there was not a soldier who remained faithful to the Khedive, and every station, with its ammunition and provisions, passed into the hands of the Arabs.

At Lado, on the 27th of May, the three Europeans

received a letter from Lupton, making them aware of
his misfortune. At the same time came a message
from a certain Emir Karam-Allah, a *soi-disant* lieutenant of the Mahdi's, calling on Emin, as Governour of
the province, to appear personally before him and
make submission. Emin was in perplexity, but was
anxious above all things to gain time. He sent word
to the Emir that, being desirous to avoid useless bloodshed, he would not refuse to appear before him, but
that the hostility of the natives against him was so
great that he could not venture to leave his quarters ;
he represented that his departure would be the signal
for a general mutiny, and added that, while he was
thus careful to protect the lives of his soldiers, he was
nevertheless willing to hold the province as being under the Mahdi's authority ; finally declaring that he
could not think of quitting his post until a successor
had been appointed, and that he should accordingly
wait for further instructions.

Without loss of time, however, he concentrated all
his force. Abandoning all outlying stations, he gathered his troops into one body, and proceeded to make
preparation for an attack which he foresaw was imminent.

At the close of the year 1884 things had indeed become serious, and a report was spread that a large
force, commanded by the Emir Karam-Allah in person, was marching upon the station of Amadi, just
five days' journey from Lado.

The rumour was only too true. Amadi had to sustain a siege, and for nineteen days its gallant little
garrison, composed entirely of negro soldiers under
Soudanese officers, maintained a resistance. At last,
coming to the end of their resources, they made a desperate dash, and breaking through the line of the besiegers, succeeded in effecting a retreat into the Makraka country.

In recounting this feat of arms, thus valorously accomplished by negroes, Emin Pasha wrote to his friend,
the Rev. Robert Felkin, in Edinburgh :— " Ever since
the Arab occupation of the Bahr-el-Ghazal—I will not
say its conquest, since everything that has been gained
has been gained by treachery—we have been most
vigorously attacked ; and I feel that I cannot give you

an idea of the admirable devotion of my black troops throughout this long war, in which for them at least there can be no advantage. Destitute of the barest necessaries of life, and with their pay long in arrears, they fought most resolutely, and when at last, after nineteen days of hardship and privation, weakened by hunger—the last shred of leather, the last boot having been devoured—they forced a gap in the enemy's ranks and made good their escape.

" These brave fellows endured all this misery with perfect disinterestedness, without prospect of reward, simply because they were prompted by a sense of duty and were desirous of exhibiting their bravery to the foe. Whatever doubts I may ever have had of the negro, the history of the seige of Amadi has convinced me that in resolute courage the black race is inferior to none, and in the spirit of self-sacrifice is superior to many. Without any highly skilled officers to direct them or give them orders, they performed miracles, and it will be difficult for the Egyptian Government to give them any worthy proof of its gratitude."

The emergency became more pressing, and another change of headquarters was soon imperative. In the north-west of the province the Mahdi's force continued to advance, while the prospect of an attack by Karam-Allah upon Lado seemed more threatening. Accordingly Emin Bey resolved upon a fresh concentration of his men upon the Nile, and hastened to transfer the seat of his government from Lado to Douflé, whither were conveyed all the Coptic and Egyptian officials, as well as all the Government papers and records.

Shortly after this a message was received from the victorious Emir announcing that he was on his way to Lado. It was accompanied by a transcript of a letter written by the Mahdi at Khartoom, dated the 28th of January, communicating the intelligence of the fall of that town and the death of Gordon.

" *Copy of a gracious order of our Lord the Mahdi— may he be blessed!—to his representative Karam-Allah, Emir of the Bahr-el-Ghazal and of the Equator:*—

"The devoted slave of God, Mohammed-el-Mahdi, son of Abdallah, to his dearly beloved representative, Karam-Allah, son of the Sheik Mo'hammed:—

"My son, receive my greeting! The blessing of the merciful God be upon thee!

"I bid thee know that according to the infallible predictions of God, and by his immutable goodness, the town of Khartoom, by the aid of the living and immortal, was taken on Monday the 26th of Jany. in the present year.

"Early in the morning, the troops of the faithful applied themselves to their task, and, confident in God, they made an assault. In less than half an hour the enemies of God were in their hands; they were annihilated to a man; so too their fortress.

"Strongly prepared for defence though they were, they yielded at the first onslaught, dispersed by the hand of the Lord. Then they sought safety in flight, crowded into the courtyards, and closed the gates. Our army pursued them, put them to the edge of the sword, attacked them with lances until their cries were heard aloud, their tears outpoured, and they were stricken with consternation. Not long were the faithful in getting the upper hand of the survivors who had closed the gates; they captured them and slew them, so that none but women and children remained to defend the place.

"Gordon, the enemy of God, so long a rebel and insurgent, so often warned by us and invited to place himself under the hand of God, refused to submit; wherefore he has found his fate; he has reaped in sorrow what he sowed in guilt; God hath sent him to hell, there for ever to abide.

"Thus has the might of the unbeliever been destroyed. Thanks be to God, the Lord of all the earth!

"On our side, ten died the death of the believer; not another was wounded or even bruised in the encounter. Behold the Divine mercy! The victory is from God; before him we prostrate ourselves in adoration. Do likewise; and accept my greeting.

"12 REBI ACHIR, 1302."

This mournful intelligence, confirmed by the non-arrival of the ordinary Khartoom steamer, and coming so quickly after the tidings of the Emir's successes in the south, thoroughly opened Emin Bey's eyes to the gravity of the situation in which he was placed. The loss of Amadi, following upon Lupton's retirement from his various stations, and the menaces which he now received from Karam-Allah, showed him only too plainly that he was in danger of being immediately attacked.

It soon transpired that the Emir was advancing with the design of attacking Remio, a station near the Yeï, north-west of Doufilé. Fearing lest the little garrison should share the fate of that of Amadi, Emin resolved to make a venture in its defence. Taking several bat-

talions of his troops, he set out and arrived at the
spot in April, in time to await the appearance of the
Arabs; and on their approach, his troops, assisted by
the Monbuttoo, made a rush upon them, and inflicted
such a sanguinary defeat, that they withdrew in all
speed back again to the north. Thus for the time all
danger was warded off the stations on the Nile.

Whether it was this fortunate exploit of the Egyptian troops that rescued the Equatorial provinces from
further incursions by the bands of the Arabs, or
whether the Emir was recalled by the Mahdi, who was
concerned at the presence of an English expedition
near Khartoom, there are now no means of judging;
but certain it is that Lado, where the rebels had been
daily expected to appear before the fences, was left
undisturbed, and it was soon ascertained that the Emir
had led his men by forced marches towards Kordofan.

Obviously it was still the duty of Emin Bey to be
on his guard against any fresh surprise. He came to
the conclusion that it was desirable that he should for
the third time change the seat of his government, and
issuing orders for the evacuation of his western stations
in the Makraka country, he proceeded to draw off all
his force and his last reserve of ammunition to Wadelaï, his most southern station on the river.

Further than this, as all hope of succour from the
north had been dispelled by the gloomy tidings that
had reached him of the fate of Khartoom, he began to
turn his eyes towards Zanzibar, whither it was agreed
that Dr. Junker should be despatched with the object,
if possible, of opening communication with the coast.

The Doctor started. Ascending the Nile from Doufilé to Meshra, he reached the residence of Anfina, the
Lango chief, a faithful ally of Emin's, whence he endeavoured to enter into negotiations with Uganda.
His efforts were vain. The road to the south, like the
road to the north, was closed not only to the white
men themselves, but also to the transit of their messengers and despatches.

Thus was Emin Pasha isolated from the world, and
thrown back upon himself and the fidelity of his
followers.

For ten months, from January to November 1885,
did Dr. Junker persevere in his wanderings amongst

the Lango, between Anfina's quarters and Fauwera, once a station of the Egyptians; and then, finding all his proceedings futile, he made his way back to Wadelaï.

At that period the situation may be thus described. The province, after having been for six months relieved of the presence of the Mahdi's troops, was comparatively quiet. So far as regarded the natives everything was satisfactory; the Bari alone had shown any symptoms of rebellion, and these were promptly suppressed. At Emin's disposal there were about 1500 regular troops armed with Remington rifles, the whole of these being negroes, except about forty Egyptians who were specially told off for the artillery; they were commanded by ten Egyptian officers and fifteen Soudanese, and all remained staunch in their allegiance.

"In spite of their utter destitution," wrote Emin, "in spite of their being without pay and almost without clothes, these soldiers continue dutiful and obedient. This is far more than could be expected."

The 1500 soldiers, parcelled out into companies varying from one hundred to two hundred men, garrisoned ten stations; nine on the Nile, namely, Lado, Redjaf, Bedden, Kirri, Muggi, Laboré, Chor Aju, Doufilé, and Wadelaï; the tenth, Fatiko, being in the Shooli country, on the road from Doufilé to Mrooli. *

Communication between the different stations was maintained by two steamers, the *Nyassa* and the *Khedive*, which had been brought into service during the time when Gordon was Governour for the first time, and which could upon occasion be fitted out for defence. The officials (Egyptian and Coptic) numbered somewhere about two hundred; and if for each official, officer, and soldier there were reckoned an average of not less than three women, children, and slaves, the total would amount to a population of at least 10,000 souls, constituting what the English newspapers have designated "Emin Pasha's people."

Since 1885 the protection of Emin Pasha has by no means been the chief difficulty. In one of his letters he writes:—"Since the retreat of Karam-Allah and

---

* Since then five other stations have been reoccupied. These are Makraka-Sugnire and Uandi in the Makraka country. Mahagi on Lake Albert, and Faloro and Fatibek in the interior, east of the Nile.

the dispersion of his troops by the natives on the Kordofan frontier, peace has been unbroken; and I may also add that the war has had the beneficial result of clearing the whole province of the Bahr-el-Ghazal of slave-hunters." What has given the greatest cause for anxiety is the lack of stores and goods for barter, combined with the fear of running short of ammunition and the impossibility of holding communication with Europe.

In another letter Emin wrote:—" We have undergone terrible trials; happily, however, we have proved the truth of the proverb, ' Necessity is the mother of invention,' and we feel that we may well be proud of the way in which we have managed for ourselves since we have been deprived of all external aid. At all our stations agricultural work is progressing well. We have grown cotton; we have learned both to spin and to weave; as a specimen of what we can do I send you a pretty little handkerchief of our own manufacture. We have introduced the craft of shoemaking, and you would be surprised at what we have produced. We make our soap of fat and ashes, and our candles of wax. Hibiscus seed we find a fair substitute for coffee; we sweeten it with honey. I must not forget also to tell you that we have grown some splendid tobacco in our gardens. Except that I miss books, newspapers, and materials for my scientific work, personally I am in want of nothing."

But it is remarkable how even in the times of his greatest anxiety, Emin never failed in his scientific interest; in all the letters sent by him, at various times, to Schweinfurth, Junker, Felkin, Hassenstein, Behm, Allen, and others, detailing the circumstances under which he was living, he speaks of his constant desire to make his long residence in Africa profitable for the advance of science.

In one of these letters, addressed to the late Dr. Behm of Gotha, after saying that he anticipated that the Nueir, the Agar, and the Dinka were on the point of breaking out in an insurrection which it would be a long and difficult task to suppress, he thus continues:—" To myself, my residence in the Monbuttoo country has been very satisfactory. I have worked hard and made many new and interesting notes; I have put together a vocabulary, and have tried generally to be as useful as possible. Your suggestion that I should make an ethnological chart is never out of my mind, and with reference to the work I have already begun to collect some examples of the dialects."

At a later date he wrote to Dr. Schweinfurth:— "Thanks to the many newspapers and pamphlets which have reached me by way of Uganda, I have now an ample stock of paper, and shall be able to resume the preparation of the herbarium which I promised you."

In another letter to the Rev. Robert Felkin, he writes :—"I have not forgotten Professor Flower ; according to his desire I have collected several human skulls, also some skulls of chimpanzees, and some skeletons of animals and Akka ; . . . I have likewise a collection of shells from Lake Albert."

Such for three years, amidst incessant care and anxiety, was the life of the three Europeans who were fated thus to be brought together and blockaded on the Upper Nile.

When the attacks of the Arabs had ceased, and the revolts of the natives had been suppressed, they deliberately set themselves to meet their difficulties by developing the natural resources of the country, and, though without means, contrived to get food, clothing, and sustenance for the 10,000 men, women, and children over whom they presided as protectors.

It was now the end of 1885 ; they had had no communication with Europe since 1883, and they began to fear that they had been forgotten. Their eyes were still towards Zanzibar, and although Dr. Junker had failed in his first efforts to go there, it was deemed advisable that he should again leave Casati to assist Emin in maintaining friendly relations with the surrounding tribes, and once more endeavour to accomplish his purpose. This time he would set out by way of Unyoro. The experiment was full of hazard ; yet all things considered, a white man accompanied only by a small escort would have a greater chance of success than any larger or armed expedition, which would assuredly rouse the alarm and suspicion of the natives.

As to an exodus *en masse* of the 10,000 officials, soldiers, women, children, and slaves that made up the population of Wadelaï, Lado, and the other stations, that was a scheme not for a moment to be entertained. Northwards, the way would be barred by the army of the Mahdi; southwards, were unknown tribes in the lands watered by the Welle and the Upper Congo, that had been reached indeed by the civilising mission of the King of the Belgians, but of this of course Emin had no intelligence, and was utterly ignorant; and lastly, on the east was Uganda, where the bloodthirsty tyrant who ruled would be certainly opposed to any passage of an armed expedition through his domain.

Circumstanced as Emin was, it would have been madness to make such a venture—unsupplied with either provisions or ammunition, to face hostile tribes in a desert and unexplored country was simply to court disaster; before his caravan had made much progress on its way, a large proportion of his people would have succumbed to fatigue and privation, even if they escaped being the victims of a bloody foe. Emin was not foolhardy enough to think of conducting another " retreat of the ten thousand."

As to any thought for himself, of taking advantage of any opportunity for escape, it would never enter his mind. As a Governour placed by Gordon in command of the province of the Equator he could never for a moment contemplate either forsaking the men who had so faithfully adhered to him, or abandoning the country that had been committed to his charge "in the cause of progress and civilisation." "I shall endeavour," he writes to Mr. Felkin, "to bring to a good issue the work for which Gordon sacrificed his blood; if not with his energy and genius, I will at any rate labour in conformity with his instructions, and ideas. When he, my lamented chief, confided to me the oversight of this province, he wrote 'I nominate you in the cause of progress and civilisation.' Hitherto I have done my best to merit that confidence which was reposed in me. The simple fact that I have been able to maintain myself here in the midst of thousands of natives, with only a handful of men of my own, is a proof that I have to a certain extent succeeded, inasmuch as I am thoroughly trusted by the indigenous population.

" I am now the sole surviving representative of Gordon's Soudan staff. Consequently, I hold it my

stern duty to follow the path which he pointed out.
Moreover I am persuaded that there is a bright future
for these countries; sooner or later they will be included within the ever-widening circle of the civilised
world."

It was therefore no way of personal escape for
which Emin was looking; at the same time he longed
most earnestly for the opening of an avenue of communication with Europe, by means of which his true
situation might be known, and along which materials
might be brought, so that he could continue his work
on the scene where for so long he had maintained his
independence.

This was the general aspect of affairs when Dr.
Junker again undertook, at the peril of his life, to
endeavor to reach Europe, there to plead the cause of
Emin and the Equatorial Soudan.

CHAPTER VI.

RETURN OF DR. JUNKER.

Dr. Junker's departure from Wadelai—The Bahr-el-Gebel and Lake Albert—Salt pits at Kibiro—Unyoro—King Kabrega—Mohammed Biri—Correspondence with Mr. Mackay—Marches in Unyoro—Arrival at Roubaga
—Uganda and its inhabitants—King Mtesa and King M'Wanga—Murder of
Bishop Hannington—Emin Pasha relieved—Passage of Lake Victoria—Arrival at M'salala mission-station—Appeal to Europe—Arrival at Zanzibar.

On the 2nd of January 1886 Dr. Junker left Wadelaï. He went on board one of the steamers belonging
to the station, accompanied by Vita Hassan, an Egyptian doctor, who was on his way to Unyoro.

The two travellers ascended the Nile, at that part
of its course known as the Bahr-el-Gebel, and measur-
ing nearly three miles across from bank to bank. As
far as Lake Albert navigation is unimpeded by rapids,
although it is rendered somewhat difficult by numerous islets of reeds and papyrus, and by shallows where
hippopotami congregate in considerable numbers.

On the west the river is bordered by a chain of
mountains, clothed with sparsely-grown forest; on the
eastern side the shore is flatter, extending in wide
prairie tracts dotted over with trees. Large herds of

elephants and antelopes seem to abound, as they come down to the river-bank in the evening to drink.

The most important district on the western shore is Fanikoro, the residence of the chief Okello. On this side of the river the population is composed of the Aloori tribe ; on the other side, which is equally well inhabited, the country is occupied by the Shooli.

A short distance to the south of Fanikoro is the northernmost point of Lake Albert (Mwootan Nzigé) which was discovered by Sir Samuel Baker on the 14th of March 1864. Gessi Pasha was the first to complete its circumnavigation in March and April 1876, since which date it has been explored successively by Mason Bey and Emin Pasha. At its north-eastern extremity, the Lake receives the Somerset Nile, the channel of the overflow from Lake Victoria, and at its extreme south it receives the Kakibibi, a stream also recently investigated by Emin.

After a few days' sailing Dr. Junker and his companion reached Kibiro, on the east of the lake, where three large villages, the property of a chief, Kagoro, are built close to the base of the mountains.

Kibiro is the leading trade-depôt of the district, and the sole occupation of the people is the procuring and preparation of salt, for which a demand is found not only in Unyoro, but likewise among the Uganda on the east, and the Aloori on the west.

The main centre of the salt industry is almost adjacent to the villages, in the midst of natural gorges and ravines, where blocks of stone and masses of debris lie in fantastic disorder. Little streams of water permeate the heated soil, so that jets of vapour are seen rising all around, the warm water being carried away by means of troughs supported on stones. Groups of women and children are seen gathering the earth impregnated with its saline particles into baskets, which they fill up with water. The mud thus formed is filtered, with the result that a pure white salt is extracted, which is made up into cylindrical blocks, and wrapped in dried banana leaves. The salt-pans render the district comparatively wealthy.

Having landed at Kibiro, Junker and Vita Hassan started off on foot, eastwards, to the quarters of Kabrega, the Unyoro king.

Overhanging the villages is a series of terraces surmounted by two isolated peaks, known as Rougoï and Kjente, between which a steep footway leads to the abode of the monarch. The path is all amongst blocks of stone and jagged points, the successive terraces rising like bastions crowned with grassy plateaux, on which trees of any sort are singularly rare. It was a task of ten hours' perseverance to reach the royal residence, which lies eastward of the river Kjahi, a little affluent of Lake Albert.

In these unsettled regions the capital is continually being changed according to the caprice of the ruler. At the time of Baker's expedition in 1872, the headquarters were at Masindi; five years later, when Emin Pasha made his first visit, they had been removed to Nyamoga; and now quite recently they have been fixed at Ginaïa.

Altogether Unyoro is one of the most important dominions in the country of the great lakes. It includes the whole land to the south of the Somerset Nile along the west boundary of Lake Albert; it consists almost entirely of vast plains, broken by marshes, and studded with acacia-woods. Bananas, prepared in various ways, are the staple food of its people, and constitute the crop upon which they mainly depend. Pasturage is good, and cattle abundant, as likewise are antelopes and elephants.

In their commercial matters, the inhabitants seem active and adroit. Unlike other Nile tribes they wear clothes, and the women of the Lango districts are the best-looking and best-proportioned to be found throughout the region.

Speke and Grant were amongst the earliest European travellers to penetrate to Unyoro. In 1863 they stayed for several weeks at the court of the king Kamrasi, a crafty character, who in the following year caused Baker no inconsiderable trouble.

In 1872 Baker visited the country again, going this time with a commission from the Khedive to annex Unyoro to the Egyptian Soudan. He found the throne occupied by Kamrasi's son Kabrega, who afterwards became an ally of Emin's, and afforded aid and protection to Dr. Junker on his homeward way.

Concerning this young ruler, however, whose name is

frequently occurring in recent letters and despatches, there would seem to be a wide diversity of opinion. After staying with him in 1872, Baker writes :—" On the 26th of April I made my official visit to Kabrega, my officers being in full uniform, and headed by a band of music. I found him in his divan, a roomy, well-built structure, with hangings of inferior printed calico brought from Zanzibar. He was himself dressed in a piece of black striped bark. This son of Kamrasi, the descendant of the victorious Gallas, and the six-teenth king of Unyoro, is a lout about twenty years of age, awkward, unpleasant, cowardly, cruel, cunning and perfidious to the last degree. He is nearly six feet high, his complexion fair. His eyes are large, but too prominent; he has a low forehead, projecting cheek-bones, and a wide mouth, with teeth as white as ivory. His hands are well-shaped, the finger-nails, as well as toe-nails, being clean and carefully cut. He wears sandals of raw buffalo-hide, which are neatly made and turned in at the edges."

This, certainly, is not a flattering portrait; but, in justice to the original, it should be stated that Dr. Junker, who saw him fourteen years afterwards, when he was consequently thirty-four years of age, says that he " was very favourably impressed by the chief's ap-pearance, and should consider him to be of a very amiable disposition."

Latterly, no doubt, Kabrega has shown himself friendly to Europeans, having not only several times sent Emin contributions of material to assist him in his straits, but having done all in his power to facili-tate the conveyance of his correspondence to the coast.

Nevertheless, Casati, after staying at Giunaïa for nearly a year, seems, like Baker, to have formed a mean opinion of Kabrega. In a letter to M. Cam-perio, dated May 2, 1887, he writes :—

" Kabrega makes no secret of his evil intentions; nothing but falsehood is on his lips. I shall, how-ever, persevere in my mission, although Emin urges me to abandon it. If I leave here, the road is closed behind me; and unfortunately no other way is open."

At Giunaïa Dr. Junker found some Arab traders who for some time had settled in Kabrega's domain, but he failed for a while to enter into negotiations with them, because they were afraid that they should be compromised by having transactions with him. One day, however, he received a letter written in French from one of them, a certain Mohammed Biri, which resulted in a subsequent interview.

This Mohammed proved to be a servant who had once been attached to the Belgian station of Karema, having followed Captain Ramäckers to Lake Tanganyika. After that officer's death, he had returned to the coast, and was now engaged in the ivory-trade in the districts in the neighbourhood of the great lakes. He gave the doctor the latest news of the Soudan, telling him that it had been abandoned by the British troops; and he described the condition of Uganda, mentioning that some European missionaries were resident here.

This was a statement that could not fail to arrest Junker's attention. It raised his spirits, and he wrote off at once to the Uganda missionaries. Not that it was an easy matter to get into correspondence with them, and he had to wait six weeks in anxious suspense before an answer was brought back. At length, in February, a messenger arrived from Mr. Mackay of the English mission, bringing the most recent intelligence from Europe, Egypt, and Zanzibar.

"That day of the arrival of the courier," writes the doctor, "was truly a red-letter day to me!" For three years he had had no communication with the civilised world.

Mr. Mackay confirmed and related in detail the disastrous tidings from the Soudan; he represented as still very critical the situation of the missionaries in Uganda, where on the 31st of the preceding October Bishop Hannington had been murdered at the instigation of the king; and he likewise stated that a relief-expedition had been organised, and had started from Zanzibar in August under the charge of Dr. Fischer, but that it had been prohibited from passing through Uganda, and had been compelled to return. His advice to Dr. Junker was to use the greatest caution, and by no means at present to venture without permission into the territory of the bloodthirsty M'Wanga, as the life of any European was there in perpetual peril. Finally, he enclosed three letters addressed to Emin Bey; one from Nubar Pasha, the Egyptian

Prime Minister, instructing him to abandon the province of the Equator; one from Sir John Kirk, the English Consul at Zanzibar; and the third from the Sultan, Saïd-Bargash.

Then followed three weary and disheartening months. Acting on Mr. Mackay's counsel, Junker applied to M'Wanga for permission to pass through his dominions. He knew well enough that elsewhere there was no chance of purchasing materials for the relief of Emin, nor any chance of finding for himself means to reach the coast. Pending the receipt of a reply, he made a move nearer to the Uganda frontier, but on the way he had the misfortune to injure himself seriously by a fall, and at the same time found himself in perplexity through the desertion of his porters, whilst to add to his difficulties it was discovered that hostilities were recommencing between Unyoro and Uganda.

This state of warfare may be said to be chronic. The two kingdoms are only separated by a small intervening tract which is overrun by troops of armed marauders. Across this runs the natural route for caravans, and all the Arab and native traders, travelling between Lake Victoria or Lake Albert and the Soudan, have to be protected by an escort, and so dangerous is the country that the march is most frequently made by night.

After meeting with many obstacles and effecting some hair-breadth escapes, Junker found himself safely over this debateable land, and having obtained the permission for which he had asked, he entered the Uganda territory, and arrived in May at Roubaga, King M'Wanga's capital.

Of all the large states in the basin of Lake Victoria, none is so well known as that of Uganda. It encompasses the north and north-west sides of the Lake, and its area can hardly be estimated at much less than 20,000 square miles. According to the accounts of the travellers who have gone through it, there seems little doubt that it is one of the finest parts of Equatorial Africa, its soil near the Lake being exceptionally fertile. The forests are luxuriant, containing trees of the largest growth; beyond these are plains abundant in pasturage for cattle, ba-

nanas and fig-trees flourishing in perfection. Further
west, the country changes its character, and instead
of woods and prairies, there are imposing hills rifted
into valleys, that echo with the rushing of torrents
and the roar of cataracts.

The first chief of Uganda who was ever visited by
Europeans was the notorious Mtesa, who has been
repeatedly pourtrayed by Speke, Chaillé-Long, Stanley, Linant de Bellefond, and others. Always ready
to welcome the white man with cordiality, in 1880 he
had advanced so far as to make up his mind to despatch an embassy to Europe.

Several weeks, in 1874, were spent at the court of
this negro sovereign by Stanley, who gives a very
striking account of Uganda, its ruler, and his military
power. At a review of the army to which he was
invited, he computed that there could be no less than
150,000 soldiers, who were then about to be led on an
expedition against the Vuavuma. The bodyguard was
composed of 600 picked men, all armed with rifles.
Besides the army, the chief's harem, consisting of
5000 wives, concubines, and slaves, was exhibited on
parade. In Central Africa, as well as upon the banks
of the Upper Nile and the Congo, a large number of
wives is regarded as a proof of wealth; each woman
has her market value, and may at any time be ex-
changed for stuffs, guns, beads, cattle, or other merchandise.

Mtesa's navy was hardly less imposing than his
army. On the lake were 230 war-canoes of all sizes;
the largest was seventy-five feet long and manned by
sixty-four rowers. Altogether the naval force was
eight thousand men.

Some doubts have been expressed as to the accuracy
of the foregoing figures; yet when the testimony of
such men as Wilson and Felkin, missionaries who have
resided in the country, is taken into account, stating
the population to exceed 500,000, and when moreover
it is remembered that every man is trained to arms,
so as to be ready for immediate service, the muster of
150,000 soldiers in time of war does not lie outside
the range of probability.

But whether this estimate be exaggerated or not, it
is certain that travellers are of one mind in declaring

that of all the African states Uganda is the most advanced in all matters pertaining to civilisation; and since 1862, when Speke and Grant first made their way thither, no other tribe has made so forward a stride in internal development.

Equally rich and diversified are the products of the soil; the climate is by no means variable and comparatively healthy; the inhabitants (numerous as it has been affirmed they are) are brave, intelligent, and singularly open to the influences of civilisation, whether from Arabs or Europeans. The Arabs from Zanzibar, quite as much as the English and French missionaries, are struggling hard for mastery over the minds of the people, and Islamism is making marked progress.

It has not taken much more than twenty years for Arab example to effect a complete revolution in the costume of the natives. At the date of Speke's visit, clothing was worn to the most limited extent; but now the Uganda as well as the Unyoro dress themselves from head to foot. Arab garments have gradually replaced the old "mbougou" of bark, and the very poorest of the people are seen attired in haïk, shirt, waistband and caftan, and wear tarbooshes or turbans on their heads.

Mtesa died in 1885; he was succeeded by his son M'Wanga, who is now the reigning sovereign.

No sooner was M'Wanga on the throne than he began to feel uneasy about the maintenance of his independence, and to have misgivings lest the advance of Europeans on Lake Victoria should damage or diminish his authority. Every fresh advent of an exploring party, every new arrival of missionaries, and especially any display of military strength, and—not least —the territorial acquisitions of the Germans in Zanguebar, all served to arouse his suspicion and to increase his apprehensions. As his alarm increased the position of the English and French missionaries at Roubaga grew more and more critical; and at last his fears that the white man would come and "eat up" all his lands became so intense that he gave orders for all intruders to be massacred. Hence resulted the cruel murder of Bishop Hannington, who had ventured into Uganda with the hope of establishing a Christian settlement. Out of a caravan of fifty who came with him, only four escaped.

Such was the condition of the country into which Dr. Junker now dared to enter. He was obliged to act with the utmost circumspection, and so remained unmolested for six weeks in the royal capital. More-over, as the result of his patience, and through the mediation of Mr. Mackay, he succeeded in effecting a purchase of stuffs for Emin Bey to the value of 2000 tallaris. Mohammed Biri, the merchant whom he had met in Unyoro, chanced to be in Roubaga, and under-took the conveyance of the goods to Wadelaï, a good service which he faithfully executed after some oppo-sition on the part of the king, to the great relief of Emin and his followers, who had been so far reduced towards a state of nudity, that they had been com-pelled to clothe themselves with the skins of animals.

Having thus enjoyed the satisfaction of providing in some degree for the needs of those whom he had left behind, Junker turned his thoughts to the prose-cution of his journey. He made a few hurried prepa-rations, and on the 22nd of July, embarking on one of the mission-boats, he set out to cross Lake Victoria.

The great Nyanza, discovered by Speke on the 4th of August 1858, and named by him after his own sov-ereign, is the largest lake-basin in the whole continent of Africa. Its area is nearly 24,000 square miles, so that it is twice as large as Belgium; there is only one lake in the world that exceeds it in size, namely, Lake Superior in Canada. Its vast surface is studded with islands, some 250 of which are clustered in the north-west into an archipelago known as Sesse, all of them characterised by singular beauty.

Storms and waterspouts are of frequent occurrence; and contrary winds with violent squalls compelled Dr. Junker more than once to take refuge on some of the islands, so that it was not until the 16th of August, twenty-six days after starting, that he reached the southern extremity of the lake, where he landed near the village of M'salala, the missionaries from the set-tlement there hastening to offer him hospitality, and aiding him to procure the means for continuing his journey to the coast.

Now secure from all the perils of barbarism, he

wrote a letter to Dr. Schweinfurth, expressing his emotion at his deliverance, after six weeks' sojourn in Uganda, from the hands of the bloody king who had murdered the English bishop, and, at the same time, exhibiting his deep anxiety on behalf of those whom he had left at Wadelaï, and who had been so closely associated with him in trial and danger. A copy of portions of this letter is appended :—

"ENGLISH MISSION, M'SALALA,
SOUTHERN EXTREMITY OF LAKE VICTORIA,
April 16*th,* 1886.

" DEAR FRIEND,—Escaped from the clutches of M'Wanga, of Uganda, I reached this place this morning, and hasten to take advantage of the first courier leaving the Mission for the coast, to send you a few lines.

" Forty porters and a few Zanzibaris have been already engaged, and in a few days I hope to continue my journey towards Ujiji, thence to Bagamoyo.

" Is it possible that nothing is being done for these unfortunate equatorial provinces? . . . . Write, my dear friend, write ! . . . . Let vigorous articles from your pen be at once the means of opening the eyes of the public to the truth. . . .

"For my part, I shall do what is possible. It is absolutely necessary that Emin Bey should at once have relief. At Uganda I managed to procure him 2000 tallaris' worth of cotton goods, in spite of the obstacles which M'Wanga threw in the way. These were to be conveyed to him by a certain Mohammed Biri, but had not been despatched when I was obliged to leave.

" European prestige here is already on the decline. It will be a dire disgrace if Europe makes no effort now. Let M'Wanga and his agents be put down ! Let Uganda be rescued from their power ! Let Emin Bey be delivered from danger ! Let the equatorial provinces be re-conquered ! These are the hopes that animate me as I come back to Europe. Write to me, I pray you. Send me a long letter to Zanzibar.—I close this in haste. Your affectionate friend, lost and found again,

" WILHELM JUNKER."

When, two months later, these lines were submitted
to the public in Egypt and in Europe, no one could
read them unmoved; they made the state of things so
clear, and witnessed so unmistakably to the perilous
situation of Emin, exposed, without provisions or ammunition, to the attack of hostile tribes, and especially to the treachery of the bloody M'Wanga, that the
appeal of one who had shared his imprisonment, and
had escaped only by facing terrible risks, could not
fail to arrest attention and to excite a generous sympathy.

Helped forwards on his journey by the M'salala
missionaries, Junker reached Ujiji, near Tabora, on
the 18th of September, whence he had the escort of
the renowned Tippoo Tib, the Arab trader, who had
rendered such signal service to Livingstone, Cameron,
and Stanley, and without further misadventure arrived
at Zanzibar at the beginning of December.

On the 10th of January 1887, he landed at **Suez**,
where he was met by his brother, the banker of **St.
Petersburg**, and by Dr. Schweinfurth.

He had spent seven years in the heart of Africa.

CHAPTER VII.

THE RELIEF-EXPEDITION.

Attempted expeditious of Dr. Fischer and Dr. Lenz—Geographical Society
of Edinburgh—Routes to Wadelai from the east—The Congo route—Formation of relief-committee in London—Arrival of Stanley in Europe—
Congo Flotilla placed at his disposal by King of the Belgians—European
members of expedition—Departure from London—Stanley at Cairo—Tippoo Tib accompanies Stanley—The "Madura"—Start from Zanzibar.

THREE years had passed without any direct communication with the Europeans blockaded in the
southern Soudan.

It was in 1882 that letters had been brought from
Lupton and Junker to Meshra-er-Rek, and thence
conveyed to Khartoom by the "Ismailia," the last
steamer that made the passage of the Upper Nile.
Amongst those on board on this occasion was Junker's assistant, the naturalist, Frederick Bohndorf,
who was fortunate in getting safely to Egypt.

Vague rumours from time to time reached Zanzibar, carried by the ivory traders, that some white men with troops were in the vicinity of Lake Albert; and then came the more definite tidings that Junker and Casati were safe at Lado, and at no great distance from Emin Bey. Whereupon, Dr. Junker's brother wrote from St. Petersburg to M. Rohlfs, the German consul at Zanzibar, to ascertain the possibility of despatching an expedition of relief. He was told that if the necessary funds were forthcoming such an undertaking was quite practicable, and that Dr. Fischer, who had for seven years been physician-extraordinary to the Sultan Saïd-Bargash, and was an experienced traveller, would be prepared to take it in charge.

The offer was accepted; and in August, Dr. Fischer, at the head of a large caravan, took his departure from the coast.

Simultaneously with this, another expedition was being organised on the Lower Congo, which was to be under the command of Dr. Oscar Lenz, an Austrian, who was well known as an African traveller. It was settled that he should endeavour to reach Wadelaï by way of the Upper Congo.

Both these expeditions were failures. Dr. Fischer found it impossible for any advance to be made beyond Lake Victoria; and Dr. Lenz, having been conveyed as far as the Victoria Falls by a steamer belonging to the Congo State, was unable to collect a caravan that would venture into the unknown lands to the north-east: he was obliged, therefore, to continue his journey to the south, proceeding by Nyangwé and Lake Tanganyika.

Meanwhile a letter was received from Mr. Mackay, the English missionary in Uganda, stating that he had heard that Dr. Junker, after many difficulties, had arrived in the Unyoro country, and was only awaiting his opportunity to pass through M'Wanga's territory and proceed homewards.

Another year of suspense followed, during which great anxiety prevailed; but at length tidings came from Zanzibar announcing that, safe and sound, Junker had made his way to the mission-station at M'salala. Great was the feeling of relief; and the general sympathy was stirred afresh when, a month later, letters were received from the traveller himself.

The civilised world was not indifferent to the appeal now made on behalf of the remaining prisoners of the Soudan. A general movement was felt. Dr. Schweinfurth took the lead in Egypt; Dr. Felkin, formerly medical officer to the Uganda mission, agitated the cause in England; in Germany, France, Italy and Belgium the public press and the scientific journals alike called attention to the critical situation of the surviving representatives of Europe in the district of the Upper Nile.

To the Geographical Society of Edinburgh belongs the honour of taking the initiative in reducing sympathy to practice. At a meeting, held on the 23rd of November 1886, the following resolutions were proposed and unanimously adopted :—

" That in consideration of his many services during twelve years in Central Africa, rendered not only to geography, but to science in general, and in recognition of his own personal endurance and of the assistance he has uniformly given to explorers, the Council of this Society deems that Emin Bey well deserves the support of the British Government.

" That the Council does not advocate any military expedition being sent to his relief, but believes that one of a pacific character might most advantageously be undertaken by the British Government.

" That it seems certain, in the judgment of the Council, that an expedition of this nature, traversing regions hitherto unexplored, would contribute materially to a further geographical knowledge of the interior of Africa."

A copy of these resolutions was forwarded to London, to Lord Iddesleigh, then Foreign Secretary.

Henceforth, the voice of the public did not let the matter rest. The question was no longer whether an expedition should be sent, but what route the expedition should take.

Three routes, all starting from Zanzibar, were suggested.

First of all, there was that proposed by Mr. Joseph Thomson, the Scotch explorer, who offered his own services as conductor. This route followed the direc-

tion which he had himself taken when he had gone to
the Masaï country ; on that occasion he had started
from Mombas on the coast, and passed through Taveta,
Nyongo and Njemps, reaching the eastern shore of
Lake Victoria near Wakala. The journey had occupied nine months. He now anticipated that he could
accomplish it in three months, or perhaps four, apparently forgetting how he had himself been unable to
make any advance, and ignoring the fact that Dr.
Fischer, still more recently, had been foiled in his
efforts to penetrate into the countries populated by
warlike and hostile tribes.

A second scheme was advocated by Dr. Felkin.
Anxious to keep clear of all complications with the
relentless King of Uganda, he recommended that a
long detour beyond Lake Victoria should be made in
the Mwootan Nzigé basin. It was a route that would
necessitate the passage of the caravan through regions
absolutely unknown, and would bring it into contact
with a dense population that had obstructed Stanley's
progress in 1877. It was not only very long but very
hazardous, and the voice of prudence might well ask
whether it was desirable to risk so much where all was
so uncertain.

Then, thirdly, there arose involuntarily the thought
of Stanley. Was not he the right, if not the only
man, for such an undertaking? The traveller, undaunted and renowned, who had found Livingstone in
1870, who had crossed Africa from shore to shore, and
discovered the Congo in 1878, who had formed the
independent state upon the Congo banks in 1884, was
not this the leader whose services they should seek?
Were not his experience, his energy, his reputation
amongst the native tribes the surest guarantees upon
which to rely?

Meanwhile it had transpired that Stanley himself
was ready to co-operate with the organising committee ; he would even undertake the conduct of an expedition. The route he would recommend would be
that which he had taken in 1876 ; the journey from
Zanzibar to Lake Victoria was known, by frequent
repetition, to be practicable ; beyond the Lake he
would run the risk of dealing with M'Wanga : he
would endeavour to enter into negotiations with him ;

he was sanguine that he could induce him to renew his
amic..ble relations with the white man, and thus having overcome the obstacles, and having obtained permission to pass through Uganda, he should go to
Unyoro and Lake Albert, and thence proceed to
Wadelaï by water.

Of the three routes thus suggested, the last seemed
to have most to commend it to approval. It was certainly the best known and the most direct; yet it was
not to be overlooked that it had the decided disadvantage of having to be accomplished almost entirely on
foot. Supposing the expedition to consist of 1000
men, how many, it must be asked, would hold out,
even so far as Lake Victoria? Before arriving at the
place of embarkation they would have to tramp more
than 700 miles, under a burning equatorial sun, every
one carrying a burden of over seventy pounds. How
many would desert? how many would succumb to
fatigue, and die? how many would be struck down
with fever, and become an encumbrance to the rest.

Arrived at the Lake, it had further to be considered
whether it were by any means certain that boats enough
could be secured to convey the hundreds of men, with
all the baggage, across.

But the Lake, after all, was only half way, and it
was *beyond* the Lake that the chief difficulties were
to be apprehended. Who could foretell what dangers
would be awaiting the caravan in Uganda? At the
first symptom of hostility the porters would be seized
with panic; and what was to hinder them from desert-
ing *en masse?* The way from Zanzibar by which they
had come would be open, and what could prevent them
from making their way back if they chose?

All these considerations had to be weighed.

It was while the matter was under debate, that the
writer of the present volume published an article in
" Le Mouvement Géographique" of December 6, in
which he proposed the route by way of the Congo and
Aruwimi.

The substance of the article was to the following
effect :—" Is there no other route besides those which
have been already proposed? Why not the Congo?
Not the Congo with its wide deviation to the south, by

Nyangwé, as followed by Dr. Lenz ; but *the Congo as far as and along the course of the Aruwimi.*

"From Banana to Matadi the passage by steamer takes only thirteen hours. The journey on foot to Leopoldville would require from fifteen to twenty days. Recently the steamer 'Stanley' has occupied only twenty-seven days in ascending the Congo from Stanley Pool to the Aruwimi, and when Stanley was exploring the river he got up to Yambuya in two days more.

Supposing then that the proper appliances and that the necessary porters can be secured, and that no unforeseen hindrances shall arise to prevent a continuous advance, it may be reckoned that in thirty-five to forty days, or, to take the utmost limit, in two months, an expedition might well accomplish the distance between Banana and Yambuya, which is just below the Aruwimi Falls. It would, moreover, involve no excessive exertion, as so large a proportion of the journey would be by water.

" 'True indeed it is that this point lies on the threshold of the unknown ; yet, after all, this 'unknown' may be held to be less alarming than the districts of Unyoro and Uganda, which are only too 'well known.' Upon the Aruwimi both Stanley and Grenfell fell in with peaceable tribes, and what merits consideration is, that the unexplored tract only extends to Sanga, at a distance of little over 130 miles. Sanga itself is the residence of a Monbuttoo chief who gave Junker a hospitable reception ; while the district to the east has been explored, not only by him, but likewise by Casati, and in some degree by Emin Bey. All these three would no doubt be remembered by the inhabitants, whose intentions may still be reckoned to be friendly, so that in all probability the caravan would be well received, and readily supplied both with provisions and guides.

" As to the question of time, it seems to us hardly to admit a doubt that Wadelaï would be much more quickly reached by the Congo and Aruwimi than by any other route from the east coast. In short, it may be maintained that by the way which is here proposed, it would be possible to arrive at the quarters of Emin Bey *in five months.*"

It had especially to be taken into account how comparatively easy the advance would be made by the fact of 900 miles on the upper river being by water. It was likewise an ascertained fact that food was abundant in the district, and these two facts combined demonstrated that the caravan would enter the unknown region with the men in robust health, not worn out by any previous fatigue; whilst at the same time they would have no way open by which they could be tempted to desert.

In England at first the opposition to the Congo route was very great. Every one seemed to have a preference for the eastern, or what was called "the Zanzibar route." The matter remained undecided—the Government took no step—but meanwhile private enterprise was on the alert, and active measures were being pushed forward. The wealthy Scotch philanthropist, Mr. Mackinnon, director of the British India Steam Navigation Company, was made chairman of the organising committee, and with his usual munificence, subscribed £10,000 towards an expedition. Sir Francis de Winton, formerly administrator-general of the Congo State, took the office of secretary; the Egyptian Government pledged itself to give financial support; the King of the Belgians gave the committee the warmest assurances of his sympathy, and placed at its disposal, if the Congo route should be adopted, a portion of the Upper Congo flotilla; and to crown the whole, Stanley volunteered his personal services, which of course were immediately accepted.

At that time Stanley was in America. Ever indefatigable in his vocation of advancing the cause of Africa, he was holding a series of meetings in the large towns of the United States, but he was no sooner apprised of the formation of the relief-expedition than he hurried back to London, where he arrived on the 27th of December, and from whence he proceeded on the 30th to Brussels.

Matters now advanced apace; decisions were promptly made and orders were definitely given. Communications passed rapidly between London, Brussels, Cairo, Zanzibar and the Congo. Egypt was requested to furnish a company of Soudanese soldiers, and Sir John Kirk, the British Consul at Zanzi-

bar, was instructed to engage several hundred soldiers
and porters. The Congo route had been deliberately
and finally chosen. Mr. Mackinnon sent orders to
Bombay that one of his company's steamers should be
at Zanzibar in readiness to convey the expedition to
the mouth of the Congo; and Stanley lost no time in
making up his staff of European coadjutors, returning once more to Brussels to take his leave of King
Leopold.

On the 20th of January 1887, the main body of the
staff left London by the *Navarino;* it consisted of
Major Barttelot of the 7th Fusileers, one of the bravest officers in the Soudan campaign; Captain Stairs
of the Royal Artillery; Captain Nelson of the Volun-
teers; Lieutenant Jephson; Surgeon-Major Parke;
Mr. Jameson the naturalist; Mr. Bonney and Mr.
Ward. They carried with them a large cargo of provisions and a complete supply of ammunition, one of
the specialities being a mitrailleuse worked on a novel
plan, designed by Maxim the engineer, a murderous
weapon capable of firing six hundred shots a minute,
and which might prove an effective means of defence
if any hostile attack were made upon them. Lastly,
there was a steel-plated whale-boat to be navigated
by either oars or sails, made in twelve sections, so
as to admit of being carried by hand, and designed
to facilitate the river passage and ultimately to be
launched upon Lake Albert.

In addition to the eight members of the staff who
started for Zanzibar there were two others, Mr. Ingham, and Mr. Troup, a former agent of the Free
State, who embarked at Liverpool direct for the
Congo, and were commissioned to engage 1500 natives
to act as porters in transporting all the baggage along
the line of the falls, from Matadi to Stanley Pool.

Stanley himself left London for Egypt *viâ* Brindisi,
on the 21st. By this route he gained several days'
advance upon the *Navarino*, and spent the interval in
Cairo, in consultation with Dr. Schweinfurth and Dr.
Junker, who had arrived there a fortnight previously.

It has been asserted that at this date there was an
entire lack of agreement between the three travellers
about the proper route to be taken; it has moreover
been stated that the Egyptian Government so far

adopted Dr. Junker's views, that the Zanzibar route ought to be followed, as to threaten to withdraw its support in case any other route were chosen. Such representations are by no means fair. It is true that at first Dr. Schweinfurth expressed some degree of preference for the Zanzibar route, but very soon, like Dr. Junker, he acceded to the choice of the Congo route ; while as to the Egyptian Government there was not the least foundation for what was said; it gave its financial support to the undertaking entirely unconditionally, and engaged, moreover, to provide the Soudanese soldiers for which it was asked.

On the 6th of February, Stanley left Cairo for Suez, and on the 22nd he reached Zanzibar, where he learned that the steamer *Madura*, which was to convey him to the mouth of the Congo, had arrived the day before.

An incident occurred during his brief stay at Zanzibar, which, when known in Europe, created no slight sensation. This was the engagement of Tippoo Tib as an agent of the Congo Free State.

Tippoo Tib is the wealthy Arab trader whom Livingstone and Cameron found settled at Nyangwé on the Lualaba, and who some years later accompanied Stanley through part of his descent of the Congo. Dr. Lenz and Lieutenant Gleerup during their travels visited his depôts on the Lualaba and the Manyema ; the Belgian Lieutenant Becker and the Swedish Lieutenant Webster both transacted business with him, and Dr. Junker, as has been mentioned, completed his journey from Tabora to Zanzibar under his escort. Every one of these travellers gives uniform high praise to his intelligence, his trustworthiness, and the courtesy of his manners.

His real name is Hamed-ben-Mohammed, Tippoo Tib being a nickname given him on account of a peculiar movement of his eyes.

Lieutenant Becker has written the following description of him : " The son of a Zanzibar Arab and a Mrima woman, Tippoo Tib has resided for ten years in the Manyema district, where he enjoys an unbounded popularity, not only in his own, but in the adjoining districts, where he is known as a man who would heartily disapprove of any unneighbourly acts.

TIPPOO TIB.
(From a Drawing by M. Louis Amelot.)

"From his immense plantations, cultivated by thousands of slaves, all blindly devoted to their master, and from his ivory-trade, of which he has the monopoly, he has in his duplex character of conqueror and trader, succeeded in creating for himself in the heart of Africa a veritable empire, in which, though he is nominally a vassal of the Sultan Saïd-Bargash, his authority is supreme.

"Though not of pure Arab blood, the Arab characteristic seems so far predominant in him as to dispose him instinctively to the exercise of patriarchal virtues. His self-command, his indomitable courage, his capacity for business, his far-sightedness, his rapid power of decision, his unfailing success, and a certain chivalrous attractiveness of manner, combine to make him, like Mirambo, a kind of hero, celebrated by all the rhapsodists of Oriental Africa."

Apparently Tippoo Tib is about forty-five years of age; he has short grisly hair and beard; he converses with much vivacity, his utterance being concise, energetic, and decisive. Only let the subject of ivory be introduced, and at once he is animated, and his eyes gleam with excitement; he becomes like one of the old Californian gold-diggers, who glowed with ecstasy when they told of their work, their findings, and their hopes. Ivory, in fact, may be said to be his absorbing thought. To this he owes all his wealth, and consequently his power, which, according to Wissman, who is acquainted with his territory, is much greater than is generally known. Owner as he is of numerous caravans of armed slaves, which he places under the command of his subordinates, he has cultivated large tracts of country, and in the course of time has established several very important agricultural settlements. It has been insinuated in certain quarters that his vast riches have not all been accumulated from irreproachable sources, and that a full statement of his mercantile transactions would show a somewhat intimate connection between ivory-dealing and the slave-traffic.

Be this, however, as it may, he is held in high repute by the natives, by travellers, and by the Europeans on the coast, and this reputation has been acquired by his extraordinary administrative faculty, by his prominent position amongst his fellow-traders and co-religionists, by his hospitality, and most of all, by his steadfastness to his word. Already an important character in eastern and central Africa, recent events have made him a historical personage.

In January 1885, when Captain Van Gèle, as agent of the Congo Association, arrived at Stanley Falls, he found that Tippoo Tib was established in the neighbourhood. He made a point of seeing him, and received from him the most satisfactory assurances of his peaceful intentions towards the white settlers, and his great desire to enter into amicable relations with them. It turned out, however, that eighteen months afterwards, the station, which was guarded only by a couple of Europeans and a few black soldiers, was attacked by Arabs, and deserted by its little garrison. It was true that the affair had taken place while Tippoo Tib was absent, and as subsequent inquiries showed, it was to be attributed, not so much to any positive hostility on the part of the Arabs, as to the incapability of the controller of the station, Mr. Deane, an Englishman. Yet it could not do otherwise than create considerable uneasiness in the Congo State, which was only then in process of formation.

And now, in 1887, having learned that both Tippoo Tib and Stanley were at Zanzibar together, the Congo Government took advantage of the circumstance to seek an explanation as to how it had come to pass that the station at the Falls had been assailed. In reply to Stanley's inquiry, Tippoo Tib renewed his assurances of his recognition of the Congo State, expressed his deep regret for what had happened, and declared that the assault had been made both during his absence and without his sanction.

The Congo Government had a further design. Considering that in a country so hard of access for European troops, it would be good policy to secure the aid of Arab hands towards suppressing raids and checking the slave-traffic, and, moreover, reckoning that it would be for the interests of civilisation if a recognised system of trade and agriculture could be established, they instructed Stanley to sound the Arab merchant as to whether he would be disposed to take office in the service of the Free State itself.

Accordingly, on the 23rd of February an interview

took place, as the result of which Tippoo Tib was definitely appointed Commissioner of the district of the Falls. By the covenants of the agreement he undertook to uphold the authority of the Free State along the upper river and its affluents, both at the station and lower down at the confluence of the Aruwimi, specified as the limit of his district; and to oppose the native chiefs and Arab traders, restraining them in all their raids and slave-traffic.

Criticism, keen and adverse, was awakened by the measure. Just as it had been when Gordon proposed to enlist the co-operation of Zebehr for the pacification of the Soudan, so now the idea of applying to an Arab trader for assistance in suppressing the slave-trade seemed unreasonable, if not preposterous. No doubt the circumstances were perplexing. It is an experiment; but Tippoo Tib's position is exceptional. Unlooked-for results may follow. The future alone can determine whether the policy is right or wrong. The compact with Tippoo Tib has been based solely upon his high repute for fidelity, gained amongst the most renowned and most discriminating of African explorers.

One thing which was immediately involved by this compact with Tippoo Tib was his co-operation with the relief-expedition now about to start. Accordingly it was arranged that he should accompany Stanley to the west coast and up the Congo, as far as the Falls station, there providing him with the 600 porters that would be required to bring the ivory back from Wadelaï.

At this date Stanley wrote : " When I was in Cairo Dr. Junker told me that Emin Bey has in his possession about seventy tons of ivory. At eight shillings a pound this would be worth more than £60,000. Not only would this cover all the expenses of our expedition, but would make it a financial success. Why not bring the ivory to the Congo? It would require nothing more than an adequate supply of porters ; and this consideration has determined me to negotiate with Tippoo Tib, who has contracted to provide me with 600 men, at the rate of £6 each for a journey from the Falls station to Lake Albert and back. As every porter carries a load of 70 lbs. we may reckon that each journey would bring a net value of £12,000 to the Falls."

On his arrival at Zanzibar, Stanley found that everything had been admirably arranged by Mr. Mackenzie, the agent of the British India Steam Navigation Company, who had the co-operation of the English Consul. Provisions and merchandise had been already embarked, and the auxiliaries had been gathered together, so that Stanley had only at once to go on board. During the time that Stanley was negotiating his contract with Tippoo Tib, Mr. Mackenzie was paying four months' wages in advance to the 623 Zanzibaris who had been hired for the expedition ; they were paid in detachments of fifty at a time, and forthwith sent in a barge to the *Madura*.

Thus far, including the nine Europeans, sixty-three Soudanese, and fourteen Somalis, the expedition consisted of 709 men, who were divided into seven companies ; to these had now to be added Tippoo Tib with his suite of ninety, comprising both sexes, making an aggregate of just 800.

The *Madura* left Zanzibar on the 24th of February ; on the 9th of March she passed the Cape ; and on the 18th cast anchor in Banana Creek, at the mouth of the Congo.

CHAPTER VIII.

ON THE LOWER CONGO.

The Congo—The Congo Free State—Its political and judicial organisation —Trade settlements—Instructions for aiding Stanley—Arrival of the *Madura* at Banana—Transport flotilla—Boma—Camp at Matadi—Trial-march —Start to the interior.

THE Congo claims the seventh place among the largest rivers of the world. It is nearly 3000 miles in length. In the volume of its waters it has no rival in the Eastern hemisphere, this being estimated at more than 50,000 cubic yards a second. In the magnitude of its current it is surpassed only by the Amazon. It rises in the high plateaux of Mouxinga, between 3000 and 4000 feet above the level of the sea, and forms in two different places a series of rapids. Its course through Central Africa is often obstructed by islands, and extending in width from twelve to eighteen miles, describes a vast curve which is twice crossed by the Equator. On either side it receives numerous affluents, and thus drains a river-basin, which in its area must be hardly less than half as large as the whole continent of Europe.

Long ago the Congo would have constituted the principal avenue to the interior had it not been that a succession of falls and rapids about 100 miles from its mouth completely paralysed all efforts for naviga-tion. These rapids, until recently, have had the effect of making the Congo a sort of *cul-de-sac*, a den of slavers into which European merchants hesitated to venture with any design of forming settlements. When Stanley for the first time reached the western coast on his way from Zanzibar to Nyangwé, a few trade-depôts were scattered at long intervals along the shores of the lower river, and Boma, about twenty hours' journey from the coast, was the out-post of civilisation and commerce ; for travellers who should risk any further advance there was the pros-pect of dying of hunger and of perishing in unknown districts where barbarism reigned supreme. This was ten years ago !

Such a discovery as Stanley's could not fail to awaken the keenest interest. Here was revealed to the eyes of Europe a vast region in the heart of Africa, rich, fertile, and densely populated, and per-meated by a colossal river-way, the mouth of which presented the exceptional advantage of being domi-nated by no European power. The opportunity for commercial enterprise was too fine to be overlooked, and accordingly, under the auspices of Leopold, King of the Belgians, a conference was held in Berlin, which resulted in the formation of the "Congo Free State" in the year 1885.

Since the date of King Leopold's proclamation, announcing the establishment of the new order of things, European activity has produced large results on the Lower Congo. The conditions of existence are improving with singular rapidity, and a political organisation has grown into fair proportions without provoking any serious opposition from the native

chiefs. The administration of the State is carried
on, in the name of the King, by a Governour-General
who has the control of every department with its
proper staff, consisting of about 150 European agents
distributed over twelve stations. There is a military
force of about 1000 black soldiers recruited from
the Haoussa of the Niger and the Bangala of the
Upper Congo; these are under the command of Belgian officers and subalterns. On the lower part of
the river a sort of police-inspection is maintained by
the employment of six steamboats, which are serviceable also, as occasion arises, for the conveyance of
the officials. In addition to these there are five other
steamers on the Upper Congo.

To provide against such infringements of the laws
of morality as seem to demand immediate repression
a penal code has been issued; but this is only temporary in its character, and is to be replaced, as soon as
experience will allow, by a more definite classification
of crimes and award of punishments. The present
is a transition state between the social anarchy of the
past and the future reign of law. A court of justice
is established at Banana, with a court of appeal at
Boma.

A postal service exists, and the State moreover has
entered the convention of the Postal Union. Offices
of the civil service are open in three departments.
To ensure the stability of property and to provide
security for any investment of capital, a State Register has been established. In its general principles
the Congo Land Law is founded upon the "Torrens
Act," a system which has been a practice in Australia
since 1858, and has likewise been adopted by France,
in Tunis. For the registration of titles to land plans
have already been made, by a special survey, of all
the districts on the lower river where there are any
European settlements.

All trade on the Congo, as is generally known, is
quite free. The State, by its international agree-
ments, is prohibited from levying either import or
transport duty: its only privilege is to receive an
export-duty on certain of the productions of the State
territory, but even this is very moderate, and rarely

amounts to more than four per cent. on the value of the goods.

The French were the first to establish any merchant-settlement on the Congo. In 1855, the house of Régis & Co. of Paris (now Daumas, Bérand & Co.) planted a depôt on Banana Point, which still retains the name of "French Point;" in subsequent years came the Dutch, followed by the Portuguese and English, and finally in 1885 by the Belgians.

In 1876, just before the date at which Stanley first arrived at Boma on his way from the interior, there were upon the banks of the Lower Congo thirty-three factories and branch-factories. Ten years later, resulting mainly from the impetus given by the enterprise of the Congo Association, this number was nearly tripled, so that in 1886 there were eighty-five establishments on the Lower Congo alone. In addition to these fifteen other stations belonging to the State, either mission-stations or business-marts, completed the chain of civilising and hospitable centres along the line of the Falls from Matadi to Leopoldville. There are now nine stations upon Stanley Pool and ten upon the Upper Congo. Hence it will be seen that upwards of fifty new settlements have been made upon the banks of the river which ten years since might have been described as practically unknown.

Progress such as this bears striking testimony to the far-sightedness of those who from the very first recognised the Congo as a promising avenue for carrying civilisation into the heart of Africa, and opening the rich resources of the country to European trade.

There is no room for question that the Congo is the one great river-highway for Equatorial Africa. Either by its own proper course or by its larger affluents it leads to the confines of Katanga, Manyema, the Soudan and the basin of the Upper Nile. So great are the comparative facilities that it offers for transport, and so comparatively certain is the security that prevails along its course that, notwithstanding its wide deflections, it could not reasonably fail to be proposed and finally to be adopted as the route which should be taken by the expedition now fitted out for the relief of Emin Bey: nor was any one so likely to appreciate the advantages it offered as Stanley, who had himself been the first to make known its eligibility to the world.

Obviously all the European settlements along the river would be fresh starting-points for the expedition, while the river itself would convey their steamers and whale-boats nearly a thousand miles inland: added to this there was the assurance of co-operation of the local government, to which the following instructions had been sent from Brussels by General Strauch, the Minister of the Interior:—" His Majesty the King, having been requested to authorise the State to aid the relief-expedition, undertakes to place at its disposal the *Stanley* and two steel-plated barges for two, or if need be, for three months. It was with reference to this that I sent you the telegram on the 15th of January, desiring you to give orders that the *Stanley* should be at Leopoldville on the 1st of April ready to ascend the river.

" In addition to the agreement, the conditions of which I now forward, the King has likewise promised the English committee that Mr. Stanley shall receive whatever assistance our agents in Africa can give him, saving all detriment to the interests of the State.

" This is no legal contract in the full sense of the word; it is simply a promise made upon the part of the King; but His Majesty is most anxious that it should be fulfilled; he does not entertain a doubt that our agents in Africa, many of whom are devoted men, will exert themselves, within the limits specified, to give their co-operation, even though it should entail upon them a certain amount of trouble; and he trusts that all of them will be desirous of saying that they have contributed to the success of an undertaking designed to relieve valiant soldiers who are so endeavouring to retain the last corner of the Soudan that it may not fall back into the grasp of barbarism."

In due time the expedition arrived. At eight o'clock on the morning of March 18th the *Madura* steamed into the harbour of Banana and cast anchor in front of the French factory. Two hours previously she had been signalled in sight, and the entire population of the place, white and black, thronged to the quay to await the arrival of the ship and to give her welcome. In the harbour was an exceptionally large concourse of steamers; there were the *Heron* and the *Prince Baudoin* of the Congo State Navy; the *Cacongo* of the Portuguese Royal Navy; the *Serpa Pinto*, belonging to the Portuguese firm of Valle and Azevedo; the *Nieman*, to the Dutch factory; the *Albuquerque*, to the British Congo Company; the *Angola*, to the English firm of Hatton & Cookson; a steamer belonging to the line of Woermann & Co. of Hamburg; and lastly the *Lys*, of the line of Walford & Co. of Antwerp, which was lying in melancholy plight on one of the sand-banks of the creek, where she had run aground two days before, through the carelessness of her captain.

No time was lost. Scarcely had the *Madura* made good her holdings, when the leader of the expedition proceeded in a pilot-boat to shore, intent upon satisfying himself at once as to what means of transport were available. Stanley is not only a bold and enterprising explorer, but it would seem as if the star of his good fortune never fails him; and now again it was shining favourably, inasmuch as it was a most fortuitous circumstance that so unusually large a number of steam-vessels should be assembled at one time at Banana. Not the least difficulty arose in securing the necessary assistance; the controllers of the factories and the commander of the Portuguese gunboat were equally ready and courteous in helping to forward men and baggage to Matadi.

The arrival of Tippoo Tib on board the *Madura*, and his appointment as agent of the Congo State, was the cause of as much surprise in Banana as in Europe. He did not land with Stanley, but remained on the ship, where the hundreds of men that formed the expedition were drawn up in perfect order and discipline, singularly in contrast with the usual habits of negroes when associated in any numbers. Good training was already beginning to tell.

Next day the change of ships was effected without commotion or accident, and the flotilla commenced the ascent of the river past Boma to Matadi. The *Albuquerque* and the *Nieman* took the lead with the Zanzibaris and the Somalis on board; the *Serpa Pinto* followed, carrying Stanley and Tippoo Tib; then came the *Heron*, and lastly the *Cacongo* with the Egyptian detachment.   In this order the steamers arrived on the 20th in the roadstead of Boma, where they stayed awhile, without shutting off their steam, to allow Stanley to make a short visit on shore.

For about a year Boma has been the seat of the local administration of the Free State, removed from Vivi where it had been originally established.   It is also the residence of the Governour-General.   The roadstead is very fine, more than half a mile in width and varying in depth from three to ten fathoms.   The whole settlement is rapidly extending.   Already its buildings of wood and iron, scattered along the river-bank and running up to the high ground at the back, present an appearance that is exceedingly picturesque. Factories of various nations, Dutch, French, Portuguese and English, are erected on the shore, where also are to be seen the different departmental offices of the land-survey, the post, the customs and the shipping.   Upon the high ground of the plateau, which is before long to be connected with the quay-level by a short railway, stand the house of the Governour-General, the residences of the public officials engaged in the works or connected with finance, the sanatorium, and the barracks for the garrison.   Over the intervening slopes are scattered the quarters of the black dependents, little villages of Haoussa, Bangala, Kabinda, Krooboys, Kaffirs and B congo.   Close to the river there is likewise a mission served by French priests; and a little lower down on the island of Mateba is a Belgian agricultural settlement founded by M. Roubaix of Antwerp.

It is but a few years since the white population of Boma was under twenty-five in number; now, including Mateba, it must amount to about 120, of whom nearly half have some share in the administration of the State.   Its black population, composed exclusively of soldiers and labourers on the Government works or in the factories, numbers not less than 500.   The garrison is 200 strong, and is composed of one company of Haoussa recruits from the Niger basin and another of Bangala from the Upper Congo : they wear uniform and are armed with Schneider rifles.

Stanley's stay on shore at Boma was very brief, and having received some of the chief Government officials who visited him on the *Serpa Pinto*, he resumed the voyage to Matadi, arriving there about five o'clock the same evening.

Matadi is a group of little European settlements on the left bank of the Congo, almost exactly opposite Vivi. There is a Government station, and a Dutch and a Portuguese factory. It is the starting point on the pedestrian route along the south bank to Stanley Pool, and will in all probability be the site of the terminus of the railway which is in project.

In due order the disembarkment was made on the following day. The expedition took up its quarters on an open plot of ground not far from the Portuguese factory. It was the first drill in the way of encampment. All the different burdens were collected together, including the sections of the whale-boat and the mitrailleuse. Besides these there were the Zanzibar donkeys provided as mounts for the Europeans and Arabs, and the herd of Cape sheep and goats that were destined to supply the table of the officials along the way.

Before starting for good along the roadway past the rapids, which Stanley knew by personal toil to be extremely arduous, he resolved to make an experimental march out, and to have a preliminary practice in the method of encamping. Accordingly he gave the necessary instructions to his coadjutors, and the whole caravan being divided, as it has been said, into seven sections of over one hundred, each under the command of a European, it was conducted, baggage and all, to an open place that seemed suited to the purpose.

Mounted on a donkey that had been handsomely caparisoned for the occasion, Stanley took the head of the column. By his side marched one of his boys, bearing the stars and stripes of the American banner; an overt demonstration that notwithstanding his English birth, and in spite of his being in the service of the ruler of the Congo and in command of an Anglo-Egyptian expedition, he does not forget, nor intend it to be forgotten, that he is an adopted citizen of the United States.

Everything was done well and in order. The caravan unwound itself like a huge serpent along the river bank, and received orders to make a second encampment near the station.

On another day, a trial was made of the Maxim mitrailleuse, which was pointed across the river and discharged with startling effect.

Four days were passed at Matadi, partly in organisation, partly in rest, the actual start for the interior being made on the 25th of March.

In the early morning, at half-past four, the camp was aroused by the sound of a shrill and piercing blast. This proceeded from a kind of marine fog-horn provided with a huge gong and worked by a piston, designed to be used for the daily reveillé. Instantaneously every one was on the stir, and for a quarter of an hour the hubbub and confusion of 800 negroes rushing about everywhere, shouting and gesticulating, were inconceivably great. Hard work had the eight Europeans of the staff, as they galloped backwards and forwards on their donkeys, to bring about anything like method; but they ultimately succeeded, and gradually calmness was restored, and the caravan was duly arranged in marching order.

In the vanguard were the Soudanese soldiers; then followed the Somalis, the Zanzibaris and the porters with their loads; Tippoo Tib and his people fell into their allotted place; the twelve sections of the whaleboat were distributed, each to be carried by two bearers, and the flocks were sent to the rear of the column. Then the various banners were unfurled and floated gaily along the line; the standard of the "Emin Relief Expedition" was in front side by side with Stanley's American flag; then there were the standards of England and of Egypt; and besides these the Arab oriflammes, glittering with their inscriptions from the Koran. Thus was the caravan marshalled ready to start.

Another blast from the horn and the caravan was on the move. The Emin Pasha expedition had indeed set out for the interior!

It was now two months since Stanley had started from London; he had reckoned that if no impediment should arise to hinder him, he should in about five months arrive where he would be close to Emin's quarters. Immediately before him now lay a journey of hardly less than 2000 miles, well nigh the same distance as there is between Madrid and St. Petersburg.

CHAPTER IX.

THE DISTRICT OF THE FALLS.

The Congo in the district of the Falls—Progress of European occupation—Proposed line of railway—The rock of Palaballa—Caravan route—Passage of the Luvu—A native market—Passage of the Kuilu—Mount Bidi—Station of Lukungu and adjacent settlements—The Bakongo—Service of porters—Mr. Ingham and Mr. Rose Troup—The River Inkissi—Arrival at Stanley Pool.

PARALLEL to the coast of Africa, and at no great distance from it, there lies a range of low mountains, formed on the edge of the plateaus, the uniformity of which is broken at intervals by some isolated peaks. Across this coast-chain the waters collected in the central plains have hollowed out for themselves channels along which they escape towards the sea, and these channels are shut in by rocky cliffs between which the streams roll on with an impetuous rush.

Of these water-courses none is so noted, nor at the same time so wild and romantic, as that along which pours the enormous volume of the waters of the Congo. Between Matadi and Leopoldville the stream is interrupted by no less than thirty-two falls or rapids, every one of which presents a spectacle of real magnificence.

Imagination may well conceive of the river-bed as a gigantic staircase, some 200 miles in length, descending from an altitude of 800 feet, and divided by thirty-two steps all differing in width and height; it is enclosed on either hand by rocky banks, and ever and again obstructed by dark projecting reefs and blocks of stone of every size and shape. Such is the Cyclopean channel along which rushes the Congo. It is the monarch of the Old-World rivers, here in its infant course spreading out into an expanse of water some 2000 or 3000 yards wide, and here again contracting itself to a breadth of 300 yards, but continuously gaining in its depth and velocity what it loses in its

superficial extent. At every angle of the channel
through which it rolls it seems to assume a different
character; in one place it appears to be possessed
with a furious rage that is indomitable, as it precipi-
tates itself into an amphitheatre of rocks where the
waters whirl in tumultuous eddies and dashing themselves against the granite crags are mingled in terrific
chaos; at another place, after having continued its
wild career for some miles (as at the rapids of Nsongo
and Lumba), the foaming billows of the river gradually subside and are lulled to rest, till they spread
themselves out in the tranquillity of a placid lake.

The calm, however, is all a delusion; soon again the
still waters are animated with redoubled fury; once
more they dash forward with increased velocity, and
finding a yet steeper slope, they hurl themselves into
another of the romantic gorges, where they renew their
ebullitions with an awful roar.

On either side of the river, as thus it tears along its
impetuous course, are lines of hills, often rising into
peaks with bare summits, broken either by sloping
valleys or by deep ravines, the sides of which are
clothed with tall rank grass, except in parts where
they are marshy, or covered with dense forests.

Such is the region of the Falls; such is the giant
barrier which Nature has erected almost adjacent to
the mouth of the Congo, as though she desired to
throw every impediment she could in the way of access to these regions of Africa, and to do her utmost
to provide a bulwark to defend the wealth of the interior. For three centuries every effort of the intruder
has been baffled; the barrier has been effectual to re-
buff every expedition that has been taken in hand, and
has defied each successive attempt to penetrate the
secrets of the mysterious land.

It was reserved for Stanley to overcome the obstacle, but the achievement was accomplished at the cost
of enormous labour and large sacrifice of life.

In 1877, when he was in command of the expedition that had been started under the joint auspices
of the *New York Herald* and the *Daily Telegraph*, he
took no less than five months in descending the river
from Stanley Pool to Boma, his progress being perpetually impeded both by the practical difficulties of

the road and by the hostility of the natives. On the way he lost fifteen of his men, including Frank Pocock, the last of his European associates.

Two years later he again appeared upon the scene, this time under commission from the King of the Belgians, and at the head of an expedition for " the survey of the Upper Congo." Carrying sections of steamers and buildings, as well as a variety of materials in his train, he spent a further two years in making his way up from Vivi to Stanley Pool. During this time six Europeans and fifty natives died, whilst fifteen other white men became so unwell that they were obliged to return. Such was the original balance-sheet of that memorable enterprise that bears so striking a testimony to the unwavering confidence, the rare courage, and the indomitable energy of its leader.

At present no less than twelve European settlements mark out the new route, and more than 5000 native porters are at the service of the white men, making a journey in perfect safety from Matadi to Leopoldville in twenty days, conveying European merchandise to the Pool, and bringing back large cargoes of ivory from the upper districts to the steamers on the river below.

Considerable, however, as is the progress made within the last six years, it does not yet satisfy the requirements of the pioneers of civilisation. Looking to the fertile lands of the interior, and taking account of the vast regions, alike wealthy and populous, that are drained by the immense navigable network of the Upper Congo, they cannot fail to realise that so long as these districts are unconnected with the sea by some quick and easy means of communication, they must necessarily continue, in spite of their rich promise, to be comparatively uncultivated and unproductive.

It was in view of this that Captain Van de Velde took upon himself to say : " Even for the organisation of a transport service either of horses and mules or of waggons drawn by oxen, it would be necessary to make a wide and substantial roadway, as well as to throw permanent bridges over the ravines and torrents, a system entailing large importations of draught cattle, which would further involve the establishment of farms, studs, and places of pasturage. But the time for all this is

over! The day of vans and waggons is gone; it is
only steam that can be adopted as an economical
method of traction. Locomotives do not suffer from
the climate; they require no veterinary skill, a native
smith can suffice; meanwhile for fodder all they want
is wood, of which the district of the Congo supplies
ample store; and even this may be dispensed with
when they are worked by electricity generated by the
motive power of the cataracts."

It has been resolved accordingly that a railroad
should be constructed. Already a party of French
and Belgian engineers, under the direction of Messrs.
Cambier and Charmanne, is engaged in the survey of
the land between Matadi and the Pool, with the design of ascertaining the best route and of estimating
the cost. If Stanley could have had these locomotives
of the future at his disposal a few days would have
sufficed for the transport of his 800 men with their
1500 packages to Stanley Pool without fatigue, an undertaking which on foot, along the rough tracks of the
caravans, could only be accomplished by a month's
hard marching.

Beyond Matadi, after the passage of the Mpozo,
the first obstacle on the way is the rock-wall of Palaballa. This is crossed by a steep path bordered by
blocks of white quartz. At its summit, which is about
2000 feet above sea-level, is a flourishing settlement
founded by the English Baptist Mission; and the vast
mountain panorama viewed from thence opens before
the traveller some idea of the country he has to cross,
and indicates the difficulties he must have to encounter.

The caravan road is a mere footpath, rarely more
than thirty inches wide, winding through a stifling
labyrinth of grass several yards high. Long and
toilsome ascents under the glare of the African sun
are succeeded by descents equally wearisome leading
to the marshes in the hollow of the deep ravines.
At intervals along the slopes there are extensive
groves of palm-trees or bananas, baobabs also being
not uncommon. On the lower ground the way pro-
ceeds through fine forests, thick with trees of various
species, connected one with another by wreaths of
creepers that form verdant arches overhead, and are
the resort of the widow-bird, with its black plumage

and long tail, as well as of countless smaller birds resembling bengalis, which rise in swarms as their solitude is disturbed. Only in single file is it possible for any caravan to make advance, so that the expedition with its 750 men would be extended for a length little short of half a mile.

On the 29th of March Stanley reached the Luvu, one of the affluents of the Congo on its southern bank. Across this river the agents of the Free State have formed a suspension-bridge of iron rods attached to baobabs on either bank, a structure of which white men and Zanzibaris avail themselves, but so frail that the natives, as a rule, hesitate to trust their feet upon it, as it oscillates so suspiciously under their weight.

Beyond Palaballa the country is almost reduced to the condition of a desert, mainly in consequence of the withdrawal of the natives from the neighbourhood of the caravan routes. This they have done not from any fear of the white man, whom they are disposed to trust entirely, but through the depredations of the negro porters, who have no sense of any rights of property save the rights of the strongest. With the recent increase of the caravan traffic between Matadi and Leopoldville the damage done to the plantations adjacent to the line of route became more and more intolerable; while in addition to this, the soldiers, Haoussa, Zanzibari, or Bangala, who were engaged for escort, would perpetually commit outrages which the European was powerless to repress. The natives, therefore, recognised the expediency of retiring further off; they removed their huts, and re-erected them at such a distance from the line of thoroughfare as they concluded would render their homesteads safe from the attacks of such marauders. It followed, as a consequence of this migration, that on entering the district Stanley's 750 men had nothing to depend on from the products of the place. They found themselves without the opportunity of providing their requisite supplies, because there were no longer any of the accustomed markets to which the inhabitants of the villages within reach of the route had hitherto been sending the produce of their fields, their hunting-grounds, and their fisheries. Even in the interior of

the country when the report was circulated that the
notorious Boula Matari was advancing with 1000 men,
all armed with guns, the alarm was so great that for
a week the ordinary market-places were quite deserted.

Very notable are these markets as demonstrating
the commercial capabilities of the natives, which are
quite surprising. A visit to one of them, that of
Kuzo-Kienzi, is described by Captain Thys : " Here,"
he says, " is a gathering of between 200 and 300
salespeople of both sexes, with their variety of goods
displayed either in baskets or spread out on banana
leaves, a throng of purchasers meanwhile moving to
and fro and inspecting the commodities. The women,
who are more numerous than the men, squat down in
front of their goods and exhibit a peculiar aptitude
for their occupation ; they solicit the attention of the
passer-by, they eulogise the quality of what they offer
to sell, they exclaim indignantly when a price is tendered below the proper value, and with insinuating
smile beguile their customers to make a purchase.
The sale of vegetables is entirely committed to the
women.

" The enumeration of the articles exhibited for sale
comprises a long list. At Kuzo-Kienzi I have myself
seen goats, pigs, fowls, fish (both fresh and smoke-
dried), hippopotamus-meat and hides, rows of spitted
rats, locusts, shrimps, sweet potatoes, maize, haricot
beans, green peas, yams, bananas, earth-nuts, eggs,
manioc (cooked as well as raw), manioc-bread, made
up both into rolls and long loaves, pine-apples, sugar-
cane, palm-nuts, tobacco-leaves in considerable quantity, palm-wine supplied either in jars procured from
the coast or in their own native calebashes, cabbages,
sorrel, spinach, pimento, and punnets of mixed salad
arranged very much as in our European market-gar-
dens. In addition to these I noticed a few small lots
of ivory, strong ropes of native manufacture, mats,
European stuffs in considerable variety, powder, glass,
pottery, beads—in short, almost every conceivable
kind of ware.

" Avenues run through the market-place, which is
divided into sections each appropriated to its own
kind of merchandise ; in one place is the ivory-mart,

in another the tobacco-mart, by far the greater allot-
ments being assigned to the vegetable department.

"There are three kinds of currency in use—the
handkerchief, the mitaku, which is brass-wire, and the
blue bead known as 'matare.' A class of men who
may be described as a sort of money-changers have
their own proper quarters, effecting such exchanges as
the business of the market may require.

"As an ordinary rule traffic would commence about
ten in the morning and be continued till nearly four in
the afternoon ; and the close of the market I must re-
luctantly report is characterised by those scenes of
disorder which not unfrequently are witnessed in the
like circumstances at home. Immoderate drinking as
ever provokes angry disputes, the intoxicating palm-
wine being here the substitute for beer and gin."

To fall in with such a bustling market as this would
have been an inestimable boon to the caravan which,
with the exception of a few porters who had succumbed
to illness or fatigue, safely reached the Lukunga, in
good order, on the 8th of April.

A pleasing exception is the Lukunga to the general
aspect of the Congo-banks in the region of the Falls.
Its valley is fertile, and the soil well adapted to the
cultivation of any kind of tropical produce, so that at-
tempts have been already made to promote the growth
of mountain-rice, coffee, eucalyptus, and other crops.

Stretched across the landscape on the far side of the
Lukunga lies the Ndunga range, the loftiest in the entire district, from the middle of which, rearing itself
some 800 feet above the surrounding eminences, is a
quartzose projection, known as Mount Bidi. The summit of this commands an extensive view. At the base
of the mountain, between the Congo on the north and
the village of Lutete on the east, are valleys rich in
vegetation and abounding in plantations, from which
the requirements of many villages are supplied. Further off is a succession of extensive plains, on which
dark green tracts indicate the position of other villages
nestling in the shelter of their venerable " safos."

It is here at the Lukunga that the second portion of
the Falls district is reached. Here, too, seems to be
the boundary beyond which the grasping, idle native,
brutalised by alcohol, is no longer to be seen as he is

on the lower river ; he is replaced by the negro, sturdy
and industrious, who for centuries has maintained business relations both with the Pool and with the Portuguese colony of Angola.

There are six European settlements in the district.
One station belonging to the State is at Lukungu, and
another at Manyanga-South ; at Lukungu, too, there
is an American mission ; an English Baptist mission
has been settled at Lutete ; a Rotterdam firm has a
store at Ndunga ; and the Belgian Society for trade
with the Upper Congo, of which the headquarters are
at Brussels, maintains a station at Manyanga-South.

The country generally is well-populated. Neither
caravans nor negro porters are objects of terror to the
natives, who, living as they do in such near proximity
to the white men, feel themselves assured of adequate
protection.

The indigenous population mainly belong to the
Bakongo tribe. They occupy the southern bank of
the river from the Congo-Portuguese frontier near
Nokki as far as Stanley Pool. Chiefly agriculturists,
they, however, do a considerable trade in ivory, palm-
oil, caoutchouc, and earth-nuts. To procure their
ivory they make long journeys eastward, and thus
become intermediate agents between the tribes of the
interior and the factories that have been planted on
the lower river and on the coast. Although their own
country abounds in elephants, they rarely hunt them,
apparently not having weapons sufficiently strong to
attack such pachydermata.

Distinct communities are formed by the various ag-
glomerations of huts. In the districts near the river
the hamlets are somewhat scattered and small ; but in
the interior where the population is more dense, villages of considerable magnitude exist; for instance,
Mwala, in the Inkissi basin, visited by Lieut. Hack-
inson of the Congo State in 1886, might without im-
propriety be called a town, as it reckons 2000 inhabitants.

Throughout the region there are very few chiefs
possessing anything like absolute power or authority,
either on account of their wealth or of any terror they
can inspire. Formerly there were some leaders with
pretensions to be potentates who succeeded more or

less in establishing a kind of sovereignty and in exacting tribute, but these have now disappeared. As matter of fact the title of "prince" which is now given to the ostensible village chief on the Lower Congo is quite inaccurate. Sovereignty, as we in Europe understand it, does not exist among the Bakongo. The recognized chief is generally the oldest freeman ; the others consult him, respect his opinion and yield him homage, but they pay him no tribute and are under no obligation to obey him. It might almost be said that with certain limitations every Bakongo is his own chief.

This peculiar political organisation, and, combined with it, the singular aptitude for trade exhibited by the natives, constitute two highly important factors in the future of the new State ; and it was these considerations that led Colonel de Winton, the former Administrator-General, to maintain that he did not believe that throughout the uncivilised world there existed a territory which for security to Europeans and for commercial prospects offered such advantages as the basin of the Congo. It is noteworthy that during the ten years or more in which Europeans have been exploring the country, neither in French Congo nor in Free State Congo has *one single white man* lost his life by any assault on the part of the natives.

Agriculture amongst the Bakongo is on a somewhat advanced line ; and they have a large variety of crops, such as maize, manioc, yams, sweet potatoes, earthnuts, egg-plants, cabbages, and beans. They also grow palms, sugar-canes, cotton, and tobacco, as well as many kinds of fruit-trees, including bananas, guavas, and citrons. Each village is surrounded by its own plantation, and the inhabitants never suffer from deficiency of food.

Cotton is used for sewing purposes ; and a kind of grass, as well as the fibre of the pine-apple, which grows very abundantly, furnishes material for the manufacture of some serviceable fabrics.

A strong, industrious race are the Bakongo, thoroughly alive to the conviction that they must work if they would live. They are very keen in their desire to obtain goods of European make ; and it is for the sake of procuring them that the young men are ready

to be hired as porters, an occupation in itself far more
toilsome than field labour. Already the people are
beginning to develop a certain amount of taste approaching to luxury in the construction and internal
arrangements of their dwellings, so that a chief will
replace his hut by a house of plaster or of wood. More
than in other districts the women are in a subordinate
position, for as the men themselves do the field-work,
they are more exacting of their wives in other duties.
All the valleys being under cultivation, there are comparatively few of the wooded gorges that are frequent
in other parts of the country.

It is especially in the district between Manyanga,
Lukungu, and Lutete that the natives are recruited as
porters for the transport service which has now regularly established itself, and is in active operation
between the Lower and the Upper Congo.

For the service between Matadi and Manyanga,
Lukungu is the chief hiring centre. The " Capitas,"
or conductors of caravans, are engaged there. These
agents, having first received their " Mokande " by way
of license or permit, present themselves with their
men to the Controller at Matadi. Here the loads are
given out, an average weight of seventy pounds being
assigned to each porter. The Capita takes charge of
the whole, superintends the transport all the way to
Manyanga, where upon due delivery of the goods he
receives a form of acknowledgement, which he carries
back to Lukungu, where he obtains his payment for
the transaction.

Manyanga itself is the centre for engaging porters
to proceed to the Pool. They come chiefly from the
environs of Lutete and the neighbourhood of the river
Inkissi, and do not fail in numbers. At present
there are several thousand young men from eighteen
to twenty-five years of age who are not unwilling to
be hired by the month, and this in a country where
seven years ago the representatives of the Congo Association were almost baffled in their efforts to get any
help whatever. The explanation of the altered condition of things is found in the fact that during the interval children have not only grown to be young men,
but have had such peaceable associations with Europeans, learning the value of their commodities, that in

order to procure them for themselves they are anxious
to engage themselves in their service. Thus it has
been brought about that Lukungu, Lutete, and Manyanga all contribute towards the supply of porters, so
that for some time to come there is no likelihood of
any deficiency of labour of this kind. Every day the
" wants " of the native population are increasing ; clothing is becoming general, the use of sandals is getting
more and more common, and in this region, where the
nights and early mornings are chilly, there is nothing
more prized than a rug or blanket of some kind. To
become the owner of such novelties the native is ready
to undertake almost any task upon which the white
man may employ him : at present he is only a porter ;
but there is nothing in the way of his becoming a navvy
or an artisan.

Lieutenant Franqui, who for two years had been in
charge of the station of Lukungu, has demonstrated
the extraordinary impulse given to the transport service between Matadi and Leopoldville in 1887, which
was just the date of the passage of the expedition.
His figures speak for themselves.

"Some internecine wars," he says, " and more
especially the discontent of the natives, who had misgivings about the competition which would arise from
rival commercial establishments being settled at Leopoldville, caused a temporary check in the supply of
porters.

" At the beginning of 1887 loads were accumulat-
ing on the lower river, and the condition of things was
becoming more serious because further large transports were known to be on the way. Already the
storehouses at Matadi contained upwards of 4000
packages, representing over 100 tons weight, whilst
the arrival had been notified of the steamers *Ville de
Bruxelles* and *Roi des Belges* bringing 6000 loads
more ; and besides this there were 1800 loads of supplies for the Congo Company. Meanwhile there was
a standing contract for the transport of 400 loads a
month ; and now, to crown it all, came the announcement of the approach of Stanley's Expedition for the
relief of Emin Pasha, which would necessitate the
conveyance of 1200 loads more, and which demanded
the utmost despatch.

"At that time the entire direction of the transport service was in my hands. First appealing to the zeal of my European staff, I endeavoured to make the natives understand that it would be for their own interest that they should work for the Government, and in a month the State was informed that 7000 men had been engaged. During March I had the satisfaction of despatching over 5000 porters with their loads.

"The business firms who managed transport on their own account suffered considerably from the recruiting thus effected on behalf of the State, as in addition to the 5000 porters there were at least 5000 natives employed in the various stores. So that, during a single month, more than 8000 men were engaged for carrying on the caravan traffic between Matadi and Leopoldville.

"All through the ensuing months recruiting went on briskly, and porters flocked in, with the result that by the end of October nearly every one of the loads had been forwarded from Matadi. I am thus in the position to testify that within an interval of eight months more than 30,000 loads were transported, and, reckoning the porters who undertook the work as far as Lukungu, not less than 60,000 men were employed. "

Nor again could any one better attest the remarkable progress that had been made in the facility of securing porters than Messrs. Ingham and Rose Troup, who were sent direct from Liverpool to provide for the transport of Stanley's baggage. The state of things had become altogether different since the time when they were first in the service of the Congo Association. They had now no difficulty in finding 1500 men to carry out the required task. Mr. Ingham took charge of the transport between Matadi and Manyanga, Mr. Troup undertaking the arrangements between Manyanga and Leopoldville. Both of them accomplished their mission with complete success. On the way to the Pool one gang of porters met other gangs returning to Matadi to bring up the baggage that had been left behind; but everything was well ordered, and in a month all was safely deposited at Leopoldville.

On the 8th of April, at 11 A.M., the first to arrive at

Lukungu was Tippoo Tib, with his troop. He made himself known to Lieutenant Franqui, who invited him to his verandah and offered him coffee. Tippoo Tib mentioned Boma, saying that it had appeared to him to be a place of some importance, and regretting that lack of time had prevented him from landing to inspect it. He likewise spoke highly of the caravan route beyond Banza-Manteka, and pronounced it well adapted for the transport of ivory. He then exhibited the contract that had been signed by himself and Stanley at Zanzibar, and had been deposited in a box containing various documents and photographs of Van Gele, Wissmann, Wester, Gleerup, and others.

Stanley, with the main contingent of the party, arrived about two hours later, and mounted on their fine white donkeys, all the Europeans made their entry. Out of the flock of fifteen merino sheep which had been brought from the Cape only one was missing, which had yielded to fatigue on the previous day. As chief of the expedition, Stanley, for himself and his staff, accepted an invitation to dine at the station, where he spoke in high spirits, and declared that he was full of confidence in the ultimate success of his enterprise.

Next morning the whole force mustered for an inspection of their arms and equipment. There were four companies, each numbering about 200 men. The Zanzibaris were under the charge of Messrs. Nelson, Stairs, and Rose Troup, the Soudanese and Somalis being assigned to the control of Major Barttelot. The companies were again subdivided into three groups, each under the supervision of a nyampara, and provided with a red banner.

On a square of about one hundred yards Stanley had the entire force drawn out in double file, and proceeded with the utmost care to investigate every detail, making the inspection with a calmness that betokened the presence of a competent, conscientious, and far-seeing leader.

In the evening the whole camp was *en fête*. All the Europeans, those attached to the station as well as those belonging to the expedition, joined in the merriment, Stanley himself at first leading off one of the national dances of the Zanzibaris, and afterwards

beating time for their movements. The enthusiasm
was great, and Stanley was borne along in a frenzy
of delight.

Trifling as it may seem, this is an instance of the
adroitness with which Stanley attracts to himself the
devotion of his men. Those who speak of him as un-
popular with his followers must speak without war-
rant: he is strict, but he is kind; and, what is more,
while he knows how to make the negroes submissive
to his authority, he succeeds in securing their attach-
ment to himself.

When, at 10.30 A.M. on the following morning, the
expedition, in good order, made a start, it was only
requisite to leave seven men behind as invalids. Of
these one died, two returned to Matadi, the remaining
four being able to rejoin the force before reaching
Leopoldville. Two months afterwards, several European newspapers, professing to have trustworthy information, actually announced that the expedition had
been decimated by famine and that its line of march
was strewn with bodies of the dead!

Two whole days were occupied in the passage of the
river Inkissi; the whale-boat was launched, and had
to go backward and forward, from bank to bank, no
less than eighty times. At the village of Nsello, near
the point of confluence, the river is 160 yards wide,
and enclosed by wooded cliffs varying from 50 to 100
yards in height. A few miles higher up it is much
broken by rapids, but further on, beyond the village
of Kilemfi, its course is perfectly free, and runs through
plains pleasing in aspect and populous with agricultural communities. The country on the right bank is
occupied by the Wambundu, a tribe mainly engaged
in the cultivation of the soil, and dependent on the
Matoko of Wazanzi, whose authority extends from
the Inkissi to the Pool. It is through this region that
the projected railway would pass.

When, on the 27th of April, the expedition crossed
the wooded rock of Yombi, it was with no small feeling of relief that the announcement was hailed that
Stanley Pool could be distinguished in the distance, its
placid waters glistening between the trees,

CHAPTER X.

STANLEY POOL.

Stanley Pool; history and description—River network of the Upper Congo —Mangale and Mense—European settlements—Leopoldville—Arrival of the relief-expedition—Means of transport—The *Stanley* and the mission-boats—Contention with the American Baptist Mission—Letter from Stanley to London Committee—Intervention of Commissary at Leopold-ville—Transport assured—" Better than could be expected "—Deficiency of food and reported famine—Vanguard despatched under Major Barttelot —Embarkation at Inchassa—On the way to the Aruwimi.

A GLANCE at the map at once makes it evident that the Congo, before making its way to the wild ravines of the falls, opens out into a large expanse of about nine square miles, approaching to the circular in form, on which Stanley has bestowed his own name, designating it " Stanley Pool."

In all the narratives of the Congo exploration no name is of more frequent occurrence than that of this important lake; no place has been more repeatedly the subject of dispute, as none can have a greater political significance, whilst nowhere has the progress of European occupation been more rapid. Stanley Pool, in fact, is the common port of all the navigable highways above it; it is the terminus of what is one of the finest network of rivers in the world, offering for the development of steam navigation a course which in various directions has been surveyed for over 8000 miles.

Hence steamers can have access to not a few of the most fertile and populous regions of Central Africa. To Stanley Falls and the Aruwimi the route lies along the Congo itself; by the Kasai and Sankullu the way is open to the territory of the Bashilangé and the Baluba; by the Chuapa to the heart of the Balolo country; by the Lomami to the confines of Nyangwe and Urua; and by the Mobangi-Welle to the land of the Niam-niam. A survey is about to be made of the Bounga, through French Congo, and there is little doubt that it will be proved to lead to the foot of the

high plateau of the Adamawa, of the fertility of which
Bart and Flégel have said so much.

It was on the 12th of March 1877 that Stanley,
while on his way from Nyangwe, discovered the Pool.
Four years later, when he was in command of the first
expedition sent out by the Society for the Investiga-
tion of the Upper Congo, he returned thither accompanied by Captain Braconnier and Lieut. Valcke, and
finding the right-hand bank occupied by a French
station that had been established some months previously by M. de Brazza, he crossed over to the
southern side and founded Leopoldville.

The route now lay open. Missionaries and merchants have not been slack in keeping pace with the
explorers, and this they have accomplished with such
effect that in a district where twelve years ago the
white man was unknown, there are now eight European settlements ; while the waters of the river which
had hitherto borne but the rude craft of the natives
are now navigated by no less than nineteen steamers,
seven belonging to the Free State, three to the French
colony, two to missionaries, and seven to various mercantile firms.

"There are few more charming sights," Captain
Thys has written, "than that enjoyed after a tedious
and toilsome march of seventeen days through the region of the Falls, when on attaining the height of
Leopoldville the wide panorama mirrored in Stanley
Pool bursts upon the view. The lake lies expanded as
an inland sea, and is enclosed by wooded hills of
which the outline becomes indistinct in the blue per-
spective. First, turning to the far extremity of the
widespread water, the eye rests upon the island of
Bamu, looking like an elongation of the Kalina point ;
the landscape beyond is bounded by the heights on
the French shore, which are clothed with verdure, and
which are in close proximity to some rugged white
rocks to which Stanley, on account of some resemblance which he traced, gave the name of 'Dover
Cliffs.' On the north shore, the French settlement
of Brazzaville comes clearly in view, as well as the
stores of the firm of Daumas, Béraud & Co. at Mfua.
The opposite bank is lower but equally wooded, and
nestling among surrounding plantations can be de-

scried the houses of Kinchassa, the Kintamo village, whose chief, Ngaliema, plays so important a part in the story of the foundation of the Free State. Nearest of all, close at our feet, are the buildings of Leopoldville."

Away to the south-east, between twenty and thirty miles, there stands a mountainous elevation of so striking a form that it cannot fail to arrest the attention of the traveller. It is the highest point of the semicircle of hills forming the southern enclosure of the Pool, and has been named " Mense Peak," in compliment to one of the resident doctors in Leopoldville. The surrounding district of Manquelê, from a geological point of view, is exceptionally curious. It is a succession of white eminences of the most rugged character—inaccessible precipices, Pyrenean circles, needle-like projections, fantastic monoliths all combine to make so wonderful a scene that the Sweedish traveller, Von Schwerin, who was the first to investigate it, has predicted it will ultimately become what Yellowstone Park is to the Rocky Mountains—an object of excursion for tourists in search of the picturesque.

All around the Pool the country is very fertile, slightly undulated, and clothed with savannahs intersected by belts of forest. Except towards the interior, where the aggregation is more considerable, it is not populous. The native residents are very much mixed. The French shore is occupied by the Bateke, with an admixture of the Babwendi; whilst on the Free State side the Wabundu, who are the true · owners of the soil, are amalgamated with the Bateke who have emigrated downwards. The former recognise the supremacy of the Makoko of Mbé, the Wabundu acknowledging the rule of the Makoko of Wazanzi.

There are four separate establishments of Europeans on Stanley Pool. Of these, the first is at Brazzaville, being the French settlement at the lower outlet, the residence of the officer in charge, and the depository of the Daumas firm. The second station is at Leopoldville, on the opposite shore, comprising the Free State settlement, and being the headquarters of the Commissioner of the district. Here also is the centre of

the American Baptist Missionary Union. The third
station is at Kinchassa, some little distance from
Leopoldville. For a while it was a Free State station,
but is now occupied by the English Baptist Mission,
under the direction of the well-known explorer, the
Rev. George Grenfell. It is likewise used by a Rotterdam association as a Dutch factory, and there is
likewise an agency of the Belgian Society for Trade
in the Upper Congo. The other settlement is that of
Kimpoko, on the southern shore, at the entrance of
the Pool, and has been appropriated by the American ·
Mission in charge of Bishop Taylor.

Of all these, Leopoldville is considerably the most
important. On the slope of a hill a kind of terrace
has been formed, where, amidst bananas, mangoes,
papaws, palms, and other fruiting trees, stand two
lines of dwelling-houses, with their accessory stores
and other erections. The hillsides and the valleys
have all been put under cultivation—fine plantations
of manioc, maize, rice, haricots, sweet potatoes, coffee, and cocoa covering an area of somewhere about
seventy acres. As to vegetables, no European gar-
den could make a much finer or more varied display—
peas, cabbages, lettuces, onions, leeks, radishes, car-
rots all flourish. A little way apart are the enclosures
for goats and for donkeys, shelters for larger cattle
being in course of construction. Beyond these are
clusters of huts of all shapes and dimensions, the
homes of the natives and the barracks of the Haoussa
and Bangala soldiers; whilst, finally, down by the
water's side, there are the carpenters', blacksmiths',
and engineers' work-sheds, in which steamers are built
and repaired with a bustle and activity that would not
discredit any European dockyard.

Regularly every morning as the day dawns, the bell
sounds and the negro trumpeter blows his matutinal
réveille. The whole settlement awakes, and both terraces and huts are at once full of animation : groups
of labourers hasten to the plantations ; the goods in
the storehouses, delivered the day before, are un-
packed ; at the forges the sturdy negroes, half naked, wield their ponderous hammers ; meanwhile, at
the military quarters, the cannibal Bangala are being

drilled by European officers, and trained in the use of breechloaders.

It only bides the time for the railway to be opened with Stanley Pool for its terminus, and a brilliant future must be before the land: the arrival of the first locomotive will be greeted with unbounded enthusiasm. Not the least occasion is there to fear that the natives, like the Chinese some years ago, will proceed to throw rails and engine into the water; the period of their initiation into the arts of civilisation has hitherto been brief, but they have already outlived the fabulous age of the dragon with the rabbit's eyes.

It was about noon on the 21st of April 1887 when Lieutenant Liebriechts of the Belgian Artillery, so recently arrived from Europe that he had only taken the command of the settlement on the preceding day, was made aware that there was an unusual commotion at no great distance along the caravan road. He hastened out and at once saw the immense throng, bearing their flags, and halting in the rear of the buildings of the American Mission. They were depositing their loads and preparing to camp out. The Commissioner without delay went to salute Stanley, under whom he had previously served as Controller of the station at Bolobo. He found the entire expedition in complete order and under good discipline, just commencing to clear the ground for the erection of their huts. Standing with the most undisturbed coolness, and with an air that might almost be said to betoken indifference, Stanley was superintending the proceedings; and to the eye of an ordinary observer it might seem as if he had never been away from Leopoldville, but was simply going on with the daily avocations that were engaging him while he was founding the settlement four years before.

His immediate inquiry was about the means of transport. Lower down the river he had been told that the *Stanley* was in dock and was undergoing repairs that it would take a month to complete. This was disquieting, because beyond all others the *Stanley* was the boat upon which he relied for the conveyance of his men. His anxiety on this point was soon relieved, when Lieutenant Liebriechts pointed out the ship lying at anchor in the harbour ready for prompt service. Alongside were the *En Avant* and the large whale-boat, both at his disposal. Thus far, then, as regarded the vessels that had been promised by the State, all was satisfactory; and just as it was at Banana, the explorer's good star was in the ascendant.

Besides these, anchored in the Pool, were two mission steamers, the *Peace* and the *Henry Reed;* and it was taken for granted that the permission of their owners would be at once obtained for the use of them for a few weeks. The application being made to the Baptist Mission at Kinchassa was immediately granted, and the *Peace* was handed over for Stanley's use. On the other hand, when the request was made to Mr. Billington, of the American Baptist Mission, for the loan of the *Henry Reed*, it was met with a point-blank refusal.

Not used to be thwarted in the uncivilised regions through which he had passed in carrying out his enterprises, and only accustomed to give the character of the means a secondary consideration, the only reply that Stanley had to give to the denial was to send an officer with some soldiers to take possession of the boat. No doubt it was a high-handed proceeding. Stanley seemed to ignore the fact that the Pool district had been brought under legally constituted authority, and had to be shown that such violent measures could not be tolerated. A warning letter from the representative of the Free State convinced him of this, and he ordered his men to withdraw.

The Commandant of Leopoldville, however, was so thoroughly impressed with the necessity of despatching this body of 750 men forward on their way, if the maintenance of general peace were to be preserved, that he himself entered into negotiation with Mr. Billington, with the result that the steamer should be hired by the State to be entrusted by them to Stanley, who made himself responsible for all risk.

All the details of this incident are given in a letter sent by Stanley to his Committee, and published in the *Times.*

" CAMP NEAR LEOPOLDVILLE, STANLEY POOL,
April 26, 1887.

.   .   .   .   .

" In 1881 I relieved two missionaries named Clarke
and Lanceley. They had suffered a misfortune, a fire
had consumed all their effects. They sent me an appeal for provisions. I provided them with a fair al-
lowance from our own stores. They belonged to the
Livingstone Inland Mission.

" In 1883 a missionary named Sims applied for a
site at Stanley Pool to establish a mission of the Livingstone Inland Mission. His colleagues had vainly
striven without aid from me to obtain permission from
the natives. I gave an order to the chief of Leopoldville to locate Dr. Sims on a site in the neighbourhood
of the station, so that, times being unsettled then, the
mission could be under our immediate protection. In
1884 I extended the grounds of this mission, and also
gave it a site for a branch mission at the Equator,
subject, of course, to confirmation at Brussels.

" By a curious event—on arriving at Stanley Pool
this time—I found myself in a position of abject sup-
pliant for favour. His Majesty the Sovereign of this
Congo State had invited me to take the Congo River
route to relieve Emin Pasha at Wadelai. Provided
the steamers and boats were at Stanley Pool in time,
without doubt this route was by far the cheapest and
best, even though food was not over abundant. I
therefore accepted the invitation and came here. But
I had not anticipated this distressful scarcity of food,
nor the absence of steamers and boats.

" To every one at Stanley Pool it was clear that a
disaster would be the consequence of this irruption of
a large caravan upon a scene so unpromising as this
foodless district. The only remedy for it was immediate departure up river. Long before arrival, I had
sent letters of appeal to the English Baptist Mission,
owners of the steamer *Peace*, and to the Livingstone
Inland Mission, which is now American, and owners
of the steamer *Henry Reed*, for aid to transport the
expedition to Bolobo immediately upon arrival at Stanley Pool. Reports confirmatory of the state of famine
in that district were daily reaching me, and immediate

departure was our only means of saving life and preventing a gross scandal.

" A few days later I received a letter from a Mr.
Billington, in charge of the *Henry Reed*, saying he
could not lend the steamer for such purpose as he
wanted to go down river—*i.e.*, overland to•the Lower
Congo—' for some purpose, and next month the Livingstone Inland Mission expected some missionaries,
and in the interval the steamer *Henry Reed* was to be
drawn up on the slip to be repainted.'

" You will observe, as I did, that there was no
question of urgency; the steamer was to lie idle on
the slip for repainting while Mr. Billington should go
down river. . . .

" Meantime the starving people would be tempted
to force from every native or white the food which
they could not obtain by purchase ; and no one knows
to what extent disorder would spread. If I did my
duty I should have had to repress it sternly. Still,
whether my people or the natives would suffer most,
it is clear that the condition of things would be
deplorable.

" From the English Baptist Mission I received a
letter from its chief stating that unless orders to the
contrary would arrive from home that he would lend
me the steamer and be happy to help me.

" Arriving at the Pool, and seeing more fully the
extent of district suffering from scarcity of food,
I sent Major Barttelot and Mr. Mounteney Jephson
to represent more fully our desperate position to the
Livingstone Inland Mission. They saw Messrs. Billington and Sims. They tell me they urged the missionaries by all the means within their power for over
an hour to reconsider their refusal, and to assist us.
They were said to have declined. Mr. Billington
argued that he had consulted the Bible and found
therein a command not to assist us. . . .

" I consulted the Governor of Stanley Pool district
Mons. Liebriechts, and represented to him that a
great scandal was inevitable unless means were de-
vised to extricate us from the difficulty. I told him I
could not be a disinterested witness to the sufferings
which starvation would bring with it ; that therefore
a formal requisition should be made by him on the

missions for the use of their steamers for a short term of, say, forty days; that the *Henry Reed* was evidently, according to Mr. Billington's letter, to lie idle for a period over two months; that this period could be utilised by us in saving hundreds of lives; that their objections were frivolous. . . . M. Liebriechts admitted that the position was desperate and extreme; that the State was also in a painful uncertainty as to whether provisions could be procured for its people each day.

"The next morning Major Barttelot and Mr. Mounteney Jephson were sent over again to the Livingstone Inland Mission to try a third appeal with Mr. Billington, who only replied that he had 'prayerfully wrestled even unto the third watch' against the necessity there was of refusing the *Henry Reed*. He was confirmed in his opinion that he was 'acting wisely and well.' Meantime it was reported to me that Mr. Billington had furtively abstracted the valves and pistons of the engines, for the purpose of hiding them. I therefore hesitated no longer, but sent a guard of Soudanese down to the steamer and another guard with Major Barttelot to demand the immediate surrender of the steamer and her belongings. Major Barttelot kept his guard without the domain of the mission and walked in alone with the letter.

"The Commissaire of the State, seeing matters becoming critical, ordered a guard to relieve the Soudanese at the steamer, and went in person to the missionaries to insist that the steamer should be surrendered to the State.

"Our guard was withdrawn upon an assurance being given that no article should be withdrawn or hidden.

"For two days the matter continued in the hands of M. Liebriechts, who at last signed a charter in due form by which the mission permits the hire of the steamer *Henry Reed* to us for the sum of £100 sterling per month, which is at the rate of 30 per cent. per annum of her estimated value.

"But what ungrateful people some of these missionaries are! Faith they may have in super-abundance —in hope they no doubt live cheerfully; but of charity I do not find the slightest trace. However, our

matter is ended, and our anxiety has abated somewhat. . . .

"HENRY M. STANLEY."

Lieutenant Liebriechts by his tact and firm though
impartial conduct had succeeded to the satisfaction of
all parties in avoiding a conflict, thus relieving the
station from a position that was serious and might become dangerous. Without recourse to force or compulsion he had insured the prosecution of the rapid
advance of the expedition.

This testimony is confirmed by Stanley himself in a
letter which he sent to Lieutenant Liebriechts very
shortly after the start from Leopoldville. "Everything," he writes, "is going on infinitely better than
could be expected, for which we owe you much gratitude."

In fact, success so far was complete. The entire
flotilla at the Pool was at Stanley's disposal. In addition to the *Stanley* and the Government whale-boats
(which had been promised him in Brussels), the two
mission steamers and the large launch of the English
Baptists, he had the use of the hull of the *En Avant*,
of which the engines were temporarily out of repair.
Besides these, the men in the yard at Kinchassa were
working hard at the repairs of the *Florida*, a steamer
which had been lent for the occasion by the Sanford
Exploring Expedition. They completed their task by
April 29th, two days before the start. Thus, including the whale-boat, which belonged to the expedition
itself, there was an aggregate of eight vessels, of
which three were steamers.

All through this period of negotiation about the
boats, there had been the necessity of providing food
for the 750 men whose sojourn at the Pool was thus
prolonged. This was no easy matter, and the days
did not pass without some suffering of privation.

Some mention has been made, in connection with
this occasion, of dearth and famine; but the famine
was not the result of drought or of bad harvests—it
was simply the result of the difficulty of getting supplies from a thinly-populated district for so large a
force that had arrived without having any reserve of
provisions of its own.

While the population of the European settlements at the Pool was limited the adjacent country could meet its demands; but after the resident white men exceeded the number of fifty, and their negro contingent had increased in proportion, the resources of the place failed to keep pace with the augmentation. For some years past the settlers at the Pool had been consuming all the goats, poultry, and eggs produced in the neighbourhood, and no effort had been made either by the improvident negro or by the inactive European to guard against any sudden emergency. Accordingly when there was the unexpected arrival of between 700 and 800 men in a locality where there is no regular communication with the outlying districts, some idea may be formed of the anxiety that was felt as to the finding provisions for such a multitude during the ten days that the expedition was compelled to tarry at Leopoldville and Kinchassa.

On the 25th of April the *Stanley* was declared to be ready. Under the command of Major Barttelot and Dr. Parke, 153 men were embarked and sent in advance towards Msuata, a place between the Pool and the confluence of the Masai, where it was reported that there was plenty of food. Detachments of hippopotamus-hunters were sent out to scour the country, and were fairly successful in getting a supply of meat. But as for chicuangue (the manioc-bread, which is ordinarily brought in by the natives from the neighbouring villages), for some days there was absolutely none to be had. Just as in the region of the Falls, the natives here at the Pool had taken alarm at the approach of a prodigious armed force in strange costume, and had fled in consternation. The flight was so general, and the consequent difficulty of securing provisions was so aggravated, that Lieutenant Liebriechts considered it prudent to send off a detachment of about fifteen soldiers, under Lieutenant von Reichslin, his second in command, to explain the true state of things to the chiefs, and to assure them that they had no cause for alarm.

Nothing, however, quite prevailed to pacify the native mind. The people very gradually, and with a cautious hesitation, made their way back, and it was not until the entire expedition had taken its departure

that the country reassumed its ordinary quiet, and
that the accustomed supply of provisions became adequate to the demand.

The means of transport being thus happily secured,
the crisis was not of long duration ; but while it lasted the panic was considerable, and Stanley had good
reason for his subsequent message—"Everything is
going on infinitely better than could be expected."

In course of time the usual order of things was
restored, and six weeks after the disappearance of the
"Relief-hurricane," as the expedition was nicknamed
on the Lower Congo, the manager of the French store
at Brazzaville was able to send off to Matadi 100
porters loaded with ivory without a single soldier to
escort them.

At length all was ready. Stanley had moved his
encampment from Leopoldville to Kinchassa, where
the whole flotilla was collected on the evening of April
30th.

Early next morning the embarkation commenced in
front of the Dutch factory. The English mission
steamer, the *Peace*, was selected as flag-ship of the
chief of the expedition, and was made to take in tow
both the large Government launch on one side, and
the expedition whale-boat on the other, the three vessels collectively carrying 117 men and 100 loads.
The *Stanley* was attached to the steamship *Florida*,
both being placed under the command of Captain
Schnegestrom of the Free State Navy, and together
conveying 364 men, 500 loads, the nine donkeys, and
a flock of goats. Lastly, there was the *Henry Reed*,
which had in tow the hull of the *En Avant* and the
English Mission whale-boat, and was under the orders
of Captain Martini. This third contingent carried 131
men and 100 loads, Tippoo Tib and his women-folk,
to the number of fifteen, occupying the *En Avant*.

By 6.30 A.M. the last load was embarked : the Europeans went on board : Stanley gave the signal ; the
Henry Reed weighed anchor ; the *Stanley* followed ;
the *Peace* brought up the rear ; and in a few minutes
the whole flotilla was lost to view behind the islands.

This was not the first expedition that the riverside
population of the Upper Congo had seen passing between its shores. The former one in 1883, composed

of the steamers the *Royal*, the *En Avant*, and the *Association Internationale*, had borne the blue banner, spangled with gold, and had peacefully opened the way for European enterprise into the heart of Africa; and now, four years later, along that same route that had been kept open by vast effort and large sacrifice, beneath the same banner and under the same command another like expedition passes on, carrying help to two valiant champions in Africa's cause, who have been lost to sight in the far distant district of the sources of the Nile.

CHAPTER XI.

ON THE UPPER CONGO.

Between Stanley Pool and Stanley Falls—Region of the islands—Accidents to the *Peace* and to the *Stanley*—Stay at B d bo—In the land of plenty—With the Bangala—Yesterday and to-day—Reception—The advance-guard —On the Aruwimi—Arrival at the Y..mbuy . Rapids.

ALTOGETHER unique is the navigable highway which the Congo forms between Stanley Pool and Stanley Falls. The distance between these two points is over 1000 miles, or something less than the united length of the Rhine and the Rhone. Its width is nowhere less than 400 yards, and in many parts extends to several miles; between the points of confluence of the Mongalla and the Itumbiri it is over twenty miles, about the width of the Straits of Dover, and unapproached in magnitude by any other water-course in the world.

From the district of Bolobo, until it has passed the point of confluence with the Aruwimi, its course is studded with innumerable islands, and a navigator has not unfrequently the simultaneous choice of ten or more different channels, each in itself a river some hundreds of yards in breadth, and separated by islands that vary from three miles to thirty miles in length. From the entire absence of any external indications, these channels at present require very watchful navigation, and in some parts present a certain amount of danger; but there can be little doubt that when the forthcoming survey has been completed, at least one channel will be proved to exist that is perfectly adapted for rapid navigation, and available to steamers of considerable size.

All the islands appear heavily clothed with vegetation which is reflected in the waters around; palm-trees of five or six species, tamarisks, cotton-trees, acacias, calamus, cola-trees, and gigantic baobabs grow in profusion; and the ubiquitous caoutchouc creeper, with its white blossoms, of which the natives have not yet learnt the value, casts its interlacing growth over the massy forest, as if to throw an impenetrable barrier in the way of any curious intruder.

Any one navigating these narrow channels, with their bordering of flowers and verdure, might almost imagine himself on the ornamental waters of some familiar and cultivated domain. The scene is quite restful to the eye, after the imposing if somewhat monotonous panorama which the river presents when the view stretches afar across the woods and savannahs on its shores.

The banks beyond Chumbiri are for the most part low, being only broken by a few hills at Upoto. Everywhere the soil seems wonderfully fertile, and is clothed with a dense vegetation which is frequently enlivened by the more brilliant green of the banana plantations that surround the villages, and by the aid of a telescope may often be made out miles away over the plains beyond the swampy shores of the river.

The population is very irregularly distributed, some large tracts being apparently quite deserted, whilst in others an almost uninterrupted line of villages extends away for miles. Generally friendly, the people not unfrequently are quite hospitable. They come in considerable numbers in their canoes to greet a passing boat, signalling to travellers that they should stop and trade with them, and always showing themselves eager for business transactions.

Two mishaps have to be recorded as occurring to the expedition on the Upper Congo; the *Peace* lost her tiller, and the *Stanley* went aground between Chumbiri and Bolobo. Stanley describes the two accidents in a letter sent to his Committee from the Bangala station, and dated May 31st:—

"On leaving Kinchassa, the *Henry Reed* and the *Stanley* filed off and commenced their first day's passage; but the *Peace*, when it had hardly proceeded two miles, was stopped by an accident. Her tiller broke, so that she would not answer her helm. Her captain immediately lowered two anchors; a violent shock, however, sent the boat into a rapid current, and we were obliged to cut the chains in order to rescue ourselves from peril. We had to go back to Kinchassa, whence the captain and engineer had to go six miles lower down to Leopoldville to have the damaged tiller repaired, so that an entire day was lost.

"We resumed our voyage next morning, and for four days maintained a moderate speed, the *Stanley* and *Henry Reed* always making good heading, the *Peace* still continuing in the rear.

"Between Kinchassa and Msuata, a distance of eighty-eight miles, we spent two days longer than is usually enough, and when we had passed Msuata we made a still more indifferent progress. The speed of the *Peace* continued to slacken; after a while it was a hard matter for her to contend with the current, until at length she was completely overpowered and began to be driven backward. We cast anchor at once, and for a second time found ourselves in a dilemma.

"Forthwith we proceeded to land the passengers from the disabled vessel, and sent on a small boat to Bolobo to procure some assistance. Next day the unfortunate craft had to be ignominiously towed by the *Henry Reed* to the entrance of the harbour of Bolobo.

"But as though it was not vexatious enough for us that we should be thus retarded by the *Peace*, the *Stanley* must next get into trouble.

"Imagine us, as we were following on in the *Henry Reed*, coming up to discover the *Stanley*, lying in broad daylight, without steam, on the shore. The great boat had been venturing too recklessly among the shoals, and here was the result—the stern had been stove in. Happily our alarm was somewhat exaggerated; the injury was not so serious but that the engineers found they could patch on some plates of metal and make the ship fit for navigation; and all hands being set to work on the task, it was ready to proceed in a couple of days."

Bolobo, where the expedition was thus delayed, is situated on the Free State shore, a little above the Kasai. It is the most populous centre in the territory of the Bayanzi, a rich and commercial nation, trading principally in ivory. It contains about 30,000 inhabitants. It has parallel lines of streets, and public squares, and the dwelling-houses are very comfortable, their fields of manioc, maize, and sweet potatoes extending inland as far as the eye can reach. They are a fine, high-spirited race of people. The Congo Association formerly had a station here, which is now only occupied by the English Baptist Mission.

For some days after arriving on May 8th, the expedition remained at Bolobo, so as to allow the *Stanley* to go back to the confluence of the Kasai and fetch up the detachment which, under Major Barttelot, had been making its way on foot from the Black River to the mouth of the Kwa. On the 14th anchors were weighed, and an entrance was made into the island-labyrinth of the Upper Congo.

Beyond Bolobo no noteworthy incident occurred; there was no loss of life nor damage to property; the boats continued the voyage by day, being brought-to every night.

The usual rule was that anchor should be cast about 5 P.M., by which hour a distance varying from fifteen to thirty miles would have been accomplished. For two hours or more the men would be occupied in collecting wood for the engines during the following day; during the evening the clang of the hatchets chopping up the firewood would be accompanied by the shrill choruses of the men as they did their work; large fires · would be kindled; in due time the cooks would have completed their preparations, and the evening meal would be served.

No longer now was there any scarcity of provisions, such as had caused anxiety in the district of the Falls and at Stanley Pool. "Food is abundant," wrote Stanley; "the natives everywhere receive us so well, and bring us such abundance of victuals, that my people have already quite forgotten their privations. I reckon that every man must have gained from 10 lb.

to 20 lb. in weight between leaving Kinchassa and arriving at Bangala, and I am inclined to think that this sudden increase of burden must tell somewhat to the disadvantage of the speed of our boats."

On the 18th the flotilla passed Lukolela, the station of another Protestant Mission, and on the 23rd reached Equatorville, a Free State settlement, where Stanley was gratified at meeting a former associate, Captain Van Gèle, who was on the point of ascending the Mobangi, to investigate its source.

Having been successfully repaired at Bolobo, the *Peace* was now able to keep the lead, and on the 30th on emerging from the midst of the islands, the party on board sighted the extensive buildings of the station of the Bangala.

Bangala is the appellation of one of the most notorious of the tribes of the Upper Congo. It occupies both banks of the river above its confluence with the Mobangi. They are a splendid race of men, above the average in height, singularly adroit in the manipulation of their canoes, and held in terror by the neighbouring people for their courage in war.

It was in making good his passage past the numerous Bangala villages on both banks of the river, that Stanley on his first descent of the Congo, in 1877, had to engage in the sanguinary strife which he describes in his "Through the Dark Continent."

"Incessant beating of their drums," he says, "had roused the savages to the height of frenzy; they mustered their canoes; they loaded their guns; they sharpened their knives and their lances; and all simply because we were intruders, navigating their waters.

"As we drifted onwards a number of the canoes approached us. I hailed the natives; I received no reply. Immediately afterwards they fired into our boats.

"The fight thus begun was carried on with equal vigour on both sides, and lasted so long that I was obliged to make a fresh distribution of ammunition. Each village seemed to send its contingent to aid the attack, and at three o'clock the number of canoes taking part in the combat was sixty-three. It was not till half-past five that the assailants retired.

" This was the fiercest of all the conflicts which we had to sustain on this terrible river."

Twelve years have since elapsed, and in that interval the events that have transpired have completely modified the condition of the country, and the disposition of its population towards strangers. A great settlement has risen in the midst of the Bangala villages ; the chiefs who in 1877 instigated the hostilities against Stanley have become the friends and *protégés* of the white man ; human sacrifices have been abolished ; steamers make regular visits to the stations ; order is maintained by armed force ; the natives readily take service under the State and have no reluctance to go down to Boma and Banana, 1500 miles away from their homes ; and the Congo army reckons in its numbers scarcely less than 700 Bangala soldiers.

These highly satisfactory results have been brought about mainly by the intelligence and tact of the two Belgian officers who were the first to be placed in control of this remote station, Captains Coquillat and Vankerkoven, ably seconded by their subordinates Lieutenants Baert and Dhanis.

Bangala is the finest of the stations which the State owns on the Upper Congo. Stanley failed to recognise it, not having been in the country since in January 1884 he had held his palaver with the old chief Mata-Buyké.

Marvellous were the changes for the better. The river now was alive with more than a hundred canoes, filled no longer with armed warriors, but with friendly people waving their hands in welcome ; upon the river bank a crowd was cordially cheering the arrival of the vessels, whilst a goodly throng was hurrying down to the wooden landing-place. Within the settlement, enclosed by its palisades and trenches, rose tier upon tier of buildings constructed of kiln-burnt bricks, and far beyond these extended large plantations. The garrison, which reckoned in its ranks some of the old assailants of 1877, was drawn up in well-disciplined order and presented arms, not lances nor old-fashioned muskets, but modern breechloading sniders.

Stanley landed, followed by his officers, together with Tippoo Tib and his retinue. He was received under the verandah of the central building by all the

European staff, headed by Lieutenant Baert, who, in the absence of the chief Commissioner, Captain Van-kerkoven, did the honours of the occasion, and hospitably offered wine, as token of welcome. In acknowledging the courtesy Stanley spoke a few words to this effect : " On landing here to-day I cannot help recalling the very different reception that was accorded me ten years ago by the same natives who are now so confiding and enthusiastic. This prosperous station, these commodious erections, these well-cultivated fields, this orderly and well-drilled force, and all those signs of civilisation which have been so rapidly imported into the heart of a nation that was yesterday, as it were, unknown to the civilised world, make a deep impression upon me. I congratulate you on the great work that has been accomplished, and at the same time I thank you for the kind and hearty welcome that you now give me. In the face of such achievements in the past, who can entertain any doubts about the future?"

While he was speaking the artillery was thundering out a salute, greeting the advent of the former Chief Commissioner of the Congo Association.

The expedition stayed three days at Bangala.

Meantime, the *Henry Reed* was sent on to convey Tippoo Tib to Stanley Falls, Major Barttelot and forty soldiers accompanying him as an escort. The ship was then to return, without delay, as far as the Aruwimi Rapids. It was on the 2nd of June when she was despatched ahead under full steam, and on the same day, the *Stanley* and the *Peace*, with the boats in tow, resumed their onward way.

Apart from the inconvenience arising from heavy rains and smart squalls, the passage from Bangala to the Aruwimi was unmarked by any special incident. On the 16th the steamers quitted the waters of the great river for the diminished channel of its affluent. Two days later the rapids of Yambuya were in sight, and the anchors had to be lowered. Here navigation must cease. The voyage from Kinchassa had occupied six weeks ; this was about eight days more than the estimated time, a delay that was regarded as quite unimportant.

So far everything had gone prosperously, and answered to the expectation of the chief of the expedition.

CHAPTER XII.

THE CAMP AT YAMBUYA.

The Aruwimi—Formation of the camp—Stanley's plan—The arrival of the *Henry Reed*—Tippoo Tib at Stanley Falls—Composition of the caravan —Forward!

THE Aruwimi, on the right bank of the Congo, is one of its most important tributaries. In 1877 Stanley first discovered it as an affluent, and in 1883 made the ascent of its lower course as far as Yambuya, where he was stopped by the rapids. The river has since been frequently explored by the agents of the Congo State, who have recently established a large entrenched camp, protected by cannon, and garrisoned with 600 Haoussa and Bangala soldiers, under the command of twelve European officers.

The course of the river is studded with numerous small islands, some of which are covered with low bushwood, others with trees of larger growth. There are also many sandbanks which, when the water is low, render navigation somewhat dangerous. The current is by no means strong, nor is the channel anywhere very deep, and at Yambuya, where the river is over 400 yards wide, the natives ford it at low water. Both banks are picturesque and well-wooded, though not densely covered with forest like those of the Lower Congo, the Sankullu, and the Lomami. At intervals between the woods there are wide fertile plains, rising variably from 15 to 30 feet above the level of the water. At the beginning of the year, during the rainy season, the woods are adorned with masses of blossoms of exquisite hues, scarlet, pink, and snowy white. Bananas and palms are in great abundance.

On the Lower Aruwimi, the shores are tenanted by the populous tribe of the Basoko, a fine strongly-built people, resembling the Wapoto lower down the Congo, and the Mwenja round Stanley Falls. Further up the river reside the Bateku, the Baburu, and other tribes.

The building of the houses on the Aruwimi is quite of a different style to what it is on the Upper Congo. The huts are all surmounted by conical roofs, which are from 4 to 5 yards high, and reach nearly down to the ground, and these are covered over with great prickly leaves which give to these primitive abodes a very singular character.

When first the expedition was making preparations to disembark, the natives congregated on the banks, and appeared to be assuming a threatening attitude, as if disposed to prevent a landing being effected. Stanley sounded his steam-whistles, and the extraordinary noise so startled them that they took to their heels. By degrees, however, they found their way back, and being enticed by a few presents, and by kindly words, soon became on friendly terms.

The camp was pitched at the foot of the first rapids, on the slope of a steepish hill about twenty yards in height. It was enclosed by a palisade, and on the sides that were open to attack it was protected by a broad fosse, with bastions at the angles. Inside it was partitioned off into three divisions, the upper of these being occupied by the huts of the Europeans, not arranged in any symmetrical order; the centre by the Zanzibaris and the police-guard; the lowest set apart for the quarters of the Soudanese and for the powder-magazine.

Whilst Lieutenant Stairs and Mr. Jameson were superintending the construction of the camp, Stanley was engaged in organising the scheme of his expedition. The main features of his plan were these : he would form an advance caravan, consisting of some 300 or 400 porters, and of these, with the assistance of about four of his subordinates, he would himself take the command. With this caravan he would proceed towards Lake Albert, mainly following the course of the Aruwimi, and using the river, wherever it should be practicable, for the transport of baggage and invalids. The point on the lake which he contemplated reaching was Kavalli, a small village on its southern extremity.

Yambuya and Kavalli lie pretty nearly in the same latitude, and the distance between them was over 300 miles, which Stanley hoped, if no impediment arose,

that he should accomplish in about two months ; but
of course he felt it quite questionable what difficulties
he might have to contend with along a route of which
he had not the slightest knowledge.

Then, next, whilst this march was being made, the
encampment would have to be left with the remainder
of the baggage under the guard of 300 soldiers ; the
Stanley and the *Peace* would have to go down to Stanley Pool to convey up Mr. Rose Troup and whatever
had been left behind at Leopoldville, as well as to
bring on Messrs. Bonney and Ward with 125 soldiers
who were at Bolobo ; and finally, when Tippoo Tib's
promised contingent of bearers should arive, the rear
body should follow on, upon Stanley's track, which, so
long as it traversed an unknown country, should be
indicated by the blazing of trees and by the vestiges
of the abandoned camps.

On the afternoon of June 22nd, the *Henry Reed*,
with Major Barttelot on board, arrived at Stanley
Falls. It had already been there on the 17th with
Tippoo Tib, who was received with every demonstration of delight. On parting, Tippoo Tib delivered to
the Major several letters, one of which was addressed
to the King of the Belgians, assuring his Majesty of
his most devoted allegiance, and of his earnest desire
for the maintenance of peace in the district that had
been entrusted to his charge.

This was in June 1887. Since that time various ac-
cusations of treachery have been laid against Tippoo
Tib, but the conduct of the Arab chief has been in
every way honest and straightforward, entirely falsi-
fying all evil report.

The whole of the Upper Congo is now in the occupation of the agents of the Free State. The Government steamers, as well as those in the ownership
of different missions and various mercantile firms, ply
freely between the Pool and the Falls, and so active
is trade, that at the close of 1889 nearly fifty tons of
ivory purchased from the natives and Arab dealers
were sold in the Antwerp market.

Control of the camp at Yambuya, as well as the conduct of the second caravan, was entrusted by Stanley
to Major Barttelot, who would have the assistance of
Messrs. Jameson, Bonney, Rose Troup, and Ward.

CARRYING THE STEEL BOAT AND CUTTING A PATH THROUGH THE FOREST

The officers who were to accompany Stanley himself were Lieutenant Stairs, Captain Nelson, Dr. Parke, and Mr. Mounteney Jephson. The caravan altogether was 368 in number, and in addition to the sections of the whale-boat, and the large stock of provisions, it had to convey 300 loads of cartridges. A company of seventy-five soldiers, armed with Winchester rifles and hatchets, under the orders of Lieutenant Stairs, was told off, to go at the head of the column, and lay open a pathway through the woods.

All preparations were complete by the 27th of June. Stanley had the troups drawn up in marching order and subjected to a strict review. Betimes next morning the expedition left Yambuya and made its entrance upon the unknown. Who could tell what difficulties were before it ? Who could anticipate what dangers were to be met ? Who could forecast what hostility, what sickness, what famine might have to be endured ?

But these things mattered not. The grandeur of the undertaking kindled the energies of all alike ; confidence and hope were strong. Had they not, as a leader, the man who had saved Livingstone, the hero who had traversed Africa from Zanzibar to Banana, the renowned rock-breaker Boula Matari, the undaunted explorer, the keenest of diplomatists, the very founder of the Congo State?

Forward, then, forward ! Straight onward to the Nyanza !

CHAPTER XIII.

FIFTEEN MONTHS OF UNCERTAINTY.

Despatch from missionary at Matadi—Despatch from Zanzibar—Fresh relief expeditions—Telegram from Mr. Ward—The White Pasha on the Bahr-el-Ghazal—Communication from Dr. Junker—The Mahdi's expedition against Emin—Supposed death of Casati—Osman Digna to General Grenfell—Omar Saleh's report of the taking of Lado and the capture of Emin—The Stanley Expedition and the House of Commons—News from Stanley Falls—Safe!

On the 23rd of June 1887, five days before he left Yambuya, Stanley addressed a letter to Mr. William Mackinnon, which he concluded by saying : " As soon

as we can get wood enough on board the *Peace* and
Henry Reed to feed their furnaces for a few days, the
steamers will be off, and our last chance of communicating with Europe for a few months will be gone."

This letter arrived in Europe on the 20th of September 1887, and until the 21st of December 1888,
an interval of fifteen months, there was no authentic
news of the expedition. False reports of all kinds
were put in circulation ; never before had the story
of African enterprise drawn forth such a profusion
of hypothetical conclusions. At the very time when
Stanley, with his advanced caravan, was making his
way along the banks of the Aruwimi, the following
telegram was sent to Europe :—

"S. Thomas, *July* 21, 1887.

" According to a report received from a missionary
at Matadi, Stanley has been killed in an engagement
with the natives, about procuring food."

Almost while the press was commenting on this information, the report of the Matadi missionary was
supported by the announcement which found its way
into publication, that Stanley's steamer had stranded
on a sand-bank on the upper river, that it had been
attacked by the natives, and that the leader, with all
the members of the expedition, had been massacred.

These tidings were reproduced in the newspapers of
all parts of the world, so that by a considerable portion of the public Stanley was regarded as lost ; his
enterprise, it was argued, was too vast for human
power ; the terrible cannibals of the Aruwimi would
never permit him to leave their territory alive ; the
country through which he was essaying to pass presented a series of swamps in which fever must be
fatal ; or even at best, if he should succeed in over-
coming the difficulties of the way, he would be sure
to fall a victim to the treachery of Tippoo Tib, that
astute enemy whom he had been beguiled into establishing at the Falls, but who had long been looking
for an opportunity to assassinate him !

On the 17th of August, another sensational para-
graph appeared, emanating this time from the East
Coast, and sent by M. Raffray, the French Consul at

Zanzibar. It said that news had been brought from Nyangwé that Stanley, after having been betrayed by Tippoo Tib, had been attacked on the banks of the Aruwimi, and that he and his followers had all been murdered. That statement was a few days later corroborated by the *Figaro*, which specified June 28th as the day of the dreadful deed.

The report, thus become current, made the more profound impression because it seemed to come from an official source; but on further inquiry nothing appeared to confirm it; the French Consul had been misinformed by some traders who had come from the interior. Hope, therefore, again revived.

But altogether, it must be owned, these rumours were disquieting; the public confidence was shaken; and it began to be realised that Stanley's position must be very critical, and that it was quite problematical whether he would ever succeed in reaching Emin. Consequently discussion was started as to the propriety of organising a fresh relief expedition which should proceed from the East Coast, a route which many maintained would prove far easier and quicker than that which Stanley had elected to take.

Meanwhile all messengers coming from the Congo to Europe had only the same uniform report to make: " No news of Stanley."

The silence could not do otherwise than cause uneasiness. Public curiosity was aroused, and as Stanley himself supplied no information, it involuntarily sustained itself upon the sensational telegrams and reports, which although they were quite beside the mark, furnished some material for discussion.

Ere long communications were received simultaneously from Yambuya and from Wadelai, the former brought down to the coast by Mr. Ward, the latter furnished by a letter from Emin. Both were to the same invariable effect: " No news of Stanley."

What could have happened? Where is he? What is he doing? Is he a prisoner? Is he dead? Some maintained that, like Hicks Pasha, he and all his people had been annihilated, and that nothing more would be heard of him; some as confidently affirmed that he must be hemmed in by the natives of the Aruwimi, and be without food or ammunition.

Neither at the headquarters of any of the geographical societies, nor by the Emin Relief Committee, did these pessimist conjectures obtain any credence.

Dr. Schweinfurth wrote : " There is no reason to be uneasy respecting Stanley's fate."

Dr. Junker's verdict was : " The expedition is exposed to no risk on the part of the natives."

Captain Wissmann's message was : " I am sure that the expedition is not lost."

And Captain von Géle said : " Though perhaps reduced in numbers by a long rough march, Stanley and his men are assuredly in being, and we shall soon hear of their exploits."

But these high authorities did not avail to allay the general misgiving. People remained incredulous, and it began to be circulated by telegrams and otherwise that fresh expeditions were being organised for the relief of the distressed explorer. Of these expeditions, however, nothing more was subsequently heard.

No doubt the letters received in Europe from Mr. Ward gave a somewhat unsatisfactory account of the situation at Stanley Falls and at the Aruwimi camp, and the comments of the press became more and more gloomy. Mr. Ward stated that the sole news which Major Barttelot had received of the expedition was from some deserters, who reported that the caravan had been attacked by the natives, and that Mr. Stanley had been wounded by an arrow. Several newspapers asserted that a still more serious state of things was being concealed.

At length, on June 17th, the *Gaulois* announced that there had been received at Brussels official intelligence of Stanley's death ; and next day the *Journal des Debats* confirmed the account of the disaster in an article to this effect :—

" A Paris journal to-day announces that official news of Stanley's death has been received at Brussels. The truth of the report has been denied. Nevertheless the letters which we have ourselves received from Zanzibar leave little room for hope, and we believe that we are warranted in giving credence to the news. As collateral evidence, it is said that the families of the porters who accompanied the expedition have now been wearing mourning for several weeks. It is de-

clared that Tippoo Tib is responsible for the catastrophe, as it is known that he was nurturing feelings of
revenge against Stanley, and that he would take an
opportunity of gratifying his enmity. Tippoo Tib is
the real author of the disaster that has befallen the
Emin Relief Expedition."

On the same day the Brussels correspondent of the
Berliner Tageblatt wrote to corroborate the statements
made by the Parisian press, by giving details of the
effect produced by the news upon the members of the
Free State Government in Brussels. What he said
was to the following purport:—"The Congo Government now acknowledges that even if Stanley be not
dead, at any rate he must be in imminent danger.
His mission has completely failed, and his caravan is
hopelessly dispersed. For a month past the officials
have been aware of the desperate condition of things,
which probably has some connection with the recall of
M. Janssen, the Governor-General. All is consternation here. Negotiations are going on between the
English and Congo Governments as to the propriety
of sending out a fresh expedition. It is to be feared,
however, that help must arrive too late."

Yet what was the fact? All through this time the
administrators of the Free State, however persistently
they were interviewed by the Brussels reporters, adhered to the unchanging statement: "No news of
Stanley."

But now in the midst of these doubts and discrep-
ancies, an announcement which appeared in the *Times*
gave a new direction to the discussion. Attention
was drawn to unexpected quarters. The announcement in question was in substance as follows:—

SUAKIN, *June 20th*, 1888.
"According to intelligence received by the military
authorities from Berber and Khartoum, and confirmed
by deserters from Osman Digna's camp, a White
Pasha has appeared in the Bahr-el-Ghazal district,
and is advancing victoriously. The Khalifa Abdullah, the Mahdi's successor, is said to be much alarmed.
This White Pasha is probably Stanley."

This strange and somewhat startling news was confirmed in a degree by later despatches. From Suakin, on July 18th, it was reported: "Some fakirs who are on pilgrimage to Mecca arrived here yesterday, and have said this morning that in passing through Darfur they heard that a large company of strangers, with a White Pasha at their head, were in the marshes of the Bahr-el-Ghazal; and further, that the population of Darfur had received them cordially, and was making preparation to join them in attacking the Mahdi."

From Cairo, on July 23rd, it was heard that "a messenger from Omdurman reports that the Khalifa Abdullah has received news of the arrival of the White Pasha in the Bahr-el-Ghazal. Abdullah intends to march against him. The messenger adds that the White Pasha is Emin."

Later on a telegram from Suakin, dated August 17th, contained further explanation: "The reports of the appearance of a white chief on the Bahr-el-Ghazal are confirmed. The chief is designated by the natives Etlu-Digu (King of Beards). His force is said to be considerable, and composed of half-naked men, probably Niam-niam or Denka. The man from whom I received the news avows its accuracy. The population of Khartoum is taken by surprise, and is in considerable alarm, being influenced by the belief that Etlu-Digu is no other than Stanley. The Mahdi is said to have despatched 5000 infantry and 200 cavalry to Fashoda, by way of Kordofan."

And again from Suakin on August 20th:—"Some pilgrims who have arrived from Sokoro by the way of the Bahr-el-Ghazal report the appearance of a large force of white men in the Bongo country. The pilgrims left Bongoland in February, after camping for four days with the white people, who were armed with Remington rifles."

Thus it came to pass that all kinds of conjectures were rife about this White Pasha who, after establishing himself in the Bahr-el-Ghazal and making alliance with the people of Darfur, was now about making an offensive movement against the Arabs. Who was this Pasha? Whence came this bold adventurer into Lupton Bey's former province? Was it Stanley? Was it Emin?*

In order to throw some light upon the matter which had thus kept the Suakin telegraph in activity, Dr. Junker wrote, in July, to the Gotha *Mitteilungen*, that a messenger who had left Khartoum on the 25th of May, had arrived in Cairo, and stated that he had been an eye-witness of the preparations that the Mahdi had been making, during the previous two months, for a great attack upon the Egyptian Government in the southern provinces. It was stated, moreover, that the expedition was to consist of about 4000 men, and would be conveyed in four steamers formerly belonging to Gordon, and by a number of ordinary boats.

This communication caused a good deal of excitement, both amongst Emin's friends and the general public, and the dismay was considerably increased when ten days later a Reuter's telegram announced that at the beginning of April Emin Pasha's position had become exceedingly critical, inasmuch as on the 12th an envoy from the Mahdi had summoned him to surrender.

A despatch like this could not fail again to set all manner of sinister rumours afloat. Some English newspapers announced, that according to information sent from the Congo by Mr. Ward, Major Barttelot had sent out detachments of troops from the Aruwimi camp to reconnoitre Stanley's advance-route, and that the men brought back the tidings that the way was strewn with human bones.

On the 12th of October the *Standard* published a notice, detailing the circumstance of Casati's death: "All Emin's communications," it ran, "with the East Coast have been cut off by the hostility of Kabrega, King of the Unyoro, who ordered both the Tripoli merchant, Mohammed Biri, and Captain Casati, to be killed."

Within three weeks afterwards, *L'Echo du Nord*,

---

* It now seems tolerably certain that the White Pasha whose exploits were re-echoed from Khartoum was Captain von Gele, of the Congo Free State, who at the beginning of the year had been arrested in his exploration of the Welle, by the hostility of the Yakoma people, near the confluence of the Mbomo, which has its source somewhere in proximity to the sources of nearly all the principal affluents of the Bahr-el-Ghazal.

published at Lille, circulated a statement that the President of the Lille Geograpical Institute had received intelligence of the death of Stanley, who had been massacred with all his followers, two porters alone escaping.

Another month had hardly passed when the Suakin telegraph again took up the dismal tale, and matters seemed to be looking more and more gloomy, as the particulars given became more precise, and were forwarded on the authority of the English officers on the Red Sea.

The account already mentioned, as appearing in the Gotha *Mitteilungen*, and declaring that an expedition was being organised against Emin Pasha, so far aroused the interest of Colonel Rundle, the Governor of Suakin, that in the hope of obtaining accurate information he sent a special message of inquiry direct to the Mahdi.

The answer was not long in coming; it was a letter sent by Osman Digna himself, as chief of the forces of the Mahdi before Suakin; it was addressed to General Grenfell, the Commander of the English garrison; its language was to this effect:—

" In the name of the great and merciful God, this is sent by Osman Digna to the Christian who is Governor at Suakin.

" Let me inform you that a short time ago Rundle sent me a letter to ask about the man who is ruling in the Equatorial province.

" On receiving this letter I sent at once to the Khalifa, who informs me that the troops there have made prisoners of the governor and of a traveller who was with him. Both of them are now in irons and in the hands of our chief.

" The whole province has now submitted to us, and the inhabitants make allegiance to the Mahdi. We have captured all their arms and ammunition; we have carried off all the officers to the Khalifa, who received them well, and they are now living with him. They have given up all their flags.

" You may tell Rundle, therefore, what has become of the governor.

" I subjoin copies of the letters which have been sent

by our chief to the Khalifa, and by Tewfik to the governor aforesaid.

"I send also, that you may see it, some of the ammunition that has been brought from the Equator.

"I pray God to give victory to the believers and destruction to the infidels.

"OSMAN DIGNA."

Enclosed were the transcripts of the two letters. The one from the Mahdist chief who was asserted to have made himself master of the province was in this form :—

"In the name of the great and merciful God :— This letter is written by one of the lowliest servants of Allah to the Chief Khalifa. We advanced with the steamers and reached the town of Lado, where Emin, the Mudir of the Equator, had his quarters. We arrived there on the 25 Safar 1306.

"We owe our thanks to the officers and soldiers who made our victory easy. Before our arrival they had captured Emin and a traveller who was with him, and had put them in irons. The officers and men refused to go to Egypt with the Turks.

"Tewfik sent to Emin a traveller called Stanley. By Stanley he sent a letter to Emin, ordering him to go back with Stanley. To the rest of the forces he gave the option of going to Cairo, or remaining where they were. They refused to obey the Turkish orders and received us joyfully.

"I also send a copy of the letter which was written by Tewfik to Emin ; and I send besides the flags which we have taken from the Turks.

"I understand that another traveller had arrived to join Emin, but that he has left again. I am seeking for him, and if he returns, I shall certainly take him prisoner.

"I have found all the chief officers and residents delighted to receive us.

"I have taken all the arms and ammunition.

"I instruct you to send back to me the officers and the head commissioners when you have seen them and given them your directions. They will be of service to me.

"OMAR SALEH."

The excitement caused by news such as this may well be imagined. In the House of Commons on the 14th of December the First Lord of the Treasury, in reply to a question, confirmed the report that General Grenfell had received a communication from Osman Digna purporting to inform him of the capture of Emin and Stanley at Lado ; and for a couple of days the alleged disaster was the prominent event that engaged the public attention. The news now, it was presumed, did not depend upon any despatch of questionable authority, but might be taken as authentic. After Dr. Junker's announcement that an expedition was about to leave Khartoum for Lado in May or June, it was not at all impossible for Emin to be made a prisoner in October; as for Stanley, his having joined Emin was equally likely, since Osman professed to have a letter from the Khedive addressed to Emin, and it was known, as matter of fact, that Stanley had been the bearer of such a letter from Cairo.

But if the suspense was great, it was soon over.

An interval of fifteen months had elapsed in which the telegraph had never transmitted any but dubious or mournful messages, when suddenly a voice was heard that proclaimed the real condition of affairs. That voice was Stanley's own.

In the House of Commons, just a week after Mr. W. H. Smith had spoken of the letter to General Grenfell, Mr. Goschen asked leave to read a telegram that had just been received by Reuter's agency. Silence ensued, and he read as follows :—

"S. Thomas, *December* 21, 1888.

"Letters from Stanley Falls, dated August 21, 1888, state that on the previous day a letter had been received from Stanley, announcing that he was at Banalya, on the Aruwimi. He had left Emin Pasha eighty-two days previously in perfect health, and well supplied with provisions. He had retraced his steps in order to bring up his rear company and their loads. He had arrived at Banalya on the 17th of August, and expected to start again in ten days to rejoin Emin. All the white men belonging to the expedition were well."

The communication coming so speedily and so opportunely after the previous alarming reports was received with unbounded enthusiasm. The whole House rose to its feet and cheered for joy. Stanley was free !

It was now plain that Stanley could not be the Mahdi's prisoner, because on the 17th of August he was only a few days' march from the Falls, and the news of his capture was manifestly false. Was there not, therefore, reason to hope that Emin was also at liberty, and that none of Osman Digna's assertions were to be received as trustworthy?

Confirmation of the happy tidings was not wanting. The next day a telegram was received from M. Ledeganck, the vice-governor of Boma, addressed to the Central Committee at Brussels :—

"S. Thomas, *December* 22, 1888."

"Tippoo Tib has had a letter from Stanley, dated Bonalya, August 17. Stanley was well. He had left Emin at the Nyanza eighty-two days before. Emin had sufficient provisions ; he was in good health, and Casati too. He announced his intention of taking up his loads from Yambuya and returning to Emin."

Thus by the two brief telegrams now received all the misgivings and uncertainty of the last fifteen months were set at rest. The expedition had accomplished its design. Stanley had made his way and joined Emin Pasha. Only when this was done had he retraced his steps to bring up the residue of his caravan.

The details of this heroic march and of his meeting with Emin have been given by Stanley in a report sent to the Relief Committee in London, and in a letter addressed to the Royal Geographical Society. A *resume* of them will form the substance of the two succeeding chapters.

CHAPTER XIV.

YAMBUYA CAMP TO ALBERT NYANZA.

On the march—First skirmish with natives—The rapids—The Nepoko—
Meeting with Arabs—A devastated region—Famine—Desertions—In the
forest for 160 days—Through villages and fields—The chief Mazamboni—
Declaration of war—Forward for the Nyanza!

LEAVING Yambuya on the 28th of June 1887, the
caravan for the first day followed the bank of the
river. For a time the road was practicable, but a difficulty soon began to present itself from the creepers,
varying from an inch to a foot in thickness, that inter-
laced themselves in arches across the path, and had to
be cut away with hatchets.

On the following day the column made its encampment at Yankondé, a considerable village just opposite the rapids. As the river was found to be taking too northerly a direction, a course had to be made
across the manioc fields and through a teeming population. Every device that the natives could invent to
molest and impede the advance of the caravan was
adopted. Repeatedly shallow holes were dug in the
path, and these were filled with sharp spikes, cun-
ningly concealed by leaves. To those who walked
over them barefooted the agony was terrible ; the feet
were not only severely lacerated, but frequently the
spikes would remain in the flesh and cause gangrenous
sores. Ten men were so crippled·in this way as to be
almost *hors de combat*. At the approach to each village there was usually a straight, well-cleared pathway, about one hundred yards long and four yards
wide, and these were literally bristling with the skew-
ers, always artfully hidden from sight. The proper
paths would have led by a considerable *detour*, but
these were made to have the most inviting aspect.
At the entrance of each village a sentinel had been
placed with a drum to sound out an alarm.

The river-bank was regained on the 5th of July, and
as there are no rapids immediately in front, Stanley

brought his boat into requisition, and found it of inestimable service, as it not only conveyed the sick and wounded, but also carried two tons of baggage. In his first letter to Major Barttelot he wrote :—" If I had to begin over again I should collect the largest canoes I could, and an adequate supply of rowers, and I should use them for the sick and for baggage. Between Yambuya and the Nyanza the canoes are many and capacious enough, but unfortunately, the Zanzibaris are miserably poor hands at rowing. There are scarcely fifty men in my whole troop who know how to handle a paddle. We can do as much in one day by land, as in two by water."

Onwards from the 15th of July to the 18th of October the column kept continually to the left bank of the Aruwimi, making no deviation. The sufferings of the men, the vast extent of the forest with its numberless intricacies, the unwholesome atmosphere, the almost incessant rain, altogether combined to make it unadvisable to venture far away from the river, where at any rate there was a tolerable certainty of procuring food from the villages on its border.

Hereabouts, the Aruwimi varies from 500 to 900 yards in width, its course broken by islands, single and in groups, which are the resort of oyster-fishermen. Insects of many kinds, flies and butterflies especially, are innumerable ; for hours every day swarms of these butterflies may be seen crossing over the water. The villages succeeded one after another well-nigh without a break, their united population reckoning many thousands, and belonging chiefly to the tribes of the Banalya, the Bakubana and the Bungangeta. As might be expected, throughout the district there was abundance of food.

On the 9th of July the caravan reached the rapids of Gwengweré, the region being still quite populous. Although the villages are so continuous, the residents appear to belong to a number of different small tribes ; as immediately at the rapids the people are Bakoka, only little higher up they are Bapupa, Bandangi, and Banali, and further inland are Bambalulu and Baburu. These last occupy a considerable region, and give the Aruwimi the name of " Lubali."

At this period the mornings were generally dark

and gloomy, the sky obscured by heavy clouds. Occasionally everything was in a dense fog, which did
not clear off until nine o'clock, and sometimes not
much before midday. . In this dim condition of the atmosphere nothing stirred ; the insects seemed asleep ;
death-like silence reigned through the forest; the
river in its dark fringe of massy vegetation lay mute
and sombre as a grave. If rain did not follow, and the
sun began to disperse the mists, as light penetrated
the vapour everything would again start into life ;
butterflies sport in the air, the solitary ibis raise its
note of alarm, the diving-bird plunge into the stream ;
there would be movement all around. Suddenly, the
drum was heard, the natives from afar had descried
the advancing troop, and shouting vociferously had
seized their glistening spears, and were ready for hostilities.

Encampment was made, on July 17th, at the rapids
of Mariri, beyond which, on both sides of the river,
resides a large number of the Mupé. Up to this
point there is no real cataract ; the rapids are formed
by reefs of rock between which the waters force a
passage, but they so entirely prevent navigation that
boats have to be unloaded and carried, as well as
their cargoes, beyond the limits of the obstruction.

Beyond the Mupé, towards the north, is the tribe
of the Bandeya ; in the interior are the Batua, to the
east the Mabode, and on the south the Bundiba, the
Binyali, and the Bakongo.

At Mugwyé, above the Bandeya rapids, stands a
group of seven villages surrounded by magnificent
banana plantations and manioc fields, extending over
an area of some miles. Here a whole day was lost
in bartering for provisions, at very costly rates. The
distrustful and unconciliatory spirit of the natives was
very great, so that at a large outlay of cowries and
brass rods only a few ears of corn could be procured
for about a third part of the caravan.

Above Mugwyé are the Panga Falls, having a descent of about 30 feet ; and these are succeeded by
the Nejambi rapids.

During the next ten days the services of three
porters were lost, two of them having deserted, and
one having died of dysentery. These were the only

casualties since the start, so that for thirty-four days
the course, as Stanley said, had been "singularly
successful."

But the expedition had now to enter upon a wilderness, through which it took nine days to march. Sufferings began to be aggravated, so that several deaths
occurred. Fortunately, the river was available for
some distance, and canoes could be employed in relieving the disabled of their loads, and thus progress,
if not so rapid as at first, was still steady.

On August 13th the expedition arrived at Air-
Sibba. Here the natives showed an angry front, apparently resolved to oppose the passage of the caravan. Five men were killed by poisoned arrows.
Lieutenant Stairs was wounded just below the heart,
but although he suffered severely for more than a
month, he happily recovered.

The porters were obliged to take every possible
precaution against these destructive weapons, which
were here in such free use. When the poison is fresh
a wound is invariably mortal. The injury to Lieutenant Stairs was not improbably caused by an arrow of
which the poison had lost its efficacy, so that he was
nearly convalescent after some weeks, although the
wound was some time longer before it was thoroughly
healed. A man who received a slight scratch on the
wrist died in five days of tetanus; another who was
touched in the muscle of the arm near the shoulder
lived only a few hours longer; and a third, slightly
cut on the throat, succumbed in about the same time
also, a victim to lock-jaw.

Stanley made every endeavour to find out whence
this deadly poison was obtained. He observed in the
huts various packets of dried red ants. He thus
knew that the bodies of the ants, after being dried
and ground to powder, were cooked in palm-oil, and
that this was the composition that was applied to the
spear-heads, and made them such fatal missiles.

On July 25th the encampment was at Air-Jali,
the point of confluence of the Nepoko with the
Aruwimi.

The Nepoko comes from the north, and is the river
of which Dr. Junker explored the source near the residence of the Mombuttu chief Sanga. At its mouth it

is more than 300 yards wide, and falls into the Aruwimi by a cataract.

From the Congo to the Nepoko the banks of the Aruwimi are almost uniformly low, never exceeding an altitude of 40 feet; higher up their elevation becomes greater, and they are frequently crowned with forests of palm-trees, the stems of some of which are as gigantic as any of those which grow on the Lower Congo. The natives have a singular method of clearing the woods: having constructed a platform some 16 feet high, they cut down the trees, hundreds at a time, to this level, so that at first sight a tract of land that has been subject to this treatment presents very much the appearance of a city of ruined temples.

The stream seems to be a boundary line between two distinctive styles of building; below the point of confluence all the huts are conical; but above it, the villages are all composed of square huts, generally surrounded by tall logs of the Rubiaceæ wood, which form a sort of outwork, offering a good position for defence for men with firearms, and requiring a considerable force to overcome and capture.

Navigation henceforward becomes more difficult; above the Nepoko, rapids are frequent, and there are two falls of some magnitude. The country rises gradually for 400 miles from Yambuya, and at last the river is shut in by the vertical walls of a canon, and its breadth confined to a channel that is scarcely 100 yards across. All along, whatever diversities may characterise the soil, one uniform feature prevails, inasmuch as mountain peaks, plains and valleys are all covered with forest, and there is not an open space that has not been cleared by the hand of man.

For some days longer the course of the Aruwimi was followed, until it became impossible to contend with the increasing vehemence of the stream. The boat and canoes had to be unloaded.

Only after two months, at the end of August, could real misfortunes be said to begin. In choosing the Aruwimi route Stanley had been influenced by the hope that he should avoid the Arabs who so frequently entice the porters to desert. Disappointed in his design, he now fell in with one of their caravans, meeting a party of Manyema, belonging to a certain

Ugarrowwa, otherwise known as Uledi Balyuz, who had formerly been in Speke's service as a tent-boy. As if to verify Stanley's forebodings, within three days of the *rencontre* twenty-six of his followers had disappeared.

Ugarrowwa's station was further up on the right hand bank of the river. The caravan reached the spot on the 16th of September, but as he had so completely devastated the country that food was scarce, only a brief halt was made. Stanley, however, left fifty-six of his men with Ugarrowwa, engaging to pay him five dollars a month each for their keep. It would have been certain death for the men to have to proceed with the caravan in their debilitated condition, while with a few weeks' rest they were not unlikely to recover their strength. On starting again the expedition, all told, amounted to 266 men. Of the 388 men who had originally set out from Yambuya, 66 had been lost by desertion and death, and 56 more had to be left sick at the Arab station.

Another Arab settlement was reached on the 15th of October. This was the headquarters of Kilonga-Longa, once a Zanzibari slave belonging to Abed-ben-Salim, an old trader whose bloody deeds are recorded in "The Congo and the Founding of its Free State."

The month of October was, as Stanley has said, "an awful month;" no member of the expedition, white or black, will ever forget it. The entire region had been so thoroughly laid waste by the Arabs that not a single native hut had been left standing. Whatever had not been ransacked by Kilonga's slaves had been uprooted by elephants, so that the district was one vast wilderness. The reserve of provisions having been exhausted, the men were obliged, as best they could, to exist upon wild fruit and different sorts of fungus.

On attempting to renew the march, the porters were found to be so weak that they were quite unable to carry the boat and the diminished loads; and thus it was that they had to be left where they were, under the supervision of Dr. Parke and Captain Nelson, the latter of whom was incapable of proceeding farther without rest. To add to the general misfortune, the men who were in condition to go on had allowed

themselves to be so miserably cheated and plundered
by the slaves, who took their rifles, their ammunition, and even their clothing, that when they set out
afresh, they were in a state of beggary and naked.
To such distress was the expedition now reduced.

After twelve days' perseverance in a most painful
march, the caravan arrived at a native village, called
Ibwiri. It proved to be a populous place and well
supplied with provisions ; but so dire had been the
effect of the privation endured for successive weeks
that the men had become mere skeletons. Of the 266
who had made a start from Ugarrowwa's quarters,
only 174 survived to reach Ibwiri.

A halt for thirteen days was made at Ibwiri, an opportunity that was enjoyed by the men, who feasted
abundantly upon goat-flesh, poultry, bananas, yams,
and all the good things that seemed inexhaustible.
So beneficial was the effect that when mustered for
another start on November 24th, they were all sleek
and robust, and so revived in spirits that they were
ready to follow Stanley to the world's end.

It is true that there was still a journey before them
of 126 miles before the Nyanza would be reached, but
now in recruited strength and with plenty of food such
a distance counted for nothing.

On arriving on the 1st of December at the summit
of an elevated ridge, they were able to see the open
country where their endurances would all come to an
end. They were now leaving behind them the dark
interminable forest; the gloom that had overshad-
owed them for 160 days was becoming a thing of the
past ; they were about to emerge upon the open plain.

Stanley himself thus writes of this period :—" Try
and imagine some of our inconveniences. Take a
thick Scottish copse, dripping with rain ; imagine this
copse to be a mere undergrowth, nourished under the
impenetrable shade of ancient trees, ranging from 100
to 180 feet high ; briars and thorns abundant ; lazy
creeks meandering through the jungle, and sometimes
a deep affluent of a great river. Imagine this forest
and jungle in all stages of decay and growth, old
trees falling, leaning perilously over, fallen prostrate ;
ants and insects of all kinds, sizes, and colours murmuring around ; monkeys and chimpanzees above,

queer noises of birds and animals, crashes in the jungle as troops of elephants rush away; dwarfs with poisoned arrows securely hidden behind some buttress or in some dark recess; strong brown-bodied aborigines with terribly sharp spears standing poised, still as dead stumps; rain pattering down upon you every other day; an impure atmosphere, with its dread consequences, fever and dysentery; gloom throughout the day, and dark almost palpable throughout the night; then if you will imagine such a forest extending the entire distance from Plymouth to Peterhead, you will have a fair idea of some of the inconveniences endured by us from June 28th to December 5th, 1887."

In another letter Stanley further writes: "After 160 days' continuous gloom we saw the light of broad day shining all around us and making all things beautiful. We thought we had never seen grass so green, nor country so lovely. The men literally yelled and leaped for joy, and raced over the ground with their burdens. Ah! this was the old spirit of former expeditions successfully completed all of a sudden revived. Woe betide the native aggressor we may meet, however powerful he may be; with such a spirit the men will fling themselves like wolves on sheep. Numbers will not be considered. It had been the eternal forest that had made them abject slavish creatures, so brutally plundered by Arab slaves at Kilonga-Longa's."

Yet these were the very men who had turned a deaf ear to prayers and entreaties when, a few weeks previously, their intrepid leader had tried to rally them by saying: "Beyond these raiders lies a country untouched, where food is abundant, and where you will forget your miseries; so cheer up, boys; be men, press on a little faster."

A few days more and the expedition entered the territory of the Bakumu, of which the different tribes extend to the south-west nearly as far as Stanley Falls. Their chief on the Arnwimi is the powerful Mazamboni. Their villages are numerous and large. As a rule they consist of a single street, from 10 to 20 yards in width, bordered by huts that are nearly uniform in size and height, and placed so close together as not unfrequently to look like a single struc-

ture 200, 300 or even 400 yards long. Cultivated
fields and pasture-lands enclose them all.

Here the natives again had sighted the caravan from
a long distance, and at once set themselves in array
to resist its progress. It was about four o'clock in
the afternoon when Stanley led his column into the
centre of a group of villages, and at once set to work
to construct a zeriba as fast as billhooks could hack
down the brushwood. Meanwhile the war-cry could
be heard pealing from hill to hill; the natives gathered themselves by hundreds from every point; the
noise of war-horns and drums made it plain that a
struggle must ensue. Some assailants, over ventur-
ous, were soon repelled, and a brief skirmish ended in
the capture of a cow. It provided the men with the
first meal of beef which they had tasted since they left
the ocean!

The night passed peacefully, both sides making
preparations for the morrow. The natives were anxious to know who the intruders were, whence they had
come, whither they were going, and what were their
designs. The Europeans, on the other hand, wanted
all the information they could get about the country
and its resources. Hours were spent in talking, both
parties keeping at due distance from each other.

From the natives it was gathered that they were
subject to Uganda, but that Kabrega was their true
sovereign, and that now Mazamboni was holding the
country for Kabrega. As the upshot of the interview
they accepted some cloth and brass-rods to show their
chief, who would return an answer the next day.

It was somewhat startling the following morning to
hear a man proclaiming that it was Mazamboni's decision that the caravan must be driven back and ex-
pelled from the land. A vehement shouting arose from
the valleys, and two arrows were shot into the camp.
Thus war was declared. The camp was situated between two ranges of hills, one above and one below. The upper range was seen to be lined with hundreds of natives preparing to descend, and nearly as
many seemed mustering in the valley.

There was no time to lose. Forthwith Stanley hurried forth a detachment of forty men under Lieutenant
Stairs to attack the valley, whilst Mr. Jephson was

FIGHT IN MAJAMBONI'S COUNTRY, DEC. 11, 1887: BURNING OF VILLAGES.

(From a sketch by Lieutenant Stairs, R. E.)

sent with thirty men to the east. A choice body of
sharpshooters was also sent to test the courage of
those descending the mountain.

The resistance did not last long. Lieutenant Stairs
crossed a deep and narrow river in the face of
hundreds of natives, and took the first village by
assault. The sharpshooters did their work well, and
drove the descending natives rapidly up the slope, until there was a general flight. Meantime Jephson
was not idle ; he marched straight up the valley to
the east, driving the people back and taking their villages as he went. By 3 P.M. there was not a native
visible anywhere within a mile and a half.

On the morning of the 12th, the march was continued. During that day and the following day there
were some skirmishes, but only of slight importance.

The course was now due east. The Ituri, as the
Aruwimi is here called, had been left behind, and the
caravan was now on the top of the plateau. About
1 P.M. a shout was heard from Stanley : "Now, men,
look out! prepare for a sight of the Nyanza !" The
people were doubtful ; they kept murmuring : "Why
does the master keep talking to us in this way? Nyanza, indeed ! Isn't it all a plain ? and do we not see
mountains for four days' march ahead?" But it was
true, nevertheless. Within half an hour they could
see the Nyanza below them : the great goal and object
of their journey was lying expanded at their feet. A
cheer rose involuntarily : "Hurrah for the Nyanza !"
The negroes who had mistrusted the assurances of
their leader came running to kiss his hands and to ask
pardon for their incredulity.

There on the summit of Baker's Blue Mountains, on
the ridge between the basins of the Congo and the
Nile, stood Stanley to enjoy his triumph and to feel
that he had his reward. The lake which was navigated
by Emin's steamers was outstretched in front of him.
The huts of Kavalli, the objective point of the expedition, were but six miles away. With what impa-
tience had the explorer traced the lessening of the long
itinerary on his map ! With what ardour had he
mounted the elevation that overlooks the Aruwimi region ! With what eagerness had he crossed the plain
on which both Nile and Congo take their origin ! With

what anxiety had he scanned the distant view, and peered through the foliage of the palms to catch a glimpse of the lake that he knew should be close at hand! And there it was! Its waters were sparkling before his eyes. It was reached at last!

At what cost the end had been attained it is hard to realise : the endurance, the effort, and the determination by which it was achieved none but those devoted followers who undauntedly kept true to their master can actually know.

Thus on the confines of Emin's province, it became Stanley's next concern to put himself into direct communication with Emin, so that he should be apprised of the arrival of the expedition that had come out for his relief.

But where was he? Was Emin within reach?

On leaving Cairo in January 1887, Stanley had had no later news of Emin Pasha than what had been brought by Dr. Junker in the previous year. Three years therefore had elapsed, and what might not have transpired in the time? There was room for many speculations. What had been happening in the Soudan? Had the Mahdists made any fresh advance towards the south? Had the natives in the Upper Nile remained submissive? Had the black soldiers and the Egyptian officers kept faithful? Might not Emin and Casati have fallen victims to treachery, and shared the fate of Gordon? Although Wolseley had reached his goal, had he not arrived too late?

Happily, however, there was no need for these apprehensions. Although Stanley himself for seven months in the untraversed woods of Africa had been cut off from communication with the world, and was ignorant of the situation, Europe had already been apprised of the safety both of the Pasha and his companion, by letters received from them on the East Coast.

Both men were free. Since Dr. Junker's departure nothing had occurred to disturb the peace of the province, and although the store of provisions was getting low, the troops had remained faithful in their allegiance, and the Egyptian flag still floated unchallenged over the fourteen stations and two steamers on the Upper Nile.

The approach of Stanley's expedition, by the way of the Congo, had been already made known to Emin by messengers who had left Zanzibar in January, arriving at the lake in May. The arrival of the relief party was consequently expected. On August 15, 1887, Emin had written from Wadelai to his friend Dr. Felkin in Edinburgh, and mentioned that he had despatched some messengers to the south-west to make inquiries about Stanley; and in November he wrote again to Zanzibar, saying : "All well; on best terms with chiefs and people : will be leaving shortly for Kibiro, on east of Lake Albert. Have sent reconnoitring party to look out for Stanley, which had to return with no news yet. Stanley expected about December 15th."

Casati had also received information of what Stanley was doing; but less sanguine than Emin, he estimated approximately that the arrival of the caravan would be about the following March. On the 5th of December he wrote from Giuaïa to his friend Captain Camperio : "For my part, I do not believe that Stanley will arrive yet. No news even of the most vague character has yet reached us from the west. I am, in my own mind, convinced that unless fortune has signally smiled upon his enterprise, he cannot be expected here until March."

Eight days after sending his letter, If Casati had been using his telescope, and scanning the shores of Lake Nyanza, he might have descried a concourse of men on the summit of the plateau; he might have seen that the mass was in motion, and would not have been long in concluding that here was the caravan for which they were on the lookout. It had actually touched the margin of the lake on the very day that had been forecast by Emin !

Nevertheless, before the three brave adventurers were to meet, four months had yet to elapse.

CHAPTER XV.

MEETING OF STANLEY AND EMIN.

The Albert Nyanza—The camp at Kavalli—Where is Emin?—Stanley makes
retreat—Fort Bodo—Dwarfs of Central Africa—Travels of Lieutenant
Stairs—Illness of Stanley—On the march—Return to the Lake—A letter
from Emin—Jephson reconnoitring—Meeting of Stanley, Emin, and Casati
—In council.

From the ridge of the plateau whence the expedition first sighted the Nyanza the view extends to an
indefinite horizon.

The confluence of the Aruwimi is about 1250 feet
above the level of the sea ; thence the laborious ascent of the wooded terraces had to be made between
which the river runs to join the Congo, forming numerous rapids and cascades as it rolls along. The
pathway kept on a gradual rise, and eventually obtained an altitude of 5200 feet. After arriving at the
eastern limit of the basin, they soon found that the
plateau was making a sudden decline, and widening
out so as to form a great hollow, in which, some 2900
feet below them, the surface of the waters of the
southern shore of the lake lay outstretched, like a
sheet of quicksilver in the midday sun.

About twenty miles away towards the east the
peaked summits of Unyoro are conspicuous. The
hills appear to rise immediately from the water to a
height of 1000 or perhaps 1500 feet. So clear is the
atmosphere that every indentation of the outline can
be distinguished. Beyond these, in remoter distance,
are the elevated plains of Kabrega's kingdom, where
for two years Casati has been stationed in order to
keep open the route towards the East Coast.

To the southward lies the valley of the Semliki, a
river that flows at the foot of one of the most Alpine
districts in Africa, its mountains rising in domes and
peaks, some of them, like the Gordon-Bennett and
Edwin Arnold, assuming the most striking forms ;
whilst the whole region is dominated by the majestic

Ruwenzori, clad in eternal snow, and 15,000 feet in height.

Northwards the lake becomes wider; but the view in that direction is not extensive. About 250 miles from Kavalli the lake gives birth to the White Nile, which passes Wadelai as it flows towards Khartoum.

It is asserted that about a century ago the length of the lake was certainly fifteen miles more than its present measurement; its waters must therefore have covered the forests of ambatch and the tracts of reeds and papyrus which are now traversed by the lower course of the Semliki. The cause of this retreat of the water from its ancient bounds may not improbably be attributed to the gradual wearing away of sandy shoals and rocks in the Nile below Wadelai. The encroachment of the shore is greatest on the western side, and Emin asserts his belief that several islands (one in particular called Tunguru) which some years ago were at a considerable distance from the margin of the lake, are now quite contiguous to the mainland, and are tenanted by residents. In a good many places towards the southern end of the lake, the brown tint of the water indicates its shallowness, and not unfrequently, even some miles out, the bottom can be reached by a sounding pole.

As they descend towards the water the slopes of the hill-sides are somewhat steep; they are not covered with very much vegetation, except in the moist ravines and interstices where magnificent shrubs and giant euphorbiæ are sure to be found in large profusion; and if anywhere the glitter of a tiny cascade shines through the foliage, there, almost to a certainty, may be seen the date-palm rearing on high its graceful plume.

On the narrow strips of level ground between the mountain foot and the water's edge are various little groups of huts, with their adjoining fields, on which they grow their bananas, or where, on the rich short pasture, they keep the herds of cows and goats that graze peacefully together.

Occasionally the waters of the lake will lose themselves in enormous banks of reeds, floating masses of vegetation, too dense for any canoes to penetrate; elsewhere they gently ripple over beds of white pebbles where the fishing-boats are moored.

In Indian file, on the evening of December 13, the expedition made its descent along the zigzag pathway, and settled itself in an encampment at the base of the hills, about half a mile from the lake, between the villages of Kavalli and Kakongo.

Just as it had happened on the higher ground, the natives here, too, manifested considerable disquietude at the unlooked-for appearance of so large a caravan of strangers, with white men at their head. They did not proceed to any overt hostility, but it was quite evident that they did not approve of such a body of intruders coming amongst them. In the conversations into which they entered with Stanley they avowed that they had never seen any boats upon the lake, except their own. If this were so, what was the conclusion to be drawn? Was it not obvious that the couriers who had been sent from Zanzibar to prepare Emin beforehand, for the arrival of an expedition in January, must have been delayed? Otherwise Emin would have been sure to send over his two steamers to the south-west, and to make proper provision for securing from the natives a hospitable reception for the caravan whenever it should come. Every indication seemed to point to the conclusion that Emin Pasha had not been apprised of Stanley's near approach.

What now should be done? The journey from Kavalli to Wadelai was far too long and too arduous to be attempted without boats by an expedition so reduced in strength, and yet no canoes were to be had; as for Stanley's own boat, that had been left at Kilonga-Longa's, 190 miles away.

Stanley took his two officers, Messrs. Stairs and Jephson, into consultation, and after prolonged discussion arrived at the conviction that the only practicable course to be followed was to make a retreat to Ibwiri on the Aruwimi, where he would build a fort, and whence he would send a detachment to Kilonga-Longa's to fetch his boat and bring on Captain Nelson and Dr. Parke. Within the fort he determined to store every load that would be left behind, and he would arrange for an adequate garrison to defend it, and to grow sufficient maize and manioc for supplying themselves with food. He would then return to Lake Nyanza, and while encamped there he would despatch his boat with an officer and some men to go forward and institute inquiries as to Emin's whereabouts.

Such was the programme which it was resolved to carry out.

Accordingly on the 15th the retreat commenced. The movements of the caravan were more or less harassed by the ill-will of the natives of Kavalli, who succeeded during the march of the retiring cavalcade on the upward slope in killing one man and wounding a second.

By 10 A.M. on the 16th the crest of the plateau was reached, and the progress back along the plain was not interrupted by Mozamboni's people. The march was continued steadily day by day without hindrance, and on the 8th of January 1888 the caravan was once more in Ibwiri, the hospitable refuge where two months previously it had found a welcome abundance and much needed repose.

No time was lost by Stanley in setting about the construction of his fortified quarters. He named the erection Fort Bodo. He likewise hurried off Lieutenant Stairs to Kilonga-Longa's to get the boat, and to come back with Dr. Parke and Captain Nelson, who had been staying there ever since the previous September.

All the forests of this region, as well as those extending south-east to the Sankullu, are the last refuge of a race of beings of whom the two that were brought over by the Italian traveller Miani in 1873 were the only examples that have ever been seen in Europe. These are the dwarfs of Central Africa.

Ages back Herodotus had testified to the existence of dwarf races in Africa, and Aristotle had asserted that the region whence the Nile had its sources was the abode of pygmies; but of modern travellers Dr. Schweinfurth, in 1871, was the first, as an eyewitness, to verify the existence of such a race in the heart of the continent. At the court of Munza, King of the Mombuttu, south of the Welle, the Doctor for the first time beheld the living incarnation of the myth of 2000 years. This was a regiment of dwarf soldiers belonging to Munza's brother, a chief who resided further south in the valley of the Nepoko.

The existence of such dwarfs may now be said to

have been ascertained throughout the central basin of
the Congo. Stanley saw one individual of the race
on the Lualaba, below Nyangwé; Grenfell saw one
on the Lalongo; Wolf fell in with another between
the Lulua and the Sankullu; Delcommune met one on
the Lomani; and Escayrac de Lauture and Koellé
assert that they are numerous in the northern basin of
the Mobangi.

Amongst the Mombuttu they are known by the name
of Akka or Tikki-tikki; further to the south and east
they are called Batua, whilst on the Aruwimi they are
distinguished as the Wambutti.

Physically, they are well made; they are by no
means the deformities which are frequently exhibited
as dwarfs in the shows of European fairs; they are
simply small men, well proportioned, endowed with
much bravery, and by no means deficient in adroitness.   Their average height may be stated as about 4
feet 7 inches.   Their complexion is a yellowish brown,
of a lighter shade than that of the taller African
races.   They form themselves into nomad communities, devoting themselves to hunting and to the manufacture of palm-wine, rarely intermingling with tribes
of ordinary stature.   The agility they display in climbing the palm-trees to extract the sap is very remarkable, and they are exceedingly cunning in devising
artifices for setting traps and snares for game.   On
their hunting excursions they bound over the tall herbage like grasshoppers, fearlessly approaching antelopes,
buffaloes, and elephants; first discharging their arrows
at them with unerring precision, and then rushing
forward to despatch the wounded victims with their
spears.   They can hardly at present be said to constitute a nation, but it may be held as not improbable
that their communities, dispersed among other and
more powerful peoples, are the expiring remnants of
an aboriginal race.   ˉ

It was chiefly in the district of the Aruwimi, between the confluence of the Nepoko and the region of
the grass-plain, that Stanley came across the dwarfs;
but there he computes he saw about one hundred and
fifty of their villages in the recesses of the forests.

On January 14th, Lieutenant Stairs arrived back
from Kilonga-Longa's, accompanied by Dr. Parke and

by Captain Nelson, who had now regained his health; but of the thirty-eight men who had been left in charge of these two officials only eleven now remained; the rest had either died or deserted. The lieutenant had likewise brought up the boat he had gone to fetch, with the goods that had been left at the Arab settlement. Having accomplished this, he was now once more sent down the river, this time as far as Ugarrowwa's, to bring up the convalescents and a part of the baggage that had been deposited there.

While Stairs was absent on this commission, Stanley was seized with illness, having an attack of gastritis and an abscess on his arm; but though he was unwell for nearly a month, he received such careful nursing at the hands of Dr. Parke that he was convalescent before the return of the lieutenant, who was away longer than had been anticipated. Anxious to lose no more time, Stanley, without waiting, gave the order to start, and the expedition, now composed of no more than 140 men, took up an ample stock of provisions and set out a second time for the Nyanza.

Captain Nelson was placed in charge of Fort Bodo with a garrison of 43 men and lads, who would be reinforced by Lieutenant Stairs and the men he would bring with him from Ugarrowwa's.

Once more, on the 20th of April, did the expedition find itself in Mazamboni's country. The reception that awaited it was very different to what it had been before; instead of the palavers ending in a declaration of war, they resulted in a consent from Mazamboni to make blood-brotherhood with Stanley.

It may be accepted, as a general rule, that Europeans on the Congo, arriving in any unexplored district, would be received with hostilities. Whilst descending the river in 1877 Stanley found himself involved in no less than thirty skirmishes, and Wissman, Kund, Tappenbeck, Van Gèle and de Brazza have all had similar experiences. But when after a lapse of time the white man reappears on the scene, the natives are usually found to be ready to lay aside the temper of defiance, and after brief recognition to conclude peace by exchange of blood. And this is pretty sure to be followed by a solicitation that the

strangers will settle down and open traffic in the
place.

Although the strength of the expedition was now
diminished by the loss of fifty rifles, the example of
Mazamboni to desist from opposition was followed by
the other chiefs as far as the Nyanza, and no further
difficulty occurred.   Food was supplied on the easiest
terms, cattle, sheep, and poultry were brought in
abundance, and never had Stanley and his followers
lived more luxuriously.

Thus, once again, on the 21st of April was Stanley
in full view of the Nyanza.

And now once more the question arose as to what
he should hear or see of Emin.   Surely by this time
the Pasha must have been apprised of the arrival of
the expedition ; but how should he be found?

On his way down to the lake some natives from
Kavalli had met him and had told him that a white
man from the north had given their chief a packet
which was to be handed to another white man who
was coming from the west ; they had also some wonderful story to tell about "big boats, as large as
islands," which they averred had been seen near their
villages.

Stanley entertained little doubt but that these big
boats must be the steamers from Wadelai, and he in-
dulged the hope that Emin Pasha might be himself on
board, a hope that was soon changed to certainty ; for
next day Kavalli came and brought him a packet protected by a strip of black American oil-cloth and en-
closing a letter from Emin.   The letter was dated
from on board the *Khedive*, on the 26th of March, and
addressed to " Mr. Stanley, commander of the relief
expedition."   The tenour of the letter was to this
effect :—

" A report having been circulated that a large caravan had arrived from the west under the conduct of
white men, I proceeded in one of my steamers to the
south end of the lake to make enquiries ; but the natives were so afraid of Kabrega, the King of Unyoro,
with whom they are at war, that they associated every
stranger with him.   Thus, at first, I could obtain no
trustworthy information.

" Shortly afterwards, however, the wife of the

Nyamsassie chief told the chief Mogo, who is on friendly terms with me, that she had seen the white men and their caravan in Mozamboni's country. At once I felt no doubt that you were in this district and that we should soon meet.

"I entrust this letter to Kavalli to hand to you when you reach the lake.

"I am glad to know you are here. I beg you to encamp where you are until I can communicate with you.   (Dr.) Emin."

Here, then, was good news. Emin Pasha was alive and was at liberty; here he was on one of his steamers, on his way to meet the expedition. The end was on the point of being attained; here was success (about which all but a few staunch believers in Europe had despaired) coming to crown the labours of a year of toil, uncertainty, and suffering!

Stanley quickly determined that his own boat should be sent northwards by the west coast to reconnoitre, and in a few hours it was launched and despatched with Mr. Jephson and a sufficient staff of men on board. Meanwhile, the bulk of the caravan made their encampment on the shore.

Days passed without further news. Stanley and Dr. Parke, the only one of his staff now with him, scanned the distance constantly with their glasses, but in vain. For five days nothing disturbed the solitude of the great lake, and the sixth day was declining when a distant vessel was discerned, which further scrutiny made it evident was not their own boat, but a steamer. From its stern floated the red flag, with the star and crescent. To a certainty here was the *Khedive*, one of the Wadelai ships.

On the deck were white men, Emin and Casati both. Mr. Jephson had fallen in with them on the 26th at Mswa, the southernmost of the Egyptian stations.

The camp was soon in the liveliest commotion; inaction was changed to hubbub and excitement; musketry salutes were fired, and in the midst of noisy acclamations the Pasha and his faithful companion landed to exchange their mutual greetings with Stanley.

It was in the evening of the 29th of April, at about 7 P.M., that this meeting was effected.

For six years Emin and Casati had been cut off
from all communication with the civilised world; and
for the last two they had been awaiting the relief
which Dr. Junker had been despatched to Europe to
secure. Meanwhile it had fallen to Emin's lot to fight
and drive back the Mahdists, to repress the revolts of
the Bari, and to punish the insubordination and coward-
ice of his own Egyptian contingent; he had had to
encounter unnumbered dangers and to surmount enormous difficulties in providing for the sustenance of
more than 8000 men, women, and children. Yet here
he was; he had overcome every obstacle and was still
master of the situation!

Captain Casati for three years had had no enviable
'residence at the court of Kabrega, King of Unyoro.
The conveyance of any correspondence between the
two Europeans, by way of Uganda, was a perfect bug-
bear to Kabrega. Naturally cruel and suspicious, he
was ever working himself into such a temper of rage
and alarm as to render Casati's position very critical.
And now the intelligence of the approach of an armed
troop from the west, which to his mind must threaten
Unyoro, gave the finishing touch to his state of wrath,
and almost cost the white resident his life.

It was while Stanley was erecting Fort Bodo (on
the 9th of the preceding January), after his first visit
to the lake, that Kabrega treacherously caused Casati
to be arrested, bound with cords, driven on from village to village, and finally sent to the domains of the
chief Kokora, who had instructions to put him to
death. Fortunately, the prisoner succeeded in making his escape, and for eight days wandered, absolutely destitute, along the eastern margin of the lake.
Chancing to find a boat amongst the reeds on the
water-side, he sent it off by one of his servants to
Emin, who at that time was at Tunguru on the opposite shore. A few days later Emin arrived and
took his recovered friend on board the *Khedive;* thus,
when they together met Stanley at Kavalli, they had
only been re-united for a few weeks after their long
and anxious separation.

Emin's armed force consisted of about 1400 soldiers,
forming two battalions. The first of these, numbering about 750 men, was divided into seven detach-

ments, occupying the stations of Dufilé, Khor-Aju, Labore, Muggi, Kiri, Bedden, and Rejaf ; the second, consisting of 640 men, was divided into five detachments, in garrison at Wadelai, Tunguru, and Mswa. In the interior, west of the Nile, he had three more outposts, making in all thirteen stations, extending along the Nile and the Nyanza for a distance of more than 200 miles. Around these stations fields of manioc, maize, beans, and sorghum had been cultivated, and there were herds containing some thousand heads of cattle.

Asked as to whether he was prepared to quit the country, Emin hesitated. " The Egyptians," he said, " are very willing to leave. There are of these about 100 men, besides their women and children. Even if I stayed here, I should be glad to be rid of them, because they undermine my authority, and nullify all my endeavours to retreat. When I informed them that Khartoum had fallen, and Gordon Pasha was slain, they always told the Nubians that it was a concocted story, and that some day we should see the steamers ascend the river for their relief. But of the regulars who compose the 1st and 2nd battalions, I am extremely doubtful : they have led such a free and happy life here that they would demur at leaving a country where they have enjoyed luxuries they cannot command in Egypt."

In fact from the time that Stanley arrived Emin never seemed to know what course to take. From his hesitation it might appear that his position was not altogether so secure as in Europe it was generally believed to be. He wished to take counsel with his officers, to tell his troops exactly how matters stood, and to make them aware of this arrival of the relief expedition. In short, he asked for time in which he might make up his mind. It was agreed that this time for deliberation should be conceded. Stanley left Mr. Jephson with a guard of thirteen Soudanese, and sent a message to be communicated to Emin's troops. After this Emin and Mr. Jephson were to proceed and pay a visit to Fort Bodo, bringing with them, on their return to the lake, Messrs. Stairs and Nelson, with the men that had been left under their charge.

Meanwhile Stanley himself, with the rest of the

caravan, and about 100 Madi porters, with which he
had been supplied by Emin, was to set out to meet his
large contingent in the rear.

Stanley and Emin had been together for twenty-five
days when the former once more betook himself to the
weary task of making his way through the same interminable forest where so recently he had endured
sickness, peril, and privation. But he had given his
word to Major Barttelot that he would go to meet him,
and go he would.

CHAPTER XVI.

THE RELIEF OF THE REAR-GUARD.

Major Barttelot—The situation at the Yambuya camp—Arrival of Tippoo
Tib's porters—Banalya—Assassination of Major Barttelot—Death of Mr.
Jameson—Arrival of Stanley at Banalya—Stanley's letter to Tippoo Tib
—On the march again—Famine—A starvation camp—At Fort Bodo—Ar-
rival at the lake—Disastrous tidings.

MAJOR EDMUND BARTTELOT, to whom Stanley had
entrusted the command of his rear-caravan, was a
young officer, who, in the expedition to the Soudan
under Lord Wolseley, was in charge of a camel-corps
of 1000 Somalis from Aden to Abu-Klea. Throughout the campaign the major distinguished himself by
energy and courage.

But in order to succeed in an unknown land like the
Congo, and in an undertaking so exceptionally difficult as the conduct of the relief expedition, something
more than military ardour was requisite. It is necessary to have foresight and patience, and beyond all it
is indispensable to have tact and forbearance in dealing with the natives. And in these latter qualities the
major unfortunately seems to have been deficient.

The sojourn of the rear-column at the Yambuya
camp forms the most lamentable chapter in the history of the expedition.

When he started from Yambuya, Stanley had left
with the major four Europeans, Messrs. Rose Troup,
Ward, Jameson, and Bonny, and 257 men, mixed
Soudanese and Zanzibaris. According to instructions
Barttelot was to remain at Yambuya until the arrival
of the steamers from Stanley Pool, which would bring

up all the men and the goods that had been left at Leopoldville and Bolobo. Then, provided that the contingent of porters promised by Tippoo Tib had also
arrived, the whole column was to set out on their
march; or even if the porters were delayed and were
late in coming, the major might, if he thought it
advisable, break up the camp and start without them,
following on in the track of Stanley, who had promised to come back and meet him.

As events turned out, the porters did not arrive;
the major, however, continued to expect their appearance, and waited on at Yambuya for nearly a year.

It was a year of indescribable misery. The dis-
comforts of the camp, the dearth of provisions, the
maintenance of 257 men almost exclusively on the
produce of a field of manioc, the misunderstanding
between the officer in command and his own men on
the one hand, and on the other, alike with the natives
around, and with the Arabs in the remoter settlements, the distrust and dislike engendered by the
major's severity and lack of sympathy, all combined
to render the situation very painful. Sickness broke
out in the camp, and the mortality was frightful.
Decimated by fever, dysentery, and mental as well as
bodily suffering, the contingent was gradually reduced
to 145 men, little more than half its original number.
It must seem little short of a miracle that not one of
the Europeans succumbed to the miseries that they
were called to endure. It was the opinion of full
many of those who were eye-witnesses of this gloomy
episode, that Major Barttelot was not at all equal to
the large responsibility that had been imposed upon
him. Moreover, it is obvious that there was far from
a good understanding between him and his European
associates, and altogether their relations, both personal and official, were very strained.

Two Government steamers visited the camp in May,
and found its aspect very miserable, presenting a
striking contrast to an Arab encampment that was
settled a little higher up the river. The Europeans
were sick and dispirited, quartered in comfortless
huts, while their Arab neighbours were in every way
thriving, lively, and well-ordered; not living in hov-

els, but in clay houses provided with verandahs, to which the natives resorted to barter their goods.

No doubt, it must be conceded, Major Barttelot's difficulties were excessively great and trying; but if, without prolonging his stay so unfortunately, he had advanced upon the track of the van column, and so had reached the lake or Fort Bodo in time to prevent Stanley losing seven months in coming back to seek him, who can say whether the subsequent events on the Nile and all the disastrous consequences that ensued might not have been averted?

The porters for whom Tippoo Tib had made the contract put in an appearance on the 4th of June. They had been engaged with difficulty, the majority being collected from the Manyema district and brought from Nyangwé to Yambuya by Mr. Jameson, who had been to the Upper Lualaba to take part in the recruiting.

Some days were occupied in the organisation of the caravan, but it was ultimately ready to start. It consisted of 25 Soudanese, 125 Zanzibaris, and the 400 porters that had just arrived. Major Barttelot was the recognised leader, having the assistance of Messrs. Bonny and Jameson. The services of Mr. Rose Troup were lost, as his health had failed, and he had been obliged to return to the coast, whither Mr. Ward had already preceded him, because, in the absence of all communication from Stanley, it was thought proper to telegraph to London and describe the condition of the column thus left in the rear.

And now that the day had come on which they should set out, the question might well be asked what should be the fate of those who, almost destitute of provisions, were to be conducted through the most terrible of unknown lands by a young and inexperienced officer who had failed to secure the confidence either of his own personal associates or of the negro soldiers under him?

Some bickerings and squabbling had already broken out, and Captain Van. Gèle, who had been at Yambuya only a few days previously, had stated that if it had not been for the presence and authority of Tippoo Tib, an outburst of mutiny would have been inevitable. The crisis, however, was not long to be deferred ; the fatal issue was close at hand.

It was at half-past seven on the morning of June 11th that the expedition effected its start. Some preliminary difficulties having been overcome, Major Barttelot temporarily handed over the supervision of the column to Mr. Bonny, so as to allow himself an opportunity of going to the Falls to take counsel with the Europeans and to see Tippoo Tib. Resuming the route to the Aruwimi, he re-formed his caravan at an encampment near the village of Banalya on the 18th of July.

The evening of his arrival the camp was *en fete*. The porters were shouting, singing, and dancing according to their habit when they are on the march. Barttelot, disliking the uproar, gave orders for immediate silence, and for the time his orders were obeyed ; but about 4 A.M. the boisterous merriment broke out again, exuberant as ever. Furious that his directions should be thus set at defiance, the major rose and left his tent, and notwithstanding the remonstrances of Mr. Bonny, proceeded to the quarters of the bearers. A woman was singing and beating a drum in front of one of the huts ; he spoke angrily to her, and threatened her with punishment. In another moment a shot was fired and the major fell dead.

It was the woman's husband, a Manyema named Sanga, who had done the fatal act. He had resented the vengeance that was threatened to his wife, and raising his gun he killed the white chief upon the spot.

Hearing the report, Mr. Bonny rushed from his tent to find the camp all in commotion, and the porters flying in every direction and shrieking aloud : " The white man is dead ! the white man is dead ! "

At the outset of the caravan Captain Vankerkhoven, the Commissioner of the Bangala district, as he witnessed its departure, had expressed his misgivings about it. " I do not believe in its success," he said ; " its leader has no tact, and no patience with the negroes." And, indeed, it might almost seem as though the major had brought his own fate upon himself, as it is universally known that the negro, when once aroused to anger, is very revengeful.

But this was only the beginning of the misfortunes

that befell the expedition ; it had to bewail the loss of
all its leaders in succession except one.

After doing his best to assist Mr. Bonny in calming
the disorder in the camp that prevailed as the conse
quence of Major Barttelot's assassination, Mr. Jameson had to leave for Stanley Falls for the purpose of
doing what he could to fill up the deficiency in numbers made by the repeated desertions of the men.   It
had been his intention, as soon as he could rejoin Mr.
Bonny, to proceed with him along the route to the
Nyanza, but having been informed at the Falls that
Mr. Ward was at Bangala, retracing his way from the
coast, he thought it desirable to go and meet him that
they might consult together.   Accordingly he took his
passage on board a large native boat.

He had overtaxed his strength.   Shortly before
reaching the confluence of the Lomami, he had a violent attack of fever, and on the 16th of August when
he arrived at Bangala, he was already in a dying state.
Surviving only till the following day, he died without
having been able to make the Europeans at the station
understand what had been the object of his coming.

On that very date of Mr. Jameson's death, Mr.
Bonny, the solitary European now left to supervise
the camp, was standing outside his hut, expecting
Jameson's arrival with recruits, when he caught sight
of a caravan, marching on in excellent order, and
headed by a white man.   It did not take long to recognise that here was Stanley redeeming his word, and
come back from the Nyanza to bring up the contingent
from the rear.

"Welcome, Bonny, welcome! but where is the
major?"

"Major Barttelot is dead, sir.   Shot a month ago
by the Manyema."

"Good God!   And where is Mr. Jameson?"

"He has gone to Stanley Falls to try and get more
men from Tippoo Tib."

"And Troup, where is he?"

"Mr. Troup has gone home, sir, invalided."

"Hem! hem! and where is Ward?"

"Mr. Ward is in Bangala."

"Heavens alive! then you are the only one here."

"Yes, sir."

Very successfully had Stanley accomplished his journey back from Lake Nyanza to Banalya in eighty-two days, experiencing a loss of only three of his followers. He had left the lake on the 25th of May, and reached Fort Bodo in fourteen days. Captain Nelson and Lieutenant Stairs were there, and everything under their charge was satisfactory; nearly ten acres of land were under cultivation, and one crop of Indian corn had been harvested and was in the granaries. Dr. Parke was now left to act as medical attendant at the garrison, which only reckoned fifty-nine rifles.

It was by his deliberate choice that Stanley for his return down the river had left himself without any of his officers; it was his object not to be encumbered with the baggage which a retinue of European associates would entail, while he knew that every available porter would be wanted to carry up the large amount of stores that had been reserved for Barttelot to convey.

On the 24th of June he reached Kilonga-Longa's, and on the 4th of July arrived at Ugarrowwa's. This latter station he found deserted, as Ugarrowwa, having got together as much ivory as he could, had started down the river with a flotilla of fifty-seven canoes, which Stanley overtook on the 10th of August.

At Banalya, a melancholy surprise awaited him. Out of the 257 that he had left a year ago there were only seventy-one remaining, and of these not many more than fifty seemed fit for service. His own sufferings that he had endured with the advanced caravan had been sad and serious enough, but they appeared slight in comparison with the privation and mortality that had prevailed in Major Barttelot's column. At present all his own men were in renovated and even robust health, but here the majority of the survivors from the Yambuya camp were reduced to a feeble and wretched condition.

After arriving at Banalya, Stanley lost no time in communicating with Europe. He sent off a messenger with letters to be forwarded from the Falls, and likewise wrote to Tippoo Tib in the following terms:—

"BOMA OF BANALYA (MURENIA), *August 17th.*

"To the Sheikh Hamed Ben Mahomed, from his good friend Henry Stanley.

"Many salaams to you. I hope you are in good health as I am, and that you have remained in good health since I left the Congo. I have many things to say to you, but I hope I shall see you face to face before many days. I reached this place this morning with 130 Wangwana, and three soldiers and sixty-six natives belonging to Emin Pasha. This is now the eighty-second day since we left Emin Pasha on the Nyanza, and we have only lost three men all the way. Two of them were drowned and the other ran away. I found the white men whom I was looking for. Emin Pasha was quite well, and the other white man, Casati, was quite well also. Emin has ivory in abundance, cattle by thousands, and sheep, goats, fowls, and food of all kinds. We found him to be a very good and kind man. He gave numbers of things to all our white and black men, and his liberality could not be exceeded. His soldiers blessed our black men for their kindness in coming so far to show them the way, and many of them were ready to follow me at once out of the country. But I asked them to stay quiet a few months that I might go back and fetch the other men and goods that I had left at Yambuya, and they prayed to God that He would give me the strength to finish my work. May their prayer be heard! And now, my friend, what are you going to do? We have gone the road twice over. We know where it is bad and where it is good; where there is plenty of food and where there is none; where all the camps are, and where we shall sleep and rest. I am waiting to hear your words. If you go with me it is well. If you do not go it is well. I leave it to you.

"I will stay here ten days, and then I go on slowly. I move from here to a big island two hours' march from here, and above this place there are plenty of houses and plenty of food for the men. Whatever you have to say to me, my ears will be open with a good heart, as it has always been towards you. There-fore, if you come, come quickly; for on the eleventh morning from this I shall move on. All my white men are well, but I left them all behind, except my servant William, who is with me.

(Signed)   "STANLEY."

In reply to this letter Tippoo Tib sent a message explaining that he must decline the invitation to join Stanley on account of the scarcity of porters at his command; whereupon Stanley proceeded to reorganise his company, and made his start to rejoin Emin. The caravan, including his own men, now amounted to nearly 350 in all. Mr. Bonny accompanied the expedition, and the entire remaining lot of goods was taken on. It was now the 1st of September.

This was the beginning of a journey of more than four months' duration, in which the route once more lay through the impenetrable forests and the devastated wildernesses of which the dwarf people were the only tenants. It was a period which brought sad and terrible hardships.

For two months, until the caravan arrived at the confluence of the Ihuru, all may be said to have gone fairly well, except for an outbreak of small-pox which was fatal to many of the native porters. Happily the Zanzibaris escaped the scourge, an immunity owing no doubt to their having been vaccinated on board the *Madura* on their way from Zanzibar to the Cape.

Beyond the Ihuru, however, the condition of things went from bad to worse. Across the deserts by the right bank of the Aruwimi the famine became intense. Weeks of privation followed, and on the 9th of December Stanley resolved to encamp in a vast forest, and to despatch a foraging party to make their way to a populous centre, which according to his map he estimated would be found at no great distance. Day after day passed by, while the expediton, suffering the agonies of hunger, watched for the return of the foragers. Stanley has given a description of the trying time to the following effect:—

" Never in all my African experience had I been nearer absolute starvation. On the fifth day, after giving out all the flour there was in camp, and killing the only goat that had been reserved, I was obliged to open the cases of the officers' provisions, which hitherto had been untouched. In the afternoon a boy died, and the condition of nearly all the rest was most disheartening; some could not stand upright, falling down as soon as they tried to rise. The spectacle that I had before my eyes thus constantly so acted on

my nerves that I ended by sympathising with it, not
only morally but physically, just as though weakness
were contagious.

"A Madi porter died before night; the last of our
Somalis gave signs of collapse, and the few Soudanese
who were with us were scarce able to move.

"The morning of the sixth day dawned. We made
our broth as usual, abundance of water, a pot of butter, a pot of condensed milk, and a cupful of flour for
130 people! Matters had come to a critical condition.

"Mr. Bonny and the chiefs were called together for
a consultation, and surmises of every conceivable kind
were put forward as to what could account for the
prolonged absence of the party sent out to forage.
Finally, Mr. Bonny volunteered to stay at the encampment with ten men, on condition that I would
leave him provisions for ten days.

"This did not seem much; it could hardly be difficult to supply sufficient gruel to keep ten men alive
for ten days; but then there were all the sick and all
the enfeebled who would be unable to keep moving,
and must necessarily die of exhaustion and hunger unless I had good luck. Nevertheless, I accepted Mr.
Bonny's offer, and a stone of milk, butter, flour, and
biscuit was prepared and handed over for his use."

In the afternoon of the seventh day a general inspection was made; it showed that there were forty-
three individuals who were absolutely incapable of
following Stanley, and who must be left to the charge
of Mr. Bonny and his ten men. Sadi, the chief of the
Manyema, abandoned fourteen of his people to their
fate; Kibbo-Bora, another chief, left his brother; a
third chief, Fundi, left one of his wives and a little
boy. The remaining twenty-six were his own people.
The condition of all these seemed desperate, and there
was hardly a ray of hope for them unless food could
be brought to them within the next twenty-four hours.

"In a cheery tone, though my heart was never
heavier, I told the forty-three hunger-bitten people
that I was going back to hunt up the missing men.
Probably I should meet them on the road, but if I did
they would be driven on the run with food to them.
We travelled nine miles that afternoon, having passed
several dead people on the road; and early on the

CAPTAIN NELSON'S "STARVATION CAMP" AT THE CONFLUENCE OF THE ITURI AND IHURI. OCTOBER, 1887.

eighth day of their absence from camp, met them
marching in an easy fashion ; but when we were met
the pace was altered to a quick step, so that in twenty-
six hours after leaving Starvation Camp, we were back
with a cheery abundance around, gruel and porridge
boiling, bananas boiling, plantains roasting, and some
meat simmering in pots for soup.

"Twenty-one persons altogether succumbed in this
dreadful camp."

The Ihuru was crossed on the 18th of December,
and on the next day the caravan having crossed the
forest, regardless of paths, fortunately found itself
at the west angle of the Fort Bodo plantations. It
was in some anxiety that Stanley arrived there. What
tidings would he get? Would his officers still be
there? Had Emin and Jephson given any signs of
life? Had their arrival been announced?

Fort Bodo was in the same condition in which he
had left it seven months previously. Captain Nelson,
Lieutenant Stairs, and Dr. Parke were all there, and
were all well, having with them fifty-one soldiers out
of the fifty-nine who had been left in their charge.

Meanwhile of Emin and Jephson there were no tidings ; no rumours whatever about them had reached
the Fort.

What could this prolonged silence portend? What
could have transpired either at the Lake or at Wadelai
to detain Jephson, who was a man of determined energy, and who had given his word to come back?

The situation appeared to admit of no delay, and it
was resolved that the Fort must be abandoned forthwith. On the 23rd of December, therefore, the united expedition set out on its march, and taking its
eastward course, proceeded to quarters in Mazamboni's
territory, where it encamped on the 9th of January.

Here the camp was left in the care of Messrs.
Stairs, Nelson, and Parke, Stanley himself, full of
gloomy forebodings, having determined at once to
hasten forward to the Lake, taking with him Mr.
Bonny and a small detachment of men. On his arrival the Bakumu this time gave him a hearty welcome, demonstrating their goodwill by bringing in
food in abundance, by assisting in building the huts

for the night-camp, and generally by rendering whatever help they could.

Still no news was to be learnt from the Nyanza. Where could Emin and Jephson be?

And here it may be well to pause a moment and survey the task that had been accomplished by the man of amazing energy, who with sinews as of steel, had left Yambuya in June 1887, and had now returned for the third time to the Lake Albert Nyanza in January 1889.

A wonderful record is the story of his marches; the first journey from Yambuya to the Lake, 171 days; the second journey from the Lake to Fort Bodo, 22 days; the third journey from the Fort to the Lake, 20 days; the fourth journey from the Lake to Banalya, 82 days; and then this fifth journey from Banalya back to the Lake, 107 days, making a total of 402 days.

Thus it is seen how for more than thirteen months out of a year and a half the leader was on the constant move, making his way through virgin forests that had neither road nor track; forcing his path through tangled brushwood and over rushing torrents; carrying in his train many thousands of pounds'-weight of goods, provisions, and ammunition; harassed over and over again by warlike and suspicious savages; uncertain as to the means of providing food for his hundreds of followers; exposed to an unhealthy atmosphere; and personally suffering the pangs of hunger and privation. Such was the man who in spite of climate, in spite of hostilities, in spite of famine, in spite of sickness, never swerved from his line of duty and devotion, but faced all difficulties, resolved to overcome them till his work was done. Who shall say that the age of knight-errantry has passed away? Other ages have had their Xenophon, Godfrey de Bouillon, Marco Polo, Columbus, Vasco, and Magellan; the nineteenth century can boast of Stanley. The race of heroes is not yet extinct.

On January 16th, the caravan arrived at the village of Gaviras, at no great distance from the Lake, where some messengers sent by Kavalli handed Stanley a packet of letters. Stanley read them eagerly, but with profound amazement at the disastrous intelligence they contained. The troops of the Equatorial province had mutinied on the 18th of August; Emin and Jephson had been made prisoners; the Mahdists, making a fresh attack in October, had routed the Egyptian force, had taken Rejaf, Kiri, and Laboré, and were now only awaiting reinforcements to renew their advance.

It looked as if all were lost.

As Wolseley had arrived at Khartoum too late to save Gordon, it seemed as though Stanley had reached the Nyanza too late to rescue Emin.

CHAPTER XVII.

REVOLT OF THE EGYPTIAN TROOPS.

The situation in the Equatorial province –First mutiny of the troops—Emin at Mswa—Revolt of the garrison at Labore—Arrest and imprisonment of Emin and Jephson—Arrival of the Mahdists at Lado—Dervish ambassadors at Dufile—Message from Omar Saleh—Capture of Rejaf—Revolt of the Bari—Anarchy—Second battle at Rejaf—Emin and Jephson at liberty —Siege of Dufile—Defeat of the Mahdists—Emin at Tunguru.

In realising the events that occurred in the province of the Equator from the time that Stanley left Lake Albert in May 1888 to the date of his return in the following January, it is requisite to bear in mind what must have been the true relation subsisting between 1500 armed and semi-barbarous mercenaries and the solitary European, devoted by taste and education to the study of science, and only placed by adventitious circumstances in the position of a military governor. It was a position in which he was supported by no authority except the prestige of his nationality and official rank; and for four years he had been unaided and uncheered by any communication with the civilised world. Little by little his authority declined, and with it declined also the consciousness of stability on the part of the man who thus saw years pass on without bringing relief to a situation which could hardly do otherwise than continually become more difficult, embarrassing, and critical.

Possibly some stringent and severe measures adopted at first, and the enforcement of capital sentence in several cases, might have nipped the first signs of mutiny in the bud, and have obviated their reappearance. But it should be asked, was it to be expected of Schnitzer, the physician and the botanist, any more than of Livingstone, the conciliating missionary, that he should exhibit the stern energy and the sharp decision of a Stanley or a Wissman?

As a matter of fact, it is plain that for a considerable period Emin Pasha had had little beyond a semblance of power. Whenever he required anything of consequence to be carried out, he could not simply issue an order, he had to submit a request to his Egyptian and Soudanese officers that what he desired should be done. These officers, as a rule, were unfortunately nearly all of that wily and hypocritical class who had caused so much misery and disappointment to Baker and Gordon ; they were such as had recently betrayed Khartoum and massacred its valiant defender.

The position of things in the province had become worse than dubious, and an outbreak sooner or later was inevitable. The arrival of the relief expedition precipitated the event.

Report was circulated among the troops that an armed force was close at hand, coming from the south, and that it was the object of the strangers to carry Emin Pasha off by an unknown route. In consequence of this, 190 soldiers at Dufilé, instigated by their officers, entered into a compact that they would at once seize his person, and thus prevent his leaving their country, if he were to leave it at all, by any other route than the northern route, which they knew, and by which they had come.

Emin was made aware of this plot by his faithful adherent Major Awach, and by some of the officers of the second battalion, at whose suggestion he left Wadelai, retreating to Mswa, one of the other settlements on the Lake. Mswa at that time was under the command of Shukri-Aga, a brave and intelligent officer, who had been promoted to his present rank in recognition of the services he had rendered in the campaign against the Mahdists of Karam-Allah in 1884.

When a detachment of the first battalion arrived at Wadelai and learnt that the officers of the second battalion had advised Emin to withdraw, there was a vehement outbreak of wrath. The Commandant at Wadelai was seized and beaten with the kurbatch; the rebel soldiers, moreover, carrying off with them to Dufilé a number of people as hostages.

This had been the actual state of things at the time when Stanley first arrived with his expedition at the margin of Lake Albert; but Emin does not appear to have disclosed to Stanley what was the extremity to which matters were reduced. Very likely, in the kindness of his disposition, he was indulging the hope that the arrival of the Europeans would reassure his followers, and would be effectual in the restoration of order, so that the mutinous soldiers would be brought back to their allegiance. As he wrote to Stanley: "The first battalion in the northern garrisons has always been extremely averse to any proposal of retreat to the south. But now that you have come, and as several of the soldiers remember seeing you at Mtesa's court when they were there with M. Linant de Bellefond in 1876, and as others know you personally, and still more by hearsay, it is quite probable that they may change their minds. They must now be convinced that there is another way to Egypt besides that to the north, because they will see that you have succeeded in getting here by it."

But Emin had not taken account of the moral malady which was poisoning the minds of such a large proportion of the Egpytians in the Soudan army; he was not allowing for treason.

Whilst, in the middle of August, Emin Pasha and Mr. Jephson were retiring along the Nile from Dufilé to Rejaf, the troops of the first battalion were being agitated into revolt by one of their officers named Abdul Vaal Effendi. He assured them that Stanley had a commission from the English Government to carry off all the Egyptians and Soudanese in the province, with their wives and children, to Zanzibar, and that there they would be subject to punishment and reduced to slavery by the Christians. In such a land, where ignorance and fanaticism were universal, words like these acted as a train of gunpowder. There was mutiny at once.

It would appear to have been on the 18th of August, one day after Stanley's reaching Banalya, where his rear-caravan had been in camp, that Emin Pasha and Mr. Jephson were arrested and were being carried as prisoners to Dufilé.

The leaders of the insurrection next summoned the officers to a divan, where all those who ventured to oppose the movement were so insulted and abused that for their own personal safety they were compelled to acquiesce. At the meeting the Pasha was formally deposed, and all the officers who sympathised with him were deprived of their commissions.

After all the revolution was the act of hardly more than half-a-dozen disaffected Egyptians, who by intimidation succeeded in rallying around them a certain number of officers and others. The soldiers, with the exception of those at Laboré, where the flame of insurrection was first ignited, took no part in the original outbreak, and only yielded to the pressure put upon them by their leaders. Indeed, it was to the fidelity of the troops that Emin owed his life; they resolutely maintained that no one should lay violent hands upon the governor, and to the utmost of their power withstood his being removed to Rejaf, the station on the extreme north.

Only a slight modification of affairs ensued during the following month of October. Mr. Jephson regained his liberty, but on the condition that he should not leave Dufilé; the Pasha was still kept in chains and might expect day by day to receive sentence of death.

Then came the sudden and startling intelligence that a Mahdist army, about 1500 strong, under the command of Omar Saleh, had made its appearance before Lado. The troops had been brought from Khartoum in three steamers and nine boats, and had made their encampment upon the site of the now abandoned station.

A few days later three dervishes arrived at Dufilé and demanded an audience of the governor of the province. They were the bearers of a long written message, of which the substance is given in the sub-joined abbreviation :—

" From the servant of God, Omar Saleh, officer of the Mahdi, to whom we give reverential greetings.

" To the honoured Mahomed Emin, Mudir of Hatalastiva.

" May God lead him in the paths of His gifts. Amen.

" After greeting you, I would remind you that the world is a house of change and decay, and everything in it must one day perish. God is the Master of all His creatures.

" We are of the army of God. With our army is victory. Victory is to the believers. God help the Faithful. It is written in the Koran.

" The whole country is subject to the prophet, Hicks, Stewart, Gordon, all are dead. Make peace with the Mahdi.

" We have landed here with an army of the defenders of the faith. It is your duty to submit. Submit and be assured of a free pardon, of protection for your children and your property, and of the blessing of God. We bid you come and join us.

" And now be of good cheer and do not delay. I have said enough for one whose intelligence is bright as yours. Come to me and I will honour you. Become a true believer as the master wishes.

" May God bless and assist you in all you do. Salaam."

The dervishes waited for a reply ; the only answer that was vouchsafed was to seize them and put them all to death.

Preparations were at once made for resistance.

Within a few days the Mahdists had assaulted the station at Rejaf, killing five Egyptian officers, and a considerable number of soldiers. All the provisions as well as the ammunition fell into their hands. Simultaneously with the news of this disaster came the intelligence that the Bari, who had long been restless under the Egyptian rule, had revolted and joined the invaders.

From all the stations along the river there was forthwith a general stampede. The garrisons of Bedden, Kiri, and Muggi fled with their wives, children,

and servants to Laboré, forsaking their posts and all
the goods which they contained. Consternation reigned
supreme. Inevitably the position of Emin and Jephson, who were still held captive by the rebels, was
becoming more and more perilous.

On the 7th of November, Jephson wrote from
Dufilé to Stanley, urging the necessity of there being
no loss of time. "Our position here," he said, "is
extremely unpleasant; for three months everything
has been chaos and confusion; half-a-dozen conflict-
ing orders are given every day, and no one obeys.
The rebel officers are absolutely incapable of control-
ling the soldiers." He proceeded to explain that the
officers were now very much alarmed at what had happened, that they were reckoning very much on Stanley's return to the Lake, and that he believed the great
majority were quite ready to quit the province with
him. "As for Emin and myself," he added, "we are
like rats in a trap. They will neither let us act or retire. Had this rebellion not happened, the Pasha
would at least for a time have been able to hold the
Mahdists in check; but as it is he is powerless to
act." "Unless," he says finally, "you come promptly, I fear you will come too late, and that our fate
will be that of the other defenders of the Soudan garrisons. Should we not succeed in getting out of the
country, please remember me to all friends."

But sad to relate, on that very date when Mr. Jephson was writing to Stanley that he must come soon,
Stanley and Mr. Bonny had hardly reached the confluence of the Ihuru. They were some hundreds of
miles away, and had to push along for more than two
months before they could reach the Lake. The prospects of Emin and his partner in trouble were indeed
becoming desperate.

Worse still did the look-out grow. The Egyptians,
in an attempt to get Rejaf back from the Mahdists,
were repulsed with heavy loss, and six of their leaders
were killed; but the defeat had one happy result; it
brought about Emin's liberation from prison.

Mr. Jephson, writing on November 24th from Wadelai, thus describes the circumstances: "Among the
officers killed were some of the Pasha's worst enemies.
The soldiers in all the stations were so panic-stricken

and angry at what had happened that they declared they would not attempt to fight unless the Pasha was set at liberty ; so the rebel officers were obliged to free him, and sent us to Wadelai, where he is free to do as he pleases, but at present he has not resumed his authority in the country ; he is, I believe, by no means anxious to do so.

" Our danger, as far as the Mahdists are concerned, is, of course, increased by this last defeat, but our position is in one way better now, for we are further removed from them, and we have now the option of retiring if we please, which we had not before while we were prisoners. We hear that the Mahdists have sent steamers down to Khartoum for reinforcements ; if so, they cannot be up here for another six weeks. If they come up here with reinforcements it will be all up with us, for the soldiers will never stand against them, and it will be a mere walk over.

" Every one is anxiously looking for your arrival, for the coming of the Mahdists has completely cowed them."

Meanwhile the Mahdists were making rapid advances. After placing their head-quarters at Rejaf, which the Egyptian troops had failed to recover, they had successively occupied Bedden, Kiri, Muggi, La-boré, and Khor-Aju. On November 25th they appeared before Dufilé-and blockaded it for four days. The station, however, was in a good state of defence, having 500 men under the command of. Emin's lieu-tenant, Selim Bey. The garrison made a successful sortie, and the besiegers were repulsed, leaving no less than 250 dead upon the field. They then fell back upon Rejaf, and entrenched themselves, awaiting the arrival of their reinforcements.

This engagement, although it gave encouragement to the Egyptians, does not seem to have much improved the position of Emin, who retired to Tunguru, a station on a small island not far from the west shore of the Nyanza ; whence on the 18th of December Mr. Jephson wrote again to Stanley : " The Pasha is unable to move hand or foot, as there is still a very strong party against him, and the officers are no longer in immediate fear of the Mahdists.

184 ABANDONMENT OF THE SOUDAN.

"Make your camp at Kavalli, send a letter directly you arrive there, and I will come to you.

"I trust you will arrive before the Mahdists are re-inforced, or our case will be desperate."

But at the time when this urgent letter was being written Stanley was far off. He had not yet arrived at Fort Bodo, which he did not reach until December 20th. It will at once be understood that his anxiety was only too well founded, and that he had not been wrong in attributing the long silence of Emin and Jephson to something untoward.

CHAPTER XVIII.

ABANDONMENT OF THE SOUDAN.

The camp at Kavalli—Letter from Stanley to Jephson—Arrival of Jephson—Emin's letter to Stanley—Meeting of Stanley and Emin—Determination to evacuate—Concentration at Kavalli—Council of war—Emin's hesitation and Casati's scruples—Egyptian attack upon the camp—Preparations for departure.

WHEN, for the second time, Stanley reached the Lake, on January 16th, 1889, he placed his camp, not as before at Nsabé on the shore, but upon a plateau overlooking the plain, near Kavalli's village. With his usual tact he at once succeeded in gaining the goodwill of the natives, who are numerous in that dis-trict, so that friendly relations and active trade were soon established between them and the members of the expedition. The second day after his arrival Stan-ley wrote to Mr. Jephson :—

"KAVALLI, *January 18th*, 1889.

"MY DEAR JEPHSON,—I now send thirty rifles and three of Kavalli's men down to the Lake with my let-ters, with urgent instructions that a canoe should set off, and the bearers be rewarded. . . .

"Be wise, be quick, and waste no hour of time, and bring Buiza and your own Soudanese with you. . . .

"If the Pasha can come, send a courier on your ar-rival at our old camp on the Lake below here to an-nounce the fact, and I will send a strong detachment to escort him up to the plateau, even to carry him, if he needs it. I feel too exhausted after my 1300 miles of travel since I parted from you last May to go down to the Lake again. The Pasha must have some pity for me.

"Don't be alarmed or uneasy on our account; nothing hostile can approach us within twelve miles without my knowing it. I am in the thickest of a friendly population, and if I sound the warnote, within four hours I can have 2000 warriors to assist to repel any force disposed to violence. And if it is to be a war of wits, why then I am ready for the cunningest Arab alive.

"I have read your letters half a dozen times, and my opinion of you varies with each reading. Sometimes I fancy you are half Mahdist or Arabist, and then Eminist. I shall be wiser when I see you.

"Now don't you be perverse, but obey, and let my order to you be as a frontlet between the eyes, and all, with God's gracious help, will end well.

"I want to help the Pasha somehow, but he must also help me, and credit me. If he wishes to get out of this trouble, I am his most devoted servant and friend; but if he hesitates again I shall be plunged in wonder and perplexity. I could save a dozen Pashas if they were willing to be saved. I would go on my knees to implore the Pasha to be sensible in his own case. He is wise enough in all things else, even his own interest.

"The Committee said, 'Relieve Emin Pasha with this ammunition. If he wishes to come out, the ammunition will enable him to do so; if he elects to stay, it will be of service to him.' The Khedive said the same thing, and added, 'But if the Pasha and his officers wish to stay, they do so on their own responsibility.' Sir Evelyn Baring said the same thing in clear and decided words, and here I am, after 4100 miles of travel, with the last instalment of relief. Let him who is authorised to take it, take it. Come; I am ready to lend him all my strength and wit to assist him. But this time there must be no hesitation, but positive yea or nay, and home we go.—Yours very sincerely,

"HENRY M. STANLEY."

Jephson arrived at Kavalli on February 6th. Stanley wrote to Emin on the following day, and a week
later a messenger from Nsabé brought a letter from
the Pasha, the contents of which quite electrified the
camp.

"NSABÉ, *February* 13*th*, 1889.

" *To* HENRY M. STANLEY, Esq.,
    Commanding the Relief Expedition.

"SIR,—In answer to your letter of the 7th inst.,
for which I beg to tender my best thanks, I have the
honour to inform you that yesterday, at 3 P.M., I
arrived here with my two steamers, carrying a first lot
of people desirous to leave this country under your
escort. As soon as I have arranged for cover of my
people, the steamships have to start for Mswa station, to bring on another lot of people awaiting transport.

" With me there are some twelve officers anxious to
see you, and only forty soldiers. They have come
under my orders to request you to give them some
time to bring their brothers—at least, such as are willing to leave—from Wadelai, and I promised them to do
my best to assist them. Things having to some extent now changed, you will be able to make them
undergo whatever conditions you see fit to impose
upon them. To arrange these I shall start from here
with the officers for your camp, after having provided
for the camp, and if you send carriers, I could avail
me of some of them.

" I hope sincerely that the great difficulties you
have had to undergo, and the great sacrifices made by
your expedition in its way to assist us, may be rewarded by a full success in bringing out my people.
The wave of insanity which overran the country has
subsided, and of such as are now coming with me we
may be sure.

" Signor Casati requests me to give his best thanks
for your kind remembrance of him.

" Permit me to express to you once more my cordial thanks for whatever you have done for us until
now, and believe me to be, yours very faithfully,

"DR. EMIN."

The *Khedive* and the *Nyanza* were now at anchor off Nsabé, and their crews were preparing a camp upon the shore. Emin landed next day, accompanied by Captain Casati, the physician Vitu Hassan, Selim Bey, the defender of Dufilé, and seven other officers, who were a deputation from the troops of the Equatorial province. The Pasha was in mufti, but the deputation were in uniform. They were attended by about sixty-five people, consisting of soldiers and servants. The whole party mounted the slope leading to the plateau, and reached the camp where Stanley was awaiting them.

It was an affecting meeting. No longer, as in the previous April, was it a question between maintaining a footing on the Upper Nile and making a retreat; now, by the avowal of the brave but unfortunate governor himself, the idea of evacuation was already to the fore; the first signal of retreat had already been given.

In order that his force should be concentrated in the event of any hostile attack, Stanley had sent a message to the rear-guard that he had left in Mazamboni's country with Messrs. Stairs, Nelson, and Parke, ordering them to come on at once to Kavalli, and on the 18th they all arrived.

All the white men, eight in number, and the principal members of Emin's faithful staff, were now summoned to a divan to be held next day, when the plans for the future should be discussed.

The evacuation of the province was definitely decided on, but it was arranged that a reasonable time should be allowed to enable the troops in the various stations to be informed of the decision, so that they might embark themselves and their families, and all who were willing to leave, on board the steamers, and muster at the Nsabé camp on the Lake shore.

On the 25th the two steamers returned from Mswa with a fresh detachment of refugees, and about the same time Emin received a despatch from Wadelai, stating that in the absence of Selim Bey the rebels had again broken out into revolt, Selim had been deposed from his command, and several of the rebel officers had been promoted to the rank of Bey.

These tidings completely nullified any hopes that

the Pasha might have entertained of re-establishing
his authority, and made him determine to leave his
own camp and join Stanley on the plateau. It was
decided that a month would be sufficiently long to
allow the faithful troops to rally round their chief, so
that the final departure might take place in six weeks'
time, that is to say, about the 10th of April. Selim
Bey and the officers then left Kavalli in order to
collect all the people who desired to leave for Egypt.

Thirty days after Selim Bey's departure, a steamer
appeared before the Nyanza camp, bringing a letter
from that officer, and one from all the rebel officers at
Wadelai, announcing themselves ready to make submission to the "Envoy of the great Government,"
and requesting to be allowed to return to Egypt under
Stanley's escort. Emin was also informed that Selim
had already despatched one steamer full of refugees
to Tunguru, and that since that time he had been engaged in transporting people from Dufilé to Wadelai,
which he was making his rallying point. The Pasha,
when he imparted what he called this "encouraging"
news to Stanley, expressed his opinion it would require three months more to complete the concentration of the people at Kavalli, and desired to know
what Stanley had determined on under the new aspect
of affairs.

It was evident that Emin did not know how to tear
himself away from the land where he had resided for
eleven years, and which seems to have a kind of fasci-
nation for Europeans. He hesitated, too, about leaving the soldiers, who, until some foolish fancy had
warped their reason, had always served him faithfully
and well. He had scruples about following Stanley;
he seemed thereby to be breaking his promise to Gordon, his venerated chief, that he would shed the very
last drop of his blood in the Soudan in the cause of
civilisation and progress.

Stanley, however, was not so much enthralled by
the fascinations of a country in which his experiences
had been so rough, where he had run so many fatal
risks, and where he had seen his companions die
around him by the score. He was fully sensible of
the import of the events that had transpired, and he
represented, with much show of reason, that in the

present state of anarchy, a handful of Europeans, however valiant they might be, could do nothing for the cause of civilisation at Wadelai, which by this time was probably in the power of encroaching Mahdists, mutinous soldiers, or hostile natives.

Moreover, his mission was to rescue Emin from danger, and he considered that it was the Pasha's duty to take advantage of the deliverance that was offered him. As a practical man, he saw no good in a useless sacrifice. The difficulties that had to be overcome in persuading Emin and Casati to make their retreat, and the incidents attending them, may best be told in the explorer's own words :—

" I summoned the officers of the expedition together —Lieutenant Stairs, R. E., Captain R. H. Nelson, Surgeon Parke, A.M.D., Mounteney Jephson, Esq., and Mr. William Bonny, and proposed to them in the Pasha's presence that they should listen to a few explanations, and then give their decision, one by one, according as they should be asked.

" Gentlemen, Emin Bey has received a mail from Wadelai. Selim Bey, who left the post below here on the 26th February last, with a promise that he would hurry up such people as wished to go to Egypt, writes from Wadelai that the steamers are engaged in transporting some people from Dufilé ·to Wadelai; that the work of transport between Wadelai and Tunguru will be resumed upon the accomplishment of the other task. When he went away from here we were informed that he was deposed, and that Emin Pasha and he were sentenced to death by the rebel officers. We now learn that the rebel officers, ten in number, and all their faction, are desirous of proceeding to Egypt; we may suppose, therefore, that Selim Bey's party is in the ascendant again.

" Shukri Aga, the chief of the Mswa station—the station nearest to us—paid us a visit there in the middle of March. He was informed on the 16th of March, the day that he departed, that our departure for Zanzibar would positively begin on the 10th of April. He took with him urgent letters for Selim Bey announcing that fact in unmistakable terms. Eight days later we hear that Shukri Aga is still at Mswa, having only sent a few women and children to the Nyanza camp, yet he and his people might have been here by this if they intended to accompany us.

"Thirty days ago Selim Bey left us with a promise of a reasonable time. The Pasha thought once that twenty days would be a reasonable time. However, we have extended it to forty-four days. Judging by the length of time Selim Bey has already taken, only reaching Tunguru with one-sixteenth of the expected force, I personally am quite prepared to give the Pasha my decision. For you must know, gentlemen, that the Pasha having heard from Selim Bey 'intelligence so encouraging,' wishes to know my decision, but I have preferred to call you to answer for me.

"You are aware that our instructions were to carry relief to Emin Pasha, and to escort such as were willing to accompany us to Egypt. We arrived at the Nyanza, and met Emin Pasha in the latter part of April 1888, just twelve months ago. We handed him his letters from the Khedive and his Government, and also the first instalment of relief, and asked him whether we were to have the pleasure of his company to Zanzibar. He replied that his decision depended on that of his people.

"This was the first adverse news that we received. Instead of meeting with a number of people only too anxious to leave Africa, it was questionable whether there would be any except a few Egyptian clerks. With Major Barttelot so far distant in the rear, we could not wait at the Nyanza for this decision. As that might possibly require months, it would be more profitable to seek and assist the rear-column, and by the time we arrived here again, those willing to go to Egypt would probably be impatient to start. We, therefore, leaving Mr. Jephson to convey our message to the Pasha's troops, returned to the forest region for the rear-column, and in nine months were back again on the Nyanza. But instead of discovering a camp of people anxious and ready to depart from Africa, we find no camp at all, but hear that both the Pasha and Mr. Jephson are prisoners, that the Pasha has been in imminent danger of his life from the rebels, and at another time is in danger of being bound on his bedstead and taken to the interior of Makkaraka country. It has been current talk in the province that we were only a party of conspirators and adventurers, that the letters of the Khedive and Nubar Pasha were forgeries concocted by the vile Christians, Stanley and Casati, assisted by Mohammed Emin Pasha. So elated have the rebels been by their bloodless victory over the Pasha and Mr. Jephson, that they have confidently boasted of their purpose to entrap me by cajoling words, and strip our expedition of everything belonging to it, and send us adrift into the wilds to perish.

"We need not dwell on the ingratitude of these men, or on their intense ignorance and evil natures, but you must bear in mind the facts to guide you to a clear decision.

"We believed when we volunteered for this work that we should be met with open arms. We were received with indifference, until we were led to doubt whether any people wished to depart. My representative was made a prisoner, menaced with rifles, threats were freely used. The Pasha was deposed, and for three months was a close prisoner. I am told this is the third revolt in the province. Well, in the face of all this, we have waited nearly twelve months to obtain the few hundreds of unarmed men, women, and children in this camp. As I promised Selim Bey and his officers that I would give a reasonable time, Selim Bey and his officers repeatedly promised to us there should be no delay. The Pasha has already fixed April 10th, which extended their time to forty-four days, sufficient for three round voyages for each steamer. The news brought to-day is not that Selim Bey is close here, but that he has not started from Wadelai yet.

"In addition to his own friends, who are said to be loyal and obedient to him, he brings the ten rebel officers, and some 600 or 700 soldiers, their faction.

"Remembering the three revolts which these same officers have inspired, their pronounced intentions against this expedition, their plots and counterplots, the life of conspiracy and smiling treachery they have led, we may well pause to consider what object principally animates them now—that from being ungovernably rebellious against all constituted authority, they have suddenly become obedient and loyal soldiers of the

Khedive and his 'great Government.' You must be aware that, exclusive of the thirty-one boxes of ammunition delivered to the Pasha by us in May 1888, the rebels possess ammunition of the Provincial Government equal to twenty of our cases. We are bound to credit them with intelligence enough to perceive that such a small supply would be fired in an hour's fighting among so many rifles, and that only a show of submission and apparent loyalty will ensure a further supply from us. Though the Pasha brightens up each time he obtains a plausible letter from these people, strangers like we are may also be forgiven for not readily trusting those men whom they have such good cause to mistrust. Can we be certain, however, that if we admit them into this camp as good friends and loyal soldiers of Egypt, they will not rise up some night and possess themselves of all the ammunition, and so deprive us of the power of returning to Zanzibar? With our minds filled with Mr. Jephson's extraordinary revelations of what has been going on in the province since the closing of the Nile route, beholding the Pasha here before my very eyes—who was lately supposed to have several thousands of people under him, but now without any important following—and bearing in mind 'the cajolings' and the 'wiles' by which we were to be entrapped, I ask you, would we be wise in extending the time of delay beyond the date fixed—that is, the 10th of April?"

"The officers one after the other replied in the negative.

"'There, Pasha,' I said, 'you have your answer. We march on the 10th of April.'

"The Pasha then asked if we could 'in our consciences acquit him of having abandoned his people,' supposing they had not arrived on the 10th of April. We replied, 'Most certainly.'

"Three or four days after this I was informed by the Phaas—who pays great deference to Captain Casati's views—that Captain Casati was by no means certain that he was doing quite right in abandoning his people. According to the Pasha's desire I went over to see Captain Casati, followed soon after by Emin Pasha.

"Questions of law, honour, duty, were brought forward by Casati, who expressed himself clearly that *moralemente* Emin Pasha was bound to stay by his people.

"I had to refute these morbid ideas with the A B C of common sense. I had to illustrate the obligations of Emin Pasha to his soldiers by comparing them to a mutual contract between two parties. One party refused to abide by its stipulations, and would have no communication with the other, but proposed to itself to put the second party to death. Could that be called a contract? Emin Pasha was appointed governor of the province. He had remained faithful to his post and duties till his own people rejected him, and finally deposed him. He had been informed by his Government that if he and his officers and soldiers elected to quit the province they could avail themselves of the escort of the expedition which had been sent to their assistance, or stay in Africa on their own responsibility; that the Government had abandoned the province altogether. But when the Pasha informs his people of the Government's wishes, the officers and soldiers declare the whole to be false, and for three months detain him a close prisoner. Where was the dishonour to the Pasha in yielding to what was inevitable and indisputable? As for duty, the Pasha had a dual duty to perform, that to the Khedive as his chief, and that to his soldiers. So long as neither duty clashed, affairs proceeded smoothly enough; but the instant it was hinted to the soldiers that they might retire now if they wished, they broke out into open violence and revolted, absolved the Pasha of all duty towards them, and denied that he had any duty to perform to them. Consequently the Pasha could not be morally bound to care in the least for people who would not listen to him.

"I do not think Casati was convinced, nor do I think the Pasha was convinced. But it is strange what strong hold this part of Africa has upon the affections of European officers, Egyptian officers and Soudanese soldiers! . . .

"The day after I was informed that there had been an alarm in my camp the night before; the Zanzibari quarters had been entered by the Pasha's people,

and an attempt made to abstract the rifles. This it
was that urged me to immediate action.

" I knew there had been conspiracies in the camp,
that the malcontents were increasing, that we had
many rebels at heart against us, that the people
dreaded the march more than they feared the natives ;
but I scarcely believed that they would have dared to
put into practice their disloyal ideas in my camp.

" I proceeded to the Pasha to consult with him, but
the Pasha would consent to no proposition, not but
what they appeared necessary and good, but he could
not, owing to the want of time, &c.   Yet the Pasha the
evening before had received a post from Wadelai
which brought him terrible tales of disorder, distress,
and helplessness among Selim Bey and his faction, and
the rebels and their adherents.

" I accordingly informed him that I proposed to act
immediately, and would ascertain for myself what this
hidden danger in the camp was, and, as a first step,
I would be obliged if the Pasha would signal for general muster of the principal Egyptians in the square
of his camp.

" The summons being sounded, and not attended to
quickly enough to satisfy me, half a company of Zanzibaris were detailed to take sticks and rout every one
from their huts.   Dismayed by these energetic measures, they poured into the square, which was surrounded
by rifles

" On being questioned, they denied all knowledge
of any plot to steal the rifles from us, or to fight, or
to withstand in any manner any order.   It was then
proposed that those who desired to accompany us to
Zanzibar should stand on one side.   They all hastened
to one side except two of the Pasha's servants.   The
rest of the Pasha's people, having paid no attention to
the summons, were secured in their huts, and brought
to the camp-square, where some were flogged, and
others ironed and put under guard.

" ' Now, Pasha,' I said, ' will you be good enough
to tell all these Arabs that these rebellious tricks of
Wadelai and Dufilé must cease here, for at the first
move made by them I shall be obliged to exterminate
them utterly.'

"On the Pasha translating, the Arabs bowed, and vowed that they would obey their father religiously."

From that time the evacuation was determined on, and preparations were made for an immediate start. Of Emin's people there were 84 married women, 187 female domestics, 74 children above two years, 35 infants in arms ; these with the men made up a total of about 600. The relief expedition numbered 550, and 350 native carriers had been enrolled from the district to assist in carrying the baggage, so that on the 10th of April the caravan set out from Kavalli in number about 1500.

CHAPTER XIX.

RETREAT OF THE FIFTEEN HUNDRED.

The start—Stanley's illness—Mutiny—On the march—Skirmishes with the Warasura—Crossing the Semliki—The affluent of Lake Albert—In the valley—Mountains of the Moon—Speke's geographical genius—Alpine climbing—The Usongora—Towu of Kative—Lake Albert Edward—Sources of the Nile.

IN the history of antiquity there is the record of a retreat above all others great and glorious. It was that of the 10,000 Greeks who after the battle of Cunaxa, through perils and dangers of every kind, without food, without guides, through wild and ter-, rible country, pursued and harassed by Artaxerxes and his Persians, at last attained their native land. A thousand miles from the sea which they had thought never to behold again, they accomplished their march in 120 days, mainly owing to the skill and courage of their leaders. Of these Xenophon, who was one of the heroes of this memorable campaign, afterwards became its immortal historian.

We are now face to face with an achievement of a similar kind, which cannot fail to take its place in the pages of the world's history, and which will have for its narrator the man who has accomplished the deed.

It is true there were not 10,000 men that Stanley had to convoy to the shore of the Indian Ocean ; but his caravan included many helpless women, children, and slaves.   Instead of brave and well-disciplined forces, he had to control artful and cowardly Egyptians, timid negroes, and Zanzibaris, who though loyal, were lazy. On the other hand, it was not 1000 but more than 1500 miles that he had to travel before reaching the harbour of safety, a distance equal to that covered in Napoleon's retreat from Moscow.

Moreover, he was in the heart of the dark continent, beneath the burning rays of an equatorial sun, on the threshold of that mysterious region, the birthplace of the Nile, of which centuries of research failed to unveil the secrets.

And whilst he has thus thrown the achievements of the 10,000 into the shade, he has revealed an unknown country to the eyes of science, has introduced new nations to the world of history, has found the solution to the long-tried problem of the origin of the "Father of rivers."

On April 10th, 1889, the camp at Kavalli was raised, and the caravan started, an interminable file of soldiers, porters, women, and children, carrying provisions, ammunition, and baggage of all sorts, and accompanied by all the cattle that could be procured. The retreat had commenced.

They encamped at Mazamboni's on the 12th. The same night Stanley was struck down with severe illness, which well-nigh proved fatal. For some time his life was in danger, but thanks to his good constitution, and the careful nursing and attention of Dr. Parke, the disorder was overcome, and the patient was convalescent.

Stanley's illness delayed the advance of the caravan for twenty-eight days. During that time several conspiracies were afloat in the camp amongst Emin's soldiers. Only one, however, was attempted to be realised. The ringleader, a slave of Awach Effendi's, whom Stanley had made free at Kavalli, was arrested, and after court-martial, which found him guilty, was immediately executed. From that time there was no further breach of discipline.

By May 8th, the column was able to resume its march. The route was to the south, skirting the region of the forests, which Stanley with his present party would not have dared to face, as the Egyptians seemed to have very vague notions about the journey. Besides, there was the question of food, which would prevent a company of 1500 people from attempting a passage through a district where caravans of only 200 or 300 had sometimes narrowly escaped perishing with hunger. Nevertheless, though much has been said to the contrary, Stanley never regretted that he went to Emin's relief by way of the Aruwimi, instead of from Zanzibar through the Masai country. This may be seen from the following extract from a letter that he wrote to Sir William Mackinnon :—

" By-the-bye, Emin Pasha said it was very lucky I did not approach him from the east by way of the Masai and Ukedo, or Langgo as he calls it. The Langgo land is a great waterless desert for the most part. Even if we had been able to pierce through the Wakedi, it is doubtful if the want of food and water had not annihilated the expedition. . . . Now that we know the Ituri so well, I feel convinced that we could not have chosen a better route."

All the district extending southwards to the Muta Nzigé has recently fallen under the sovereignty of Kabrega, the rapacious potentate of Unyoro, who has made a bold push in this direction, his bands of marauders keeping the entire neighbourhood in a state of agitation.

In making his advance, Stanley did not escape the necessity of using powder and shot. First, the warlike Warasura, the name given to the Wanyoro in that district, congregated near the village of Buhobo, and endeavoured to waylay the caravan. They were routed, and fled in all directions.

Then two days later, whilst crossing the Semliki, the war-cry was heard again, and a well-directed volley of arrows was discharged upon their rear. Guns were again brought into use, and the natives were chased for some distance. Henceforward the course was clear.

Stanley was now on the threshold of a land of wonders. The valley of the Semliki lay outstretched before him, extending to the south-west far as the eye could reach. In its midst, bending now to the north-east, now to the north-west, 80 to 100 yards wide, and averaging 9 feet in depth, flowed the river, its rapid current bearing the ample volume of its waters towards the Albert Nyanza. On either hand were fertile plains, dotted over with villages, groves of bananas and acacias, well cultivated fields, and splendid pastures. These are bounded east and west by ridges of hills rising from 300 to 900 feet above the level of the valley, and crowned by vast plateaus that slope gradually eastwards to the Congo, and on the north-west join the tableland of Unyoro.

In the central portion of this latter region the hills rise ridge upon ridge, and there is one great mountain chain that culminates in a snow-clad peak, probably 17,000 feet in height, the Ruwenzori, known by the natives as the "Cloud-King."

Ancient writers were well aware that beyond the sands of the desert lay a system of inland lakes connected by streams that together formed the Nile; behind these lakes, they averred, was a chain of mighty mountains, to which they gave the name of "Mountains of the Moon." The earliest explorers of Eastern Africa imagined that in Mounts Kenia and Kilima-Njaro, those other snow-peaks of the equatorial regions, they had discovered these mountains of the moon; but Captain Speke, with the marvellous clairvoyance of which he gave so many proofs during his short career, marked them on his map as lying between Lake Albert and Lake Tanganyika. Utilising with a rare sagacity the information that he picked up from the natives along his route, he came to the conclusion that away to the north-west was a lake—Muta Nzigé—and that this lake was bounded by a lofty mountain range that could be no other than the ancient Mountains of the Moon.

Twenty years ago this hypothesis was the cause of much scientific discussion. Speke's assertions were violently attacked, especially by Captain Burton, his fellow traveller. Then the matter was forgotten.

But direct observation has proved that Speke was right. Stanley has now brought the Mountains of the Moon within the range of positive knowledge, and that in the very locality which Speke had indicated, thus rendering a striking tribute to the geographical genius of his illlustrious predecessor.

To Europeans the mysteries of this ancient range have always been the subject of much curiosity, and almost all the officers of the expedition had a keen de-

RUWENZORI.—"MOUNTAINS OF THE MOON."—NORTH-WEST PEAK, SHOWING POINT REACHED BY LIEUT. STAIRS, AND WHAT APPEARS TO BE THE CRATER OF A PEAK.

sire to distinguish themselves as climbers of these African Alps. Lieutenant Stairs succeeded in attaining the greatest altitude, but had the mortification to find two deep gulfs between him and the snowy mount proper.

Early on the morning of June 6th, accompanied by some forty Zanzibaris, he left the camp, and commenced the ascent of the mountain. For the first 300 yards the climbing was fairly good, the path being through long rank grass. At 8.30 the thermometer registered 75° F. The aspect of the country here became different, and on all sides there could be seen dracænas, and here and there an occasional tree-fern and Mwab palm.

At 10.38, after some sharp climbing, the mountaineers reached the last settlement of the natives. The thermometer then read 84° F. Beyond the settlement the way led through a forest of bamboos, which became denser as they ascended. They now noticed a complete and sudden change in the air; it became much cooler and more pure and refreshing, and in another two hours the thermometer had fallen to 70°. It was now past midday. Right ahead of them, rising in one even slope for 1200 feet, stood a peak, which they now started to climb. The ascent was most difficult, as in some places it was covered with arborescent bushwood some 20 feet high, and in others with a thick spongy carpet of wet slippery moss, studded with blue violets and lichens.

Shortly after 4 P.M. they halted to encamp for the night at an altitude of 8500 feet. On turning in, the thermometer registered only 60°, and the Zanzibaris, who were lightly-clad, felt the cold very much.

The ascent was continued on the following day, and persevered in until 10 A.M., when Lieutenant Stairs found his progress stopped by an immense ravine, at the bottom of which there was dense bush. Here he had his first glimpse of a snow-peak about two and a half miles away, and he estimated that it would take at least a day and a half to reach the snow-line. Unprovided as he was with food and warm clothing for his men, he thought it better to return, hoping that at some future time a more favourable opportunity for making the ascent would present itself. The altitude reached by the party was 10,677 feet above the level of the sea.

By about 3 P.M. Stairs and his men had rejoined the expedition. His excursion had convinced him that the Ruwenzori range is of volcanic origin, the extreme top of the peak having a distinct crater-like form.

A march of nineteen days brought the caravan to the south-west angle of the range. On June 26th it left the Awamba, as that part of the Semliki valley is called, and entered the plains of Usongora. These at present are almost a desert, but there are traces of the recent existence of a large population, which has been driven off by the raids of the Warasura. The freebooting tribe here showed some signs of hostility. But no fighting was necessary; the report that the caravan was invincible had already preceded it, and on its appearance the Warasura were seized with a panic and fled.

On July 1st the caravan made its entry into the important town of Kative, well known for its salt-pit, which supplies not only Usongora, but also Toro, Ankori, Mpororo, Ruanda, Ukonju, and many other districts with salt.

Near Kative, Stanley found a definite solution to the problem of the sources of the Nile. The Semliki, of which he had just ascended the right bank, is none other than the channel which carries into Lake Albert the overflow of another lake, known upon the maps as Muta Nzigé, and of which he had a distant view in 1876. He now named it the Albert Edward Nyanza, in honour of the " first British Prince who has shown a decided interest in African geography."

Compared with the Victoria, the Tanganyika, and the Nyassa, this upper lake of the western Nile-system is small, though its length cannot be less than 50 miles. It is about 3000 feet above the sea-level, that is, 1000 feet higher than Lake Albert. Between the two lakes, the Semliki forms a series of falls and rapids.

Henceforward, thanks to Stanley, the upper Nile-system is clearly defined. The Muta Nzigé is the reservoir of all the waters from the west that by way of the Semliki fall into the Albert Nyanza, just as the

Victoria Nyanza is the reservoir for all the waters from the east that by way of the Somerset also fall into Lake Albert.

And thus is verified the assertion of the Greek geographers—that the Nile has its sources in two inland seas. The Muta Nzigé is the *palus occidentalis*, the Victoria Nyanza is the *palus orientalis*. The outpour of the lakes, the two streams of the Semliki and the Somerset, commingle their waters in a third reservoir, the Albert Nyanza, and re-issue conjointly under the name of the Bahr-el-Jebel, which lower down is known as the Bahr-el-Abiad, or White Nile.

Speke, in 1859 and 1861, introduced an important factor into the solution of the problem by the discovery of Lake Victoria ; Baker, in 1863, by that of Lake Albert ; and Stanley has completed the work in 1889 by verifying the Semliki as the connection between Lake Albert and Muta Nzigé.

Rounding the north end of Lake Albert Edward, the caravan passed through Usongora, Toro, Uhaiyama, and Unyampaka. Stanley had visited the latter in 1876, and Ringi, the king, who was at war with Unyoro, now received him with much hospitality. The natives of this district were all friendly, as the reports of its good deeds in relieving the country of the presence of the obnoxious Warasura had preceded the caravan. It was the first really kind welcome it had had since leaving Kavalli.

Stanley speaks in high terms of the comeliness of the various tribes in this mountain district. He describes the natives of Usongora as a fine race, but in no way differing from the finer types of men seen in Karangwé and Ankori, and the Wahuma shepherds of Uganda. The Toro natives also are a mixture of the higher class of negroes, and the majority of the Wahuma can boast of features quite as regular, fine, and delicate as Europeans.

A few days later the column left the shores of the Lake, and turning south-eastwards, came on to the high table-land of Ankori. They were now about 600 miles from Kavalli ; more than 1000 had still to be travelled before they would reach Zanzibar.

Their trials were not yet at an end ; fresh difficulties had still to be overcome.

CHAPTER XX.

TO ZANZIBAR.

Ankori and Karangwe—The land of fever—Frightful mortality—Lake Windermere and Kafurro—Fresh geographical discovery—Expansion of measurement of Lake Victoria—Arrival at Msalala—First news from Europe—More fighting—Mpwapwa—A harassed march—Arrival at Bagamoyo
—Conclusion.

ALIKE from its picturesqueness and from the character of its population the region between Lake Albert
Edward and Lake Victoria is one of the most interesting in Central Africa.

It consists of a series of wide plateaux ranging from
4000 feet to 5000 feet above the level of the sea,
bounded by a chain of conical peaks. This chain
joins the Ruwenzori range on the north, and includes,
with the Kibanga, Ankori, Mpororo, and Ruanda districts, the watershed of Lake Albert Edward on the
west and Lake Victoria on the east. The highest
summits along the line are Mounts Gordon-Bennett
and Lawson on the north, and the elevation of the
Mfumbiro Mountains in the centre, which all rise to a
height of over 12,000 feet. To the west of the chain
are the plains of Ankori; to the south-east those of
Karangwé. In both these districts the people are
agriculturists, and uniformly hospitable. They are a
handsome race, many of them having regular well-de-
fined features that would bear comparison with those
of Europeans.

The Ankori country is subject to keen and search-
ing winds which are extremely trying to health, and
which proved very disastrous in thinning the numbers
of the expedition. Never all along had fever been so
prevalent; as many as 150 cases broke out in a single
day, and even seasoned veterans like Emin and Casati
more than once were prostrated by its effects. The
negroes, no matter of what tribe, fell out of the line
of march, and laid themselves down by the wayside to
" sleep off " their painful languor, whilst the Egyp-

tians, too, worn out by fatigue, ulcers, and dysentery, would hide themselves in any recess and sink down on the ground, where, unless they were picked up and carried on by the rear-guard, they would be left amongst the natives, who (however well-disposed they might be) could yet not understand a word of the language they spoke.

So terrible were the ravages of the fever that in the month of July alone the caravan lost no less than 141 of its followers.

On the 1st of August the expedition crossed the Kagera, a stream that conveys to the Lake Victoria the waters of a cluster of minor lakes. Four days later it reached Kafurro, at no great distance from the lake, which is the smallest of all these, and which was named Lake Windermere by Speke's companion, Captain Grant, because of its fancied resemblance to the English lake in Westmoreland.

Kafurro may be described as a well-known locality, an Arab settlement having been established there for more than thirty years; Speke and Grant having stayed at it for several days in 1861, and Stanley having resided there for a whole month in 1877, all three of them being hospitably entertained by Rumanika, the well-disposed sovereign of Karangwé. Now again the caravan received a cordial welcome; the chiefs were all courteous, and the supply of provisions abundant. The district altogether is very fine; rich pastures on which large herds of cattle graze alternate with swelling uplands, planted with magnificent trees, or fruitful with luxuriant crops, and frequently crowned with thickets of acacia. Rhinoceroses, both black and white, are numerous, and herds of horned antelopes are not unfrequently to be seen.

And here, in passing onwards from Karangwé to the adjacent district of Uzinja, Stanley made a remarkable discovery which was quite unexpected. He was following the route which had been taken by Speke and Grant in 1861, and relying upon the indications of his map, he was entirely under the impression that he was still a long distance away from the south-west boundary of Lake Victoria; his surprise may be imagined when on making a bend to the north-east in the direction of Msalala he saw, immediately before him, the broad expanse of the Victoria Nyanza itself.

In all existing charts the Uzinja shore is marked as taking a north-westerly direction. This presumptive coast-line, however, would now seem to be a succession of mountainous islands lying so closely one behind another, that Stanley himself, when he was making his circumnavigation of the Lake in 1876, had been misled, and had conjectured them to be the mainland. It was obvious now that such was not the case, and, moreover, it was demonstrated that the Lake extends far away beyond them to the south-west. This adjustment gives the Lake an additional area of 6000 square miles.

And as the expedition now made its progress, fresh discoveries were ever being made, even in quarters where Stanley himself did not suppose that there was anything unknown to be revealed.

At length on the 28th of August, as the eye pierced through the foliage of the banana-trees, it rested on a cross that rose above the thatched roof of a Christian church. Here was the mission-station of Msalala, in charge of Mr. Mackay; here assuredly were the outskirts of the world of civilisation!

For twenty days a halt was made at Msalala. It was a well-earned rest.

The time during the stay was mainly occupied in providing for the transport of the provisions which had been sent by the "Emin Pasha Relief Committee" a year and a half previously; and in dealing with the mass of correspondence which would have been forwarded to them by way of Uganda and Unyoro, had not those districts been closed to all Europeans. Since January 1888 Emin and Casati had received no communications from Europe, Stanley having been cut off from all correspondence since June 1887.

The next proceeding was to despatch an express courier from Msalala to the coast with letters for Europe. The letters were delivered at the coast station on November 2nd, and the substance of their contents was immediately forwarded by telegraph.

Much refreshed by the three weeks' repose, the caravan set forth again on the 6th of September upon the last stage of its march. It proceeded along the accustomed route, through Usikumu and Ihuru towards Mpwapwa.

Having twice already travelled along the greater part of this road, Stanley was sanguine in believing that no difficulties would arise, and that all hardships were at an end: but he was reckoning too fast; he had to learn that till he was actually in port, he had obstacles to overcome.

"Previously," wrote Stanley about this time, "I have seen my difficulties diminished as I have arrived nearer the coast. I cannot say so much now. Our long train of invalids tells quite a different tale. Until I can get these unfortunates on board a steamer there will be no peace for me. And the most disheartening thing about it is that after all the toil and trouble we have had in carrying them 1200 miles, and in fighting for them to protect their lives, we see so many of them die just as we are within sight of port.

"At the south of Lake Victoria, we passed four of the most harassing days of the entire journey; there was respite during the night, otherwise we had to fight continuously with scarcely a moment's freedom from attack. The natives seem to have an inexplicable hatred towards the Egyptians, and in order to repulse them we were compelled to inflict severe penalty upon them."

Mpwapwa was reached on the 11th of November, fifty-five days after leaving Msalala, and 188 days after setting out from Kavalli. On the way, the number of the white men in the caravan had been increased by two, as it had been joined by Fathers Girault and Schinze of the Algerian mission; but in the ranks of the Egyptians, Zanzibaris, and negroes the gaps were appalling. Out of the 1500 people who left Lake Nyanza scarcely a moiety survived to arrive at Mpwapwa; the other 750 had fallen off or succumbed on the route, a number which tells its own sad and impressive tale of the sufferings that had to be endured during the 240 days of that gigantic march.

No sooner was the approach of the returning expedition made known at Zanzibar than measures were promptly taken to send out provisions to meet it on its way, the organisation of the party being under the control of Major Wissmann, the German commissioner, and Mr. Stevens, the correspondent of the *New York Herald.*

The meeting with the envoys·from the civilised world occurred on the 30th at Mswa. How welcome they were needs not to be told ; they were not simply the bearers of material comfort, but the harbingers of joy, announcing the satisfaction with which it was hailed that the expedition had so happily accomplished its design.

" I feel "—this is what Stanley writes from Mswa —" just like a labourer on a Saturday evening returning home with his week's work done, his week's wages in his pocket, and glad that to-morrow is the Sabbath."

Five days more and the protracted tramp was finished. The 2nd of December was spent at Mbugani ; the 3rd at Bigiro ; on the 4th the Kinghani River was crossed ; and on the 5th Thalassa ! Thalassa ! the sea was in sight !

The Zanzibaris, catching a glimpse of the water beyond the gardens of Bagamoyo, were breathless with excitement ; their eyes filled with tears as their hearts were stirred with emotion. It was their native place ; they were at home once more.

At Bagamoyo the reception that awaited Stanley was such as had never been accorded to an explorer of this generation. The town was elaborately decorated ; triumphal arches were erected across the avenues ; the German troops were drawn up under Major Wissmann, himself distinguished in the annals of African exploration, having twice traversed the continent, and being like Stanley enlisted by the King of the Belgians for the great scheme of civilising Africa. There, too, were the consuls and representatives of various powers, bringing messages of congratulation from sovereigns, ministers, and scientific bodies. And now when Stanley and his companions, mounted on the horses which Major Wissmann had provided, made their entry in their travelling gear, their clothes in rags, their features furrowed with the sufferings they had undergone, covered with the dust of the last eight months' toil, excitement knew no bounds ; palm-branches were waved ; trumpets blazoned out their welcome ; and salutes were thundered forth by the soldiers mustered on the shore, and from the troopships anchored in the harbour.

It was a noble triumph that had been nobly earned.

Three years had elapsed since the expedition had set out from Zanzibar on its critical adventure. Unwearied skill, indomitable patience, superhuman effort, had brought it to a prosperous issue. The hero had returned, himself safe and sound, and had brought back Emin Pasha, rescued from the savage heart of Africa.

INDEX.